ONE:

FRESH STARTS

BONDS OF CONTRITION

CORE: BOOK THREE

BY

MAQUEL A. JACOB

Published by
MAJart Works
2001 NW Aloclek Dr Suite 211
Hillsboro, Oregon

www.majartworks.com

Cover Art by Dar Albert
www.wickedsmartdesigns.com

ACKNOWLEDGEMENTS

This is the end of our heroes and villains journey and I hope you enjoyed the Core of Confliction Trilogy

I would like to thank NaNoWriMo for having such an awesome platform that pushes writers to find out what they're really made of. Challenging us to kick out a novel in 30 days. Core of Confliction was born from the 2013 madness of National Novel Writing Month which happens every November. I also met my awesome author buddy Dr. Laurel Standley who is not only a scientist but writes Eco-Thrillers so please check out her books.

To all my fellow authors at NIWA, I give you great big hugs. I have learned so much about the business end of writing and publishing from you.

A big thanks to Mom who sat patiently and listened as I read book one to her and she pointed out a lot of weird mistakes. To her husband who actually came up with the title Core of Confliction, you come in handy sometimes.

Last but not least, all my friends, family and beta readers I send you my love and gratitude. Stay tuned for my next endeavor.

Also By
MAQUEL A. JACOB

Core of Confliction

Seeds of Conviction

Curve of Humanity Series

Welcome Despair

A Collection of Shorts

Blood Doctrine

****COMING SOON****

Blood Dominion

Planet Azrom: 140 Years Before

Five royal guards wearing armored helmets that kept their hair back while letting the rest flow down their backs marched down the marbled outside corridor of the palace leading towards the brothel hall. At nearly seven feet tall, in dingy battle armor with dark cloaks swaying behind them, they looked formidable and clearly on a mission. Their stride did not stop as they rounded the corner of the hall into the brothel. Nearing the center, they halted as one and the leader scanned the room. He was looking for a particular type of whore the ruler would find aesthetically pleasing enough not to reject or kill. The last few years showed his dissatisfaction with many of the choices.

Along the walls sat large canopied beds covered with vast arrays of sheer colored fabrics occupied by couplings engaged in various forms of fornication. In the middle of the hall, two feet high cushions were arranged in one large square with much of the same activity. Soldiers and royal court members were allowed to come and go at any time to release their carnal desires. Most of the whores had been well bedded over the decades.

Off to the right, a small dark-haired figure caught the leader's eye. She had unkempt hair, tanned skin, not much endowments and couldn't have been more than six feet tall. This was quite short for their race, but something about her was alluring, even to him. He motioned at one of his men then towards the bed. The soldier who was in the throes of thrusting into her like an animal, was pulled off and tossed out of the way. The guard dragged her upright by the hair.

As the royal guard hauled her out of the hall with the rest of his men in tow, the leader got a closer look and grimaced. That deadpan expression was something he had seen many times before in whores due to years of lying with scum and not knowing true pleasure. They went on to being killed or commit suicide. This may be her last day alive.

At the royal bath house, the guards shoved her into the arms of a washing servant who immediately pushed her away onto the floor. She wiped her hands on the fabric of her robes and glared at the leader.

"How dare you make me touch one of those dirty things?" The servant yelled.

"Just clean her up and have her taken to our Lord!"

He ignored the hissing sound coming from her mouth and turned away. Leaving the room he wondered if he would be back tonight with another one.

The female washing servant bent down to examine the filthy girl. Her skin crawled just looking at her.

"Such filth!" She stood and motioned the other servants to come closer. "Make sure to scrub her down completely, especially," her eyes lowered to the region between the girl's thighs, "inside there." Each servant bowed low as she left them to do their work while she observed. If the girl had been a royal or a soldier, she would have personally pampered her.

One of the male servants grabbed the girl by her hair and dragged her into the large basin built into the floor. Only one other person had been in it previously and they had no intentions of changing the water for someone like her. A soft, fluffy long rod was steam sanitized then soaked in a bowl filled with scented oil water.

All four servants stepped into the basin with her, each having a hold on her limbs. One male servant was in charge of her unruly hair while the other three scrubbed off layers of sweat built up over time. Done with the first stage of cleaning, the male held her from behind by the neck as two other servants grabbed her legs spreading them wide. The remaining servant lifted the fluffy rod out of the bowl nearby and flicked it twice. She inserted it between the girl's thighs, pushing it deep inside her, using slow circular thrusts to ensure every inch was clean. Satisfied with the completion of her task, she removed the rod and set it on a cloth outside the basin. It would be disposed of later. The girl had not struggled throughout the whole ordeal.

The male servant pulled her by the underarms out of the bath basin and laid her on the floor while the others drained it. He went over to the communication terminal and hit the call icon. Within minutes two guards came marching in to retrieve the, now clean, female for their ruler. She was treated no better as they too hauled her up roughly by her armpits and carried her out between their huge bodies into the corridor.

Halfar, supreme ruler of Planet Azrom, sat upright in his bed, wearing only a sheer black covering robe while he passed the time analyzing old battles on his holoscreen. His bed was set high nearly three feet off the floor and colored fabrics covered much of it. Plush coverings were spread all over the floor to ensure his feet never touched bare earth. Glow lamps hovered high above in each corner giving the room enough light to not annoy him.

His stark black hair hung loose draping around him in soft tendrils bringing out the strange murky green of his eyes in contrast with pale skin. He had been bored the past forty years with the steady conquests of small worlds for the sake of trade and politics. Nothing fascinated him much anymore so he resorted to reminiscing.

Hard boots striking marble from outside broke his reverie and he looked up to see two of his royal guards stop at the doorway of his bed chamber with a small naked female slumped between them, held up only by their grip. Her hair had fallen forward covering her face. One of the guards grabbed her by the chin and lifted it up so Halfar could get a good look.

What he found in her eyes as she stared directly into his intrigued him. It was a look he knew well; Resentment mixed with despair. He had seen it in many enemies right before the killing blow. In her stare, there was no intention of dying anytime soon. A strong resolve to live vibrated from her soul. He wanted to break her. With a motion of his hand, the two guards tossed her into the chamber and left.

She dragged herself up into a kneeling position and again stared   at him. It was protocol to avert your gaze when in the presence of the supreme ruler which made her boldness even more outrageous. Halfar cocked his head to one side, then threw off the bed covers.

"Come here."

His voice boomed throughout the chamber. He watched her hesitate for a brief moment before moving forward. Her steps halted a few feet from the bed but still within his reach. Grabbing her by the hair, he yanked her onto the bed.

"I am sure you understood me when I said here."

While she was still stunned from the assault, he pulled her beneath him and pinned her down. As she regained her sense of surroundings, she began to struggle. So much so, that Halfar was amazed at her strength, needing to readjust the pressure he applied as he forced himself into her. He watched her writhe in pain, refusing to give him the satisfaction of hearing her scream by stifling them. It only made Halfar want to hurt her more. He hadn't even bothered to disrobe for the occasion. Eventually, she did scream and he sighed with contentment at the sound.

"Now, isn't it better to let it out?" He switched to one hand to hold her down and used the other to smack the side of her buttocks. "Stop fighting!"

His goal was to incite the opposite and it worked. He pried one of her legs wider and held it up from underneath the knee. She was going to learn how to endure his ferocity because he decided at that moment to keep her.

Shaking uncontrollably, drenched in sweat, the female was hauled off the bed by the same two guards who brought her. Halfar was back sitting up perusing his holoscreen as if nothing had occurred. He snuck a quick glance at her as she was dragged away by her arms and their eyes locked. Seething hatred for him burned from inside hers so he let the corners of his mouth raise a little in a smirk.

After only a month of the routine Halfar made it known to his men that the female was not allowed back in the brothel and, he imagined to the dismay of the royal washers, required to be bathed in one of the royal chambers. She was never allowed to wear any coverings per his instructions and her indifference towards it fascinated him. There was no shame in her eyes or demeanor. On a whim he had her DNA analyzed and found it matched one of the warrior clans known for their intimidating size. She was obviously a runt, in the end doing royal service for the palace.

Halfar turned to her one evening while she lay exhausted and angry, pretending to seem unfazed.

"What is your name?"

It seemed appropriate to know after nearly a year since acquiring her. He could see her face muscles working.

"Rass." She didn't turn to face him.

"Hmm. It's no secret that I enjoy torturing you but I want to see something more." He saw her tense up preparing for another fight. He laughed. "If you submit to me, I will let you train with the royal guard." Her fingers clutched the bed covers beneath her. "You must come to my bed chamber whenever I request and in return, if you are able to advance, I will release you of your bond to become a royal guard."

"Why?" This time, she did turn to look at him.

"You're holding back. This halfhearted fighting you engage in with me is tiring. I want to see the full potential of your hatred unleashed." She raised her eyebrows. "All you need is training to hone the craft of battle."

"But, I have to submit to you?"

"I am your ruler," Halfar replied matter of fact.

He slipped his robe back off and forcibly pulled her to him by her legs, spreading them open around his waist. She started to struggle again as he entered her roughly but stopped after the fourth thrust. Being released from her bonds had to sound appealing and becoming a royal guard more so. Halfar saw a new resolve blossom inside her as he released his seed.

It wasn't long before Rass had beaten most of the first-year guards and killed more than a few that Halfar decided it was time to make him an official royal guard candidate. During training hours, Rass was male and in the evening, female for his pleasure. Their relationship became one of mutual respect and trust as the years unfolded with many of the battle strategies Halfar implemented coming from Rass. He had no regrets bringing the young unknown into his fold.

Since the qualification rounds were closed to all except the participants, with the trainer and Himself as judges, only those involved knew how deadly Rass had become. His speed and agility were unmatched although he did have a rival; another young candidate named Kur who stared from the shadows at Rass with disdain and lust most of the time. Halfar found it amusing.

He began to watch Kur more closely and came to the conclusion that the young soldier had a slew of pent up rage manifesting as superiority. There was a sense of making every battle refined as opposed to mindless barbarism. His attention to aesthetics was intriguing, his fighting skills, frightening.

On a battle session day, Halfar pulled one of the trainers aside determined to find out more about the strange, green haired warrior. They both sidestepped an arc of blood splatter that landed near their feet.

"Where does he come from?" Halfar asked the trainer.

"His mother was a worker in the mines. One of the commanders from the lower royal family dragged her off during an inspection for his master. She gave birth in the mines four moons later."

"You need to clarify," Halfar's eyes darkened. This disturbed him greatly.

"The lower royals found out about the child and negotiated with the council to raise him in the palace until he reached the age for military training."

"His mother?"

"Still in the mines, my lord."

"Lovely." Halfar's sarcasm was not lost on the trainer. "I'll have her moved into the palace as a handmaiden. Tell no one."

"Of course, my lord." The trainer bowed low.

Halfar returned to the arena to continue his observations of Kur. The story behind the young soldier's existent made him seethe with anger.

"Royal blood." His forehead creased.

War came soon after Rass and Kur were inducted into the royal guard. A twenty yearlong battle against another race who were on equal footing when it came to fighting superiority. In the end, most of his top warriors and generals were killed in battle so Halfar made a bold decision appointing the two rivals as his new generals. He also did this in part because their troops were one of the few left standing when the fighting ended.

With the interstellar council coming up, it would show his determination to keep Azrom's forces intact and that even the massive loss incurred hadn't lessened their reputation as one of the most feared races in the galaxy.

☀

New Lassa

"Ten years," Chardon, the leader of New Lassa, sighed.

In female form, Chardon stood leaning over the window sill of her new chamber staring out at the fairly revived landscape. The Razznian battle ships that had invaded her planet left many sectors in ruins. To ensure the planet's survival, Chardon added insult to injury by using her powers to wipe out everything. The blast traveled like a wave across the planet, disintegrating plants, flesh and machine. Most of her race were saved from it by taking refuge in underground bunkers designed to withstand it.

She forced her dark blue eyes to adjust in order to see farther across the land. Off in the distance Jaron was scolding Trinon who had to look down at his mother. He stood with that disarming smile on his face which infuriated everyone, even her.

A loud galloping sound came from the corridor outside her chamber and she hung her head in anticipation. Only one ball of energetic species made that kind of ruckus. The door flew open, banging against the wall.

Standing out of breath, black hair whipped around like snakes, was her own child Farin. He wore his usual black body tunic with cloak and shiny leather boots. His pale creamy skin and murky green eyes, which he inherited from his father, were in stark contrast. Nearly the same height as his mother, he was tall and beautiful at the age of twenty.

"Mother!"

"Yes, Farin?"

"I did it!"

Chardon turned to lean back against the window.

"Did what, Farin?"

He grinned. "I climbed the monolith!" Taking a deep breath and exhaling, he said, "And I did it just as fast as Trinon!"

So that's what happened.

Chardon now understood why Jaron was chastising Trinon. Farin was not a manbeast but he did have shiny black talons able to cut through nearly anything. Because of their sleekness, he could never get a grip on the giant slate that stood as high as a mountain. All the manbeasts practiced on it. She could only imagine the damage done to its surface by Farin's exuberance.

"Is that so?" Chardon crossed her arms and waited.

She didn't have to wait long. Her bodyguard, and Trinon's father, Modas, came into the room looking none too happy. A quick glance at her followed by a short bow was all she got before he launched into his complaint.

"Your child sliced through most of the monolith trying to climb it," Modas said through gritted teeth.

"So I heard."

"We need someone who can repair it before it starts to shift from the cracks and collapses."

"Aren't you being overdramatic?"

"No," Modas replied. His teeth still clenched. "I am not."

Farin's excited expression turned to dread and Chardon almost felt bad for her silly son. What made her not pay it any mind was Modas' behavior on the matter. He had been going off the rails lately and everyone made attempts to keep him in check. All nearly seven feet of his frame shook with indignation.

"I will see to it." Chardon pushed herself from the window sill and walked over to him. "It is a piece of slab, Modas, regardless of how many generations it has served your species."

That snapped him out of his current state and into one that Chardon found even more offensive: Disgust. It was a 'how dare you' look. A high-pitched whimper from the doorway made the manbeast jerk his head towards Farin. Chardon saw the realization in Modas' eyes and was not surprised when he turned away and strode right out the door.

"Don't worry, Farin. You did nothing wrong. Come."

Chardon opened her arms and Farin ran into them. They stood in an embrace for a moment. When they released each other, both laughed. Further down the corridor, Modas heard their laughter and fumed.

He didn't find it amusing by any means. The monolith was one of the few things salvaged from their original home world and transferred to New Lassa. It had been a training tool for manbeasts for probably centuries, maybe even millennia. No one knew where it came from or how it came to be. Even their hated head scientist, Ganna, had no answers.

Up ahead he watched Trinon walk off away from his mother, unfazed by the lecture. His older brother, Mota, met him and slapped the young manbeast on the back in jest. They had no sense of pride for their history. Both only looked forward and cared nothing for the past. Modas eyes narrowed. They would have to face the past soon enough. His agenda was coming to fruition.

An infant appeared mere centimeters from his face and he stared into the pouty lips of his newly born grandchild who his daughter, Mara, held up proudly. The litter she had been born in had three beast and two energy users. She was, of course, not a manbeast so could never under- stand the plight of man-beasts but he loved her just the same. Grabbing the Lassian child from his daughter's hands, Modas lifted him up higher for closer inspection.

⁎⁎☼⁎⁎

General Kur surveyed the palace grounds from his balcony on the fourth level. He swept his forest green hair off his shoulders and smiled at the progress that had been made. Ten years since the Razznians, attacked Azrom and the planet surface was still in near ruins. Rebuilding the in- side of the palace was complete with the outer wall being the last thing project for repairs. Off in the distance, he could see the villages beyond the barrier wall that separated them from the palace. It angered him to see the suffer-ing of his people knowing it all stemmed from Supreme Ruler Halfar's reign.

The first to be compensated should have been their people. At the council's behest, Halfar made reparations of the palace in its entirety a priority over everything else. Kur found his judge-ment lacking in reason. The same happened when he himself was duped by the royal council into launching a coup against Halfar while on Earth. Instead of finding the root cause, Halfar had commanded Rass to dispatch him, without consideration for their history together. Despite the cruelty of it and how Rass' decision would sway, Halfar had insisted. In the end, it only brought them closer physically and philosophically. Both were on the same page when their supreme ruler was involved.

Footsteps echoed behind him and he turned to see Rass stroll-ing towards him, head down in deep thought. A tightening in his groin had him trying to restrain his urges. Rass aroused him often these days by simply being near, especially now with his jet black wavy hair, now down to his waist, brushing against his hips as he walked. Those small pink lips pursed in frustration made Kur lick his own. Rass finally looked up and Kur straightened his posture.

"What troubles you, general?" Kur asked playfully.

"Halfar."

"Hmm. Is he opposing some random council agenda?"

"On the contrary, he's adopting one. It is to further restrict the royal families from the main sector of the palace."

"For what reason?" Kur was suspicious.

"No clue. I have a feeling something is coming and it won't be beneficial to our race."

"That is a given." Kur tilted his head. "Bond with me."

Rass's eyes went wide and he stared at him for a long time.

"Why did you ask that?"

"Because I want you."

"Have you gone insane?" Rass seethed.

Kur stepped closer to him. They locked eyes.

"No." He ran his fingers in Rass's hair. "I want you and no one else."

"This is not the time," Rass whispered.

"When will it be?" Kur snapped. He took a breath. "There is no reason to wait."

He watched the conflict on Rass' face then saw clarity. Rass sighed heavily.

"Then I will be yours."

Filled with a sense of relief and jubilation Kur grabbed Rass by the hair and kissed him roughly. He had waited so long to ask that he had feared it would be too late to claim him. Now there were no obstacles. Figuring out what the concept of love encompassed had given him a new understanding of his feelings for Rass.

"You do realize we cannot announce it yet?" Rass said when Kur released him from his grip.

"I know."

All too well.

Halfar would not be happy. In fact, Kur figured there would be a sense of jealousy and that was the last thing he needed; Halfar declaring war on them out of spite. He used a thumb to wipe his moisture from Rass' lips then resumed viewing the palace project.

"What are you thinking?" Rass inquired, leaning over from the side.

"Our people are suffering, yet I am glad the palace is almost complete. That means we can focus on them soon."

"Don't count on that basis, Kur. I heard no intentions in the council meetings to ensure the care of our people outside the wall."

Kur turned to him and saw truth in that statement. The ones supplying the population with rations were the First Royal House and they would be the ones to deal with. This new restriction could be as a result of it. The council's and the royal's agendas did not complement each other.

"I am disappointed. We still have not resolved the issue of the Razznians on Earth either. Halfar says it is under control, but I am not so sure." Kur drummed his fingers on the ledge.

"Halfar could care less about Earth. The humans who worked for us are just keeping tabs and making sure the Razznians don't interfere in his organizations flow of revenue."

"I always hated that concept of currency. It is only one of three planets we know of that have it and those races always end up destroying themselves because of it." Kur grinned. "So, no revenge tactics?"

"He believes we have dealt a big enough blow."

"Has he forgotten the other part of the equation?" Kur asked. Rass raised an eyebrow at him. "The Dreridians. He advised us that a plan was in the works for holding them jointly responsible for the attacks."

"That plan," Rass stood up straight, "is no longer in play."

"The council," Kur snorted.

"They believe we have more important issues to attend to."

"Then, if the Razznians regroup and come back to avenge the devastation of their home world?"

"We would be wholly unprepared," Rass finished.

Razznians on Earth

Small flickers resembling candle light shining in various windows of an old rundown building could be seen from the road. Nestled in thick brush amongst large trees, the place was in a remote part of town just on the outskirts of the city. A perfect hiding place for the illegal operations of some fifty employees housed inside: drug makers, drug runners and bodyguards.

As far as the state was concerned, the building was an abandoned shell with no electricity or active plumbing and Sars wanted to make sure it stayed that way. So far, they had been free and clear for over three years.

In the farthest room towards the back was a tiny dingy office set up with a metal desk and three chairs. Sars, Razznian commander and spy, sat behind the desk. After his team of eight fled captivity from the Azrom dungeons during the battle they arrived on Earth. He brought more of his race over the years as business boomed. He found illegal trade was the way to go and his only competition was Halfar's organization with its deep ties to the crime world.

Since his crews worked only at night, staying hidden from humans was not hard and now other aliens resided on Earth. The thing about opening gateways was that they could possibly be detected by off-worlders. Unlike the other aliens who could blend with humans more or less, their reptilian appearance, scaly skin and lidless eyes, scared most away whenever they were actually seen.

The ones who were a threat, his crew ate. Humans really were quite tasty but it wasn't about good eating. Razznian code was to eliminate your enemy and eat what you kill. Leave no remains for ceremony.

"Sir," one of his subordinates called to him.

His third officer had been on a handheld communicator

with a colleague. They had opted for low tech, voice only ones.

"Hmm?"

"We got cops sniffing around again."

"Where?"

"Our second branch in the city. There's gonna' be a raid of the apartment building tomorrow night."

Sars snorted at the Razznian's speech. Many had adopted the phonetics of the region for good reason but it still sounded odd coming from a reptile. He had done some research on the Earth species similar to theirs and the human reactions to them since alien refuse had contaminated many of the waters on the planet. It made him feel good to know, even though not evolved, his kind were above humans on the food chain.

"Who tipped them?" Sars had a good idea who.

"One of those Shadow observers working with Halfar's organization."

"Still trying to get us off this rock, huh? Make sure it's empty. I don't want any casualties this time."

"Yes sir."

He went back out into the hallway with his handheld.

Only twenty or so Razznians had lost their lives on Earth but Sars wasn't comfortable with any. For each soldier's death, another had to replace them. He kept a strict number of teams to ensure stability. Halfar ran his operation on Earth with an iron fist, inducing economic and physical fear. Sars liked to keep under the radar. There were rumors heard throughout the city about a brutal drug gang that even law enforcement feared and Sars smiled at that. No need to go out of your way to instill terror when it spread naturally.

Another subordinate peeked his head around the doorway.

"This week's batch is complete and packaged up."

"Good. Get ready to move out. Rendezvous with the second branch. They are going to have to work on the streets for a while."

"Yes sir."

Sars stood up, as did his two lieutenants. They all wore dark red hoodies, dark pants and red sneaker boots. It was the best attire for working in the cloak of night. He usually didn't go out with the runners but from time to time he liked to keep tabs on how the operation was going.

"Kill the portables," he instructed.

The remote-controlled LED lamps causing the flickers of light were distinguished with the push of a button. Throwing his hood over his head, Sars followed his crew out the door.

The city was alive for a weeknight which Sars translated into decent sales. He had expected a slow turn but was glad for the surprise. His first lieutenant, who had been with him since nearly birth, stood by, a serious look on his face as he scanned the area for threats. After the infiltration of Azrom, his team had a new level of protection for him that, in his book, bordered on possessiveness. At least one or more of them was never father than five hundred feet away.

Transactions were looking good so far. Each dealer was calm and smooth, making sure they kept their heads down so the buyer didn't accidently see their faces.

"Remember the first five years on Earth?" He asked his first lieutenant. The veteran soldier nodded.

"We have come a long way."

"It's good we figured out after a year that we needed to be in a larger populated city. We nearly ate through that one sector."

"I'm surprised the government ruled it as an unknown epidemic and not mass slaughter."

"Mmm." his lieutenant replied. "It may be because the wounds were not from human or animal bites and once infected did appear diseased."

"That may be true. But there are other aliens on this rock."

"Yes, but they don't eat humans."

Sars glanced over at him. "Not that they know of." He decided to switch the conversation. "Any word on Razzna?"

"Yes."

"Why haven't you told me?" Sars exclaimed.

He searched the soldier's face for signs of a good reason.

"The truth?"

"Obviously!"

"I felt it would distract you. We all want to go home but only a third of the planet is habitable at the moment. A sector furthest from the blast is almost ready but so much has to be rebuilt and being on the outs with the Dreridians means we can't negotiate terms."

Sars hissed in defeat. He knew it would come to this and he was still trying to come up with a solution. From the reports he had heard their ruler said as much. Since the deal with the now deceased Lassian, Sestis, went south leaving Razzna still in dire need, doing the bidding of the Dreridians seem optimal.

Sestis hated the manbeast of her race and brokered a deal that should have seen both sides happy. Halfar, on the other hand dealt a major blow by destroying the planet Lassa along with her. Being far more advanced in technology and commerce, the Dreridians agreed to continue her original plan with some minor adjustments. The successful infiltration of Azrom would have been payment for a new automated system for their mines. No need for the enslavement of Lassian manbeasts or any other race for that matter.

"I understand your concern. You're right. I will find a way to negotiate with the Dreridians. A deal that won't see us enslaved ourselves."

"And Azrom?"

"Oh, I'm sure Halfar has all but forgotten about us and the Dreridians. He will be in for a rude awakening. The Dreridians do nothing for free and when they do not get what they want," Sars didn't finished.

****☼****

Azrom

The gateway's dark pool of stars rippled before turning into a black gaping hole. Light glowed from the center of darkness and four figures emerged from the vortex onto the palace platform where Halfar stood waiting to greet them.

Chardon, Farin, Modas and Trinon, stepped onto the roof. Halfar could not believe Farin was the same child. Now twenty years old, still a baby by Azrom measure, he stood at six feet with creamy skin and long black hair, stunningly beautiful as ever. Farin smiled wide and rushed over to him.

"Father!" His voice was still an octave too high for Halfar's liking.

"Farin," Halfar wrapped his arms around him and squeezed.

Chardon walked over to him, the two manbeasts following dutifully behind her. He could see a kind of tiredness in her eyes and knew it was from the stress of the invasion of New Lassa. Even Modas seemed deflated. Azrom was not the only planet the Razznians ravaged. Farin let go and ran off across the platform then down the corridor, Trinon in pursuit.

"He's in good spirits," Chardon quipped.

"Did something happen on Lassa?"

"No. He's just glad to spend time with you. It's not something he can do often."

"I know. We are still trying to fix things."

Halfar turned his attention to Modas still standing in quiet defiance. The manbeast and he had a mutual disdain for each other so they both nodded in acknowledgement. If there was a way to get rid of him without death, Halfar had not found it yet. He caught Chardon's expression and motioned her to him.

"Come, bask in my arms." Chardon leaned into him as he gently folded his arms around her. "Are you well? I worry about you."

"Just tired trying to keep council members from murdering Ganna."

"That is a hard task." Halfar kissed her softly. "Why don't you rest for the remainder of the day?"

"I will."

Halfar saw Modas frown knowing he would not allow him to watch over Chardon in their personal chamber. He decided to give the man- beast a gift this once.

"If you could make sure she is not disturbed, I would be grateful," Halfar said to him.

Modas lifted his brow in disbelief. Halfar almost laughed at him but kept it in.

"Of course," Modas replied.

They left the platform and headed down the corridor to the main palace. Four royal guards fell in step behind them as they rounded the curve.

Reconfiguration

Azrom's colorful flowers were bustling atop high pedestals in every corner of the banquet hall. Halfar felt a wave of nausea hit him as he watched the royal families in full regal attire trying to impress each other, fawning over fabric and design. He scanned the hall and noticed the first royal house not participating in the spectacle. They appeared bored and as their first cousin, he understood their stance of just going through the motions.

At the center of the first house clan sat Romnus. Both their fathers, as brothers, fought for supremacy for nearly two centuries until Romnus' father's death in battle. Halfar knew that if Romnus had not bowed out of the fight for rulership, he would be Supreme Ruler at this moment and that alone made him wary of the first house's intentions. So far, they were silent on the new policies he had proposed regarding segregation amongst the royal families.

Another cousins, Lord Chastan, was already drinking. His eyes leered at the lesser royal females. He came from his mother's side which is why his hair was dark blond with deep waves, worn short. Halfar remembered when Chastan had stared at Chardon with the same lust and it made his blood boil. The man had no shame or restraint.

One of his advisors, Dondar, came forward and whispered, "My lord, it is almost time for the appreciation ceremony. Shall I get them lined up?"

Halfar nodded and Dondar alerted the guards with his own.

"Bow and address our Supreme Ruler!" The captain of his royal guard yelled.

The hall went silent and all in attendance turned to Halfar seated on his throne and bowed low responding with, "My Lord!" They stood waiting for him to acknowledgement their greeting.

"Resume," said Halfar waving his hand at them.

Halfar wished Chardon and Farin were in attendance but his council suggested otherwise. With the appreciation ceremony they advised it would look like he was flaunting the alliance of non Azromians. He found it a little insulting but obliged. There was no need for unnecessary strife during the rebuilding process. He barely heard the shameless drivel of his courts singing his praise as they prostrated before him.

"Well, that was a farce of a banquet," Chastan slurred.

Walking in stride together the First Royal House members made their way back to their palace. There were seven in all with two females; Chastan's sister, Kuhala and Romnus' half-sister, Reita. At the end of the banquet Romnus made sure they were the first to get up and leave by giving the signal with a glance. He kept watch on Chastan as he weaved down the corridor, the only thing stopping him from tilting over was being wedged between two bodies.

"It was quite informative," Romnus said. "I found it very telling how the third house prostrated themselves at Halfar's feet like slaves."

"Bottom feeders," Reita, scoffed.

She stood almost the same height as him and was just as deadly in combat. Her dark hair was pulled back into a tight ponytail that hung down her back.

"There is not one among them that can challenge us for the throne."

Romnus looked sideways at her and raised an eyebrow. Surely she wasn't implying that a call to overthrow Halfar was in order? If so, he would have to pull her aside and make her understand it is not something she could voice out loud. He too felt the same way but it was not time.

"I could wipe them out for you, cousin," Chastan said in a temporary state of lucidity.

"Of course you can," his sister, Kuhala, snorted.

"Let's just see how those new policies of his pan out," Romnus added.

He couldn't figure out the council's agenda knowing Halfar had not come up with the idea of segregation. Something was missing in the equation and he needed to find out before mayhem ensued.

Why are you not ruling, cousin?
Azrom's future bode ill at this junction.

Chardon could not keep her eyes open no matter how much she tried. They felt heavy along with the rest of her body. She had not been able to rest this well in a long time and it was overdue. After a few blinks, she was able to open them narrowly without having to squint. A dark blur in the corner of the room cleared up, as her vision focused, to show Modas leaning silently against the wall. He was watching over her as usual.

"Why are you so far away?" Chardon whispered.

"I was instructed not to disturb you."

"You never have. And since when did you start taking orders from Halfar?"

"It was not an order, it was a request. He is not my leader."

Something about the way he said it sent a chill in her spine. He was not being himself lately. She watched him unmoving, brooding even.

"What is wrong with you? Why are you being so distant?" She snapped.

Modas looked up at her and his face scrunched up.

"You wouldn't understand. It is an issue that only concerns manbeasts."

"Manbeasts are Lassians! So, it does concern me!"

The effort to yell made Chardon light headed and she closed her eyes. That mentality al- ways infuriated her and she had no idea where it came from. Sensing Modas move closer she felt a little relief. He was her bodyguard from childhood and knew he would always be by her side.

Modas

Lassa 150 years ago

Trails of flowers were left behind the leader of Lassa and his mate as they walked down the pathway leading to the council chamber. Two field workers on either side of them scattered handfuls from a woven basket hooked over their arms. Up ahead, two council members waited at the arched entrance to greet them.

"They seem nervous, my love," his mate whispered.

"Of course. I like to make my intentions known."

"We do need a new bodyguard, especially for our young son."

"I am sure, the council and the manbeasts will comply."

The two councilmen bowed slightly and held their arms out gesturing towards the corridor ahead. Down further was the door of the council chamber. Once inside, they made themselves comfortable on the floor cushions at the end of the table. Off to their right was the leader of the manbeasts, with two of his subordinates, his large frame taking up two places. On the left were four council members.

"Midday is a great time for negotiations," the leader stated.

"What brings us together this day?"

"I have just come from the combat trials and saw a splendid manbeast take the title. Your son, Modas. Extraordinary."

"I thank you. He has worked hard."

The leader turned to the council.

"I want to have him removed from the battle roster and placed in my entourage. I'm sure you can accept whoever was runner up."

"As can you," Modas' father retorted. "My son is fit for battle, not babysitting."

"I concur, leader," the councilman said. "We need strong

warriors like Modas. Putting him on your detail would be a waste of talent."

The leader was taken aback by the display of resistance to his request. "I am not asking for your approval! I am the leader of this race and want my family protected by the best."

"You are not being reasonable," the second councilman started to complain.

"The answer is no."

They all turned to the manbeast as he said it and the leader saw a look of resolve on his face. He would not budge, that was clear. Angry but not ready to give up, the leader stood as did his mate.

"This discussion is far from over. I will get what is to be mine."

"My son is not yours."

As the leader left the council chamber, a wicked plan crept into his head. He smiled, kissing his mate on the forehead. Not yet, but he will be. There was a small faction of Lassians who had no love for the man- beasts and he knew they would assist.

Modas rushed into his family's outdoor chamber and quickly stripped off his robes. He was covered in sweat and soil from combat training. There was very little time for him to freshen up and head for evening meal but he made haste. Still young yet old enough for battle, he was not at his full height. His father assured him many times that he would grow another foot in the coming years. With no time for washing his mane, he pulled pieces of twigs and debris out, using his fingers to comb it.

Evening meal was a din of noise. Eight manbeasts, seven of them his siblings, were seated on cushions around the table as they grabbed helpings of the steaming meat and vegetables off the serving platters. Modas squeezed in between two of his older brothers and did the same. His father turned to him, their eyes locked.

"The leader made a request for you today."

"A mission?"

"No." His father took a bite of meat and chewed loudly. When he was done, he continued. "He wants you to babysit his family."

"And you said no."

"Of course he said no," his oldest brother yelled. "You are a warrior. We need you in times of battle."

"They have been getting less over the past few decades. Nothing extreme," his younger brother interjected. "Maybe he can be on standby."

The rest of his family looked at the young one and Modas nearly laughed. They were not sure if his younger brother was kidding or just naïve. He on the other hand felt both arguments were correct. Escorting the leader's family around was not ideal. There was no adventure in that. But, with not many battles occurring, he could see why their leader made the request. The question was, 'why me?' Modas couldn't help feeling there was an alternative motive.

"I agree, father. I am of more use on the battlefield."

His father nodded in agreement and the conversation was over. It was time to eat.

Tired from a battle, Modas, along with the other manbeasts, went to their chambers to sleep. Their leader had congratulated his father with a small private meal and invited the family. It had been a short stint, lasting only a few days with worthy opponents. Modas nearly faltered as he got closer to his bed. He was satiated, full beyond reason. As his head hit the cushions, his body grow heavy and he fell asleep.

Danger!

He could feel it. His body would not move the way he wanted as he tried to lift himself off the bed. With every fiber of his being, he forced his adrenaline to push aside whatever was coursing through his veins and catapulted out of his room. Screams, along with roars of battle cries rang throughout the chamber. His speed had been cut by half but fast enough to carry him out into the night air.

Blood splattered on him, covering his whole body and he stopped cold. A Lassian warrior pulled his longsword out of the deep diagonal cut it had made across his father's chest and the great manbeast fell backwards dead onto the ground by his feet. On the sides of his family chamber other Lassian warriors held back the manbeasts who had been awakened by the sounds. Modas could see their eyes were not focused and realized they too had been drugged.

With a howl that frightened the Lassians to halt where they stood, their mission complete, Modas attacked with a new-found ferocity. Within seconds he ripped apart every Lassian warrior in his vicinity, not giving them time to prepare themselves. As he cut the last one, ready to move on to the ones holding his fellow manbeasts at bay, four darts flew into his chest. Stunned he looked at them, stopping for a moment, but resumed his advance. Four more struck him in other parts of his body and with a thud, he hit the ground. He could taste the soil as it entered his mouth, his vision blurring as a Lassian warrior knelt down beside him.

"This is an atrocity!" The head of the military council yelled.

The meeting chamber was filled to capacity with angry Lassians. There was no doubt who had facilitated the assault yet there was nothing to be done about it now that their leader was apparently out of control.

"He will be assassinated for certain," one of his colleagues said. "And I won't lift a finger to stop it!"

"How do we remedy this?" The head of the science council asked.

"We don't," he snapped.

Surprising them was the sound of the chamber door swinging open to reveal their leader standing in the doorway, his mate attached to his arm. He smiled as if nothing was amiss which they all understood he surely knew.

"Councilmen! It is such glorious weather this day! Why are you congregating in the meeting room so early?"

A councilman moved towards him and another grabbed his arm to stop him. The two men met each other's gaze and the suppressor shook his head. Sitting back down, he took a deep breath and exhaled slowly. The head of the military council looked up at his leader with disgust but decided to play his game.

"Have you not heard? A manbeast family was attacked and slaughtered."

"Oh?" Their leader raised his brow and feigned sadness. "How disgraceful. Obviously another manbeast clan over some dispute."

"That is the report from the Lassian warriors who went to assist in diffusing the situation."

"Were there any survivors?"

"One. The young warrior, Modas."

"Is that so?" The leader stepped into the chamber and tapped his bottom lip. "Well, as leader of our race, I feel it is my duty to take the young thing in under my wing."

Another councilman's hands began to glow and his neighbor swatted it, also shaking his head. The military head was at a loss for what to do. The last thing he wanted was for Modas to be in the hands of the one person who had his family murdered. He looked around at his colleagues and was surprised to see nods of approval. Then he understood.

"Yes, that may be fair. You are obligated to do so, after all."

"Indeed. He will no doubt be in grief for some time and not fit for battle. I believe he would find solace in being a personal body guard to my family."

Silence engulfed the room.

"If that is all, you should really get out and enjoy the weather."

"We have to appoint a new leader for the manbeast council."

"Oh, yes. Then get on with it. Just don't take too long. The sun can't wait forever."

With that, the leader and his mate left the council chamber.

"For the love of Lassa!" A council member slammed his fist on the table.

"I know!" Another shouted. "I know, but we must remain patient."

"If he dies, his son becomes leader," the head of science spoke.

"That's fine, we can handle him when the time comes," the head of military stated. "He's still just a child and we can mold him."

"Then we let it run its course?"

"As we concluded, someone will assassinate our leader eventually."

"Hopefully sooner than later."

A sea of darkness engulfed Modas as he sat yet could feel movement around him. Tiny sounds filtered through every now and again but he paid no heed. An emptiness had swallowed him and he had no way of filling it. Images of his family's last meal together in their home flickered in fragments. He felt the stinging of tears, unable to wipe them away.

Hands. Small ones, soft and smooth, planted on his cheeks. They didn't go away even when Modas forced his eyes open to see what and who was in front of him. Slowly, his vision came back, the light hurting his eyes and sitting in front of him was the leader's son, Chardon. His creamy slightly tanned skin and auburn hair appeared to shimmer. Blue eyes, dark as the sky at dusk, stared back at him.

"Don't cry anymore. I'll stay with you," Chardon said.

"What?" He asked.

His own voice sounded like the crunching of dry soil and deduced it was because he was indeed parched.

Before he could recover, Chardon threw his arms around his neck and hugged him. When the young teenage boy released him there was a small smile on his face and Modas still didn't understand why.

"Come along, young Chardon," a servant called. She was by the doorway waiting for him.

Chardon stood up, still smiling, then raced out of the chamber, the servant following not far behind him. Modas was left slumped on the floor with tears drying as they streaked down his face. Another servant came over and set a bowl of food in front of him.

"Please," she said. "I know you are hurting, but you must eat. You need your strength more than anyone." The servant also laid a hand on his cheek. "This was a horrible tragedy but you must endure," she looked around her then back at him, "for now."

Modas eyes went wide as he watched her leave. Alone in the room he let his gaze scan the area. It was not much, just a small chamber with a window, a bed and a chair. The washing area was hidden behind a curtain along the side wall. His stomach growled like an angry beast and he finally took a closer look at the bowl before him. Using his fingers, he dug into it and ate every morsel, wiping the bowl clean.

Rage crept back inside him. This time, he suppressed it. For now. Those words echoed in his mind and the pieces locked together, making him determined about what needed to happen.

I must bide my time. The right moment will come.

His vision blurred and the room tilted sideways. The food had been drugged. He did not fault her for doing so because if she hadn't, he might have gone and ruined everything. He needed to sleep this time, not be catatonic in a void of his own making. As he drifted off into sleep, he saw Chardon's smiling face.

On the grassy section of the leader's property, he stood waiting for the head servant to escort him into the family's main chamber. He wore a blue chi mere over a simple brown sleeved robe fastened at the waist with a black sash. No more need for his battle robes and body tunic. If one did break out, he wasn't sure he could muster the will to fight. He had to attend to Chardon and his cousin, Jaron, on most days, never really trying to know who they were as individuals. Over the past few years, he had grown fond of them, Chardon more so than the other. There was a strange form of lust that emitted from the leader's son. Modas felt their species too different even though they were all Lassians. Something about that thought jarred him and he remembered the Lassian warriors who slaughtered his family. No, they were not alike in any way. Footsteps from the hallway behind inside the door made him turn.

The night before, he had gone to check on Chardon and found the young man sitting on his darkened chamber's floor stripped naked with a bed covering barely hiding the lower half. When Chardon turned, Modas realized it was not a young man, but a female who sat before him. The initial shock was broken by Chardon's voice, dripping with honey as she asked, "Am a just as pretty?" Her skin was flushed, the hair around her temple wet with sweat and he could only imagine what she had been doing.

Contemplating her question, he remembered the day before when he told Jaron how pretty she was and Chardon was in the vicinity of the conversation. He looked down at Chardon again and felt the stirring of desire within him. This is wrong. He swiped his hands down his face.

"Yes, Chardon, you are very pretty."

Sensing a presence in the doorway he turned to see the leader standing there looking down on his child with such disgust that he flinched. It was like he wasn't in the room, the leader's gaze was so focused.

"Kila!" the leader yelled. Chardon's servant came running and stopped cold. "Get that thing covered and make sure it's back in male form!"

The stare moved to Modas and he saw it as a signal to leave. Hurrying towards the door he found the leader had somehow already left.

Now he stood waiting to be either praised or chastised, the summons not giving any details on which way the conversation would go. The head servant came out and gestured for him to follow. He had been in the family chamber only a few times, the first nearly a moon after the death of his family.

Most Lassian décor was simple with modest furniture and small vases of fresh picked flowers. The leader had a different flare. Too many colors, overly large furniture and flower petals everywhere. One day he had almost slipped on the floors from a cluster of them beneath his feet. Inside the main living area, the leader sat alone on multiple cushions at the low table.

"Sit," the leader commanded.

"I would prefer to stand. I must not be long, having to escort Chardon soon."

The leader turned and stared at him angrily but Modas didn't waver. He was not intimidated by the man and refused to show otherwise.

"We have a secret in our midst and it needs to remain so."

"I'm not sure I understand."

"Leaders are chosen because they are unchanging, resolved to their will and person."

Modas pursed his lips. Whatever the man was getting at, he felt threatened.

"That said, as much as I love my mate, her bloodline is tainted. It became apparent when Chardon was nearly twelve that he was a shifter."

Modas relaxed his face and inhaled slowly.

That's all? I'm getting a history lesson?

The leader's face conveyed something else.

"No one," the leader yelled, "is to know about this! Not even our scientists!"

The volume of his voice raised flags of danger in Modas,

especially when the leader got up and came so close they exchanged breaths, locking eyes with him.

"You think I don't know how you lust after my son and his cousin? A filthy manbeast drooling, wanting to covet the flesh of our elite? You will never," he emphasized the last word, "touch them! You'll never have them. What you will do is protect my child, always, even when he is leader. You swore an oath and it will be honored."

As the leader stepped back and returned to his cushion, Modas' eyes narrowed.

"I did make an oath, but not to you." He watched the leader move to get back up. "It was for Chardon alone and I will protect him, always."

With that, he turned and left the chamber, tuning out the outbursts coming from the leader.

In the dark of night, on a hillside far away from the village, Modas held a meeting of manbeasts. He had set the date for it nearly a moon ago and only invited those he felt would benefit his cause. There were forty in attendance, all dissatisfied with Chardon's leadership and angry about the past transgressions of his father.

"I don't need to tell you that what is said here cannot be spoken out- side this circle," he began. They nodded in agreement so he continued. "As some of you know, my family was murdered at the request of our leader's father." Loud murmurs resounded. "The cores of their bloodline and the Lassians who participated are tainted and must be eradicated."

A curtain of dark fell along with the absence of sound and Modas felt uneasy for the first time since setting his agenda in motion. He understood some manbeasts were not comfortable with the plan but it would be for the greater good of Lassa.

"I know some of you have mates who are not manbeasts, as do I, but we must be united as a race to ensure this does not happen ever again."

Lights formed on the trail below the hilltop and a group of workers strode by. Fearing what the unsuspecting Lassians may report, Modas twirled a finger in the air signaling his manbeast to disperse. He would have to set up another meeting soon.

Off in the distance, Talas stood with one leg set atop a large boulder as he stared out at the hilltop covered in manbeasts, Modas at the helm. He knew what the manbeast was up to and didn't need the earlier hint from Trinon. Sestis had told him the story of the massacre and was not surprised when Modas started to act strange. The version she told about manbeasts going on a rampage, killing Lassian warriors, did not add up so he filled in the gaps and came to the truth. Modas' vendetta was pointless and unjustified in his book. To hold something for so long against the dead and take it out on their descendants was something Talas could not fathom.

"Have you gone mad, manbeast?" he asked aloud of Modas to himself.

Below him Trinon and Und were leaning against the rock bed he stood on. They looked up at him in unison then walked off towards their family chamber that sat two miles ahead of them. Talas shook his head in exasperation. Modas was making things more complicated than need be and he wondered what the manbeast hoped to accomplish. The outcome would be a fissure between every class and a distrust like no other. Modas would lose everything; his mate, his children, loyalty.

Talas turned away from the valley and headed down, carefully climbing the cragged surface the same way he had come up. Kelin was waiting for him when he landed on solid ground.

"Did you see what you came for?" He asked.

"Plenty. I fear the worst."

"Come home. There is nothing to be done now. Our little one is asleep although," Kelin smiled. "I'm sure he wouldn't mind being awakened and held for a while."

Talas smiled back. Being a mother and warrior was not something he had gotten used to yet. Then he frowned, thinking of Modas' agenda. He was endangering everyone, including children. This made Talas' indifference turn to anger.

Oreridian Dreams

Being found out was never a big deal for the Razznians on Earth because they were able to locate and then just eat the person who may report their location. The special task forces coming out of the woodworks were making it harder. Of course, they were still no match for Razznians. Sars speculated it was Halfar's organizations doing the pushing since apparently aliens could sniff out others fairly easy.

"How are we doing on funds," Sars asked his first Lieutenant.

His unit met in the back room of a local dive they owned on the out- skirts of the city. Humans rarely entered the place because the reviews cited the atmosphere as 'bloodthirsty'. Sars nodded in agreement of the tag while he waited for a reply.

They have no idea how true that is.

"A little over four hundred million."

"Not enough. I believe Halfar controlled nearly a billion at the tail end of his so-called tenure. No, we need to take a larger chunk of the tristate area."

"We do have an in to branch out into the other states across the continent."

"Not yet, too soon. Any new raids?"

"Two. We were able to hold off the task force and," he chuckled, "it is reported that they are too scared to try again. Some of the officers quit and others are traumatized, deemed unfit for duty."

"I guess that is a plus." Sars paced the room for a bit. "How much merchandise can we create in the next two weeks?"

"About twenty kilos?"

"I may be able to negotiate a buyer." Sars smiled. His rows of sharp teeth exposed.

"For that much?"

"Our product is addictive yet does not have the same harmful side effects as human narcotics. Yes, I know a small group who would love to have it."

His crew stared at him in awe and doubt. He understood why. It was a large order and they had four really good distributors who couldn't handle that kind of load. The plan was to get on equal if not greater footing than Halfar after he learned of what the Azrom ruler was up to on Earth. This new idea of his would put them closer to that goal.

"I believe we can accomplish all our tasks at hand in the coming years."

"How will this help us get Razzna back on track?"

"Alien species like to chemically escape too."

"Ahh!" His crew replied together.

"This will be a sample shipment then?" His second officer asked.

"But will they even negotiate with us?" His first lieutenant also asked.

"Dreridians are always willing to negotiate. As long as they get something in return." Sars saw his crew relax even in the face of the daunting task of making twenty kilos on top of what their distributors had already ordered. It will work itself out.

✲

Lord Pondur, ruler of the Dreridian system, set his chalice down on the conference table. He glanced at his treasurer who in turn looked up at him.

A meeting had been called after a decade of no response from the Razznians and it was brought to his attention that the coup on Azrom was part failure and success. Both planets suffered damage but Azrom sent a devastating blow to Razzna, an overly aggressive one. He was aware of both side's inability to fight fair but this had gone too far. When it disrupted commerce and the flow of goods, it affected his worlds and he would not tolerate it.

"Payment is due, yet we cannot collect," his treasurer announced.

"And why is that?"

"At first, the Razznians seemed to have disappeared, leaving their solar system. There has been some activity on Razzna recently. It looks like they are only shipping in architects and scientists."

"That is not surprising. They need to find a way to sustain

their race until Razzna's surface can be fully repaired."

"It has also come to our attention that New Lassa's surface was nearly destroyed as well, by their leader's own power."

Lord Pondur pursed his already thin lips, the crags on his face deepening. "I could never understand Lassians." He found it fascinating that they were able to survive and relocate after Halfar so selfishly sent a planet bomb, killing the world completely. "New Lassa, is it?"

"Who should we contact for barter, my lord?" The treasurer inquired.

"All of them."

"My Lord?"

"The Lassians, Azrom and Razzna."

"But, New Lassa had nothing to do with the original negotiations and Azrom was the target. I am not following the logic, my lord. Please forgive my ignorance in this matter."

"Simple. It started with that Lassian whore, regardless of her death. She did it on behalf of her race. Azrom has essentially stopped mining operations on Razzna, which means their minerals which only come from Razzna, are now a rare commodity. Of course, Razzna accepted the goods requested by Sestis and used them. So, all of them."

"Very good, my lord. I understand now."

As the treasurer leaned over his screen to do calculations, his head of science, Lord Greggor, entered the room. Lord Pondur saw him eye the hunched over figure at the table, questioning. Lord Greggor's skin was more cragged with deeper valleys in between and thicker yellow curved talons, his girth twice the normal size of their race. Lord Pondur wondered what the scientist was eating until he remembered past experiments involving other species.

No need to continue that train of thought, he chided himself.

"Is the new treasurer doing well?"

"Hmm, he is learning quite fast. He will take some getting used to."

"My Lord," Greggor began, "we really need to send out a search unit for the Razznians. I have come up with a fail proof system."

"Have you? Then by all means, find them."

"And then?"

"Then what?" Lord Pondur watched his head scientist stare at him cruelly. "Ah. Well that poses a problem doesn't it?" He came around the table to stand in front of Greggor. "If we can repair Razzna, then it would be easy to barter a transfer of rulership. Temporary of course."

"One hundred years, maybe?"

"Sounds like ample enough time to get them back on their scaly hides and pay off their debts."

"What about Azrom? They seem to be angry at us for supplying the Razznians with the equipment. They think we had an ulterior motive."

"Which we still do."

"How about we charge them the same as the Razznians?" The treasurer asked. His slender frame came up for air from gazing intently at his screen.

"Their ores are of high grade but I would not want to be ambassador on that decrepit rock for any length of time." Lord Pondur waved his hand in defiance.

"Azrom is going through a rough change. It seems there is dissent."

"Halfar will not rule for much longer." Lord Pondur retrieved his chalice and took a sip of his drink. "Didn't I prophecy this two centuries ago?"

"Yes, my lord, you did. Very observant of you."

Lord Pondur raised his glass and tilted it towards Greggor before taking another sip.

"Let Azrom self-destruct first then we go after them for payment."

"May I, my lord?" The treasurer stood up.

"Hmm?"

"I think we should collect payment despite Azrom's troubles. We may not get it in a timely manner. Also," the officer paused, "it would further facilitate their demise making it easier for us to negotiate a rulership pact."

Both Lord Pondur and Greggor raised their brows at each other and made a small nod. Lord Greggor was the first to speak.

"Impressive."

"You may be worth more than I suspected," Lord Pondur addressed the treasurer.

"Thank you, my lord."

"See to it, then."

The treasurer sat back down and resumed his calculations. Lord Pondur smiled and Lord Greggor helped himself to a drink. It was going to be a prosperous century.

TWO:
A COMING STORM

Whispers

Lord Romnus strolled the palace corridors with his entourage which also included his handmaid, Biandra. He wore his cloak draped around his shoulders, a show of defiance against Halfar's new rule for the royal family to always be presentable. As Halfar's first cousin, Romnus had always tried to be respectful of his decisions when he took the throne, but this new rule left something to be desired. He couldn't help feeling at a loss.

Biandra, handed him a small fruit and he took it without looking down at her. He towered over her by nearly a foot and wondered she how appeared, her smaller frame amongst his large group. It had never occurred to him until recently when one of Halfar's guards smacked her down for defending him. Biandra was by no means helpless but seeing the difference in size from that point of view made him angry at himself for not protecting his own people.

Even now, he remained quiet, boiling with rage at the further segregation of the royal family from the main palace. All their movements had been restricted and Romnus had decided to not abide by it, bucking Halfar's new system at every turn. He could feel tension from his entourage.

A high-pitched laugh came from up ahead followed by a streak of cream and black rounding the corner. The stunningly beautiful Farin, in female form, was running at a side angle and not aware of her surroundings. He stopped just in time to see her screech to a halt mere inches from him. Farin quickly bowed, hitting her head on Romnus' chest. He smiled down at the top of the young one's head as he took a bite of the fruit.

"There is no need to bow to me, young Farin. You are royalty as well."

Farin's head whipped back up nearly clipping Romnus in the chin. He watched those strange green eyes go wide with embarrassment and Romnus let out a small laugh.

Oh, cute and beautiful.

He noticed how tall the young royal had grown, standing a little under a foot shy of him.

"Oh, right." Farin grinned.

Not far behind was Trinon looking bored. Romnus could see some- thing had changed in the manbeast, more so than before. A kind of gloom hung around him even though he smiled gleefully. Being Farin's bodyguard had to be tiring, the young one having endless amounts of energy.

"You shouldn't be here. Your father would be upset if you are not in the main palace," Romnus chastised him.

"I'm just exploring," Farin pouted. "Trinon's with me."

Please don't do that.

Romnus felt an aching in the pit of his stomach and took another bite of fruit to distract his desire. Farin in female form was always a pleasure to see but it made him feel not in control of his manners. Filthy thoughts of what he could do to her roamed in his mind.

"None the less, you should hurry back."

He gave Trinon a nod.

"Can I come visit later?" Farin asked.

"Welcome back to Azrom, beautiful Farin," Romnus replied, bowing slightly.

He tsked himself for the dirty thoughts as Farin blushed and ran past, barely missing knocking down his entourage. Halfar would probably try to kill him if he knew how much he wanted Farin. Try was all his cousin could do because Romnus had never been defeated in a fight; especially with regards to Halfar.

Trinon followed Farin at a leisurely pace. Romnus had seen the speed of the young manbeast at the mock battle a decade ago and knew it would take little effort to catch up to Farin.

"Shall we continue, my lord?" Biandra asked, staring up at him.

"My apologies, of course."

Romnus advanced forward. Now he really needed release and they happened to be headed towards the brothel.

✳✲☼✲✳

Tap, tap, tap.

Halfar's taloned fingers struck the throne's armrests in a slow tempo, a frown fixed on his face. He could not fathom how his child had gone off the grid in such a short time. It made him angry that Trinon did not have a tighter leash on Farin. His council had warned him about letting the two roam outside the main palace unescorted. With the new rules he implemented seeming to have only infuriate the royal family more, the council voiced fears that Farin may be targeted for retaliation.

He leaned forward on his throne, straining his ears for the sound of footsteps and within moments, heard the telltale sounds of running feet along with the steady stride of a manbeast. At the entrance appeared Farin, out of breath, with a wide grin on her face.

"Where have you been?" Halfar's voice thundered. He watched the grin turn to shock and fear. "Have I not told you to stay within the main palace walls?"

"I…" Farin began to speak. She looked over at Trinon who smiled back at her. "I'm sorry, Father," she finally sputtered after gaining what looked like a little courage.

Halfar sat back against the throne and let out a loud sigh, finding it tedious to constantly yell at his child's disobedience. Farin was ever moving and curious about everything. The council's suggestion to lock Farin in a secluded wing sounded tempting but he knew Chardon would never forgive him.

"Trinon, escort Farin to her chamber and make sure she does not leave until evening meal." He saw a darkness form on the manbeast's face as he obeyed. Something about it disturbed him. He noticed the change after the Razznian battle.

Three of his royal advisors came forward, bowing low to him and he averted his gaze to see what they wanted. The first, Mesrod, raised his head and cleared his throat.

"My Lord, as fascinating as Farin can be, you must keep that child at bay. At least until she is of mating age."

"It would be a shame for something to happen to her on the palace grounds," the second, Prevcan, added.

"What do you mean?" Halfar was getting agitated by their tone.

"She is quite beautiful and it is no secret what the soldiers have in mind," Dondar, the third member said.

"No one touches my child unless they want death."

"Yes, I agree, my lord, but that doesn't stop them from trying. Once she has been tainted there is no undoing of it," Dondar replied.

Halfar gripped the edges of his throne knowing they spoke the truth. When Farin turned fifteen, he was able to shift forms and become female like his mother. He could feel anxiety creep into him as he watched the first transformation. Farin was indeed too beautiful even for an Azromian.

"I am trying, if you haven't noticed."

"Of course." Mesrod looked over at Dondar and nodded.

"Regarding the royal bloodline," Dondar began, "I believe we should expand your house as much as possible to keep rebellion at bay."

"And you suggest what exactly?"

"Kur is a loyal servant and General of the Armada. He should be brought into the fold to claim his rightful place in the royal house," Prevcan explained.

"Isn't it too soon?" Halfar felt uneasy about telling Kur his origins. It was not a pretty story and Kur just might resent him more than he already did. "He may not be pleased."

"It will be hard at first, but I believe he will come to terms quickly."

"He has great ambition. This will be one step further towards his goal," Mesrod added.

Halfar grimaced, letting the thought stew for a moment in his mind, his eyes on the advisors to see what lay beneath their proposal. They we right about Kur's ambition. He had witnessed the lengths his general would go to firsthand. Another loyal servant in the royal house would be beneficial. His mind made up, he nodded slowly.

"Bring him here quietly. No one else is to be present except the five of us."

"The guards?" Dondar asked.

"Only two shall stay in the hall."

"As you command, my lord." They chanted in sync.

Prevcan, turned and left the hall with two royal guards in tow while Dondar, brought his attention back to Halfar. Something else was obviously on his mind and Halfar had a feeling he won't like it.

"My lord. If I may be so bold. Since you are in the mood for procreating, have you ever considered mating with our own to have a full-blooded heir?"

He fought back a blooming rage as he sat on his throne listening to the advisors' words. No, he didn't like it at all. Sitting upright, Halfar leaned forward.

"Are you suggesting a child of my loins is not of royal blood?"

"I am not implying such a thing at all. But, my lord to be honest, Farin and her young sibling are not full blooded Azromians. They are halfbreeds."

Halfar's arms turned black and sleek, growing in length as his hands morphed into shiny black pincers. The other two remaining advisors stepped away.

"As I said, my lord, I mean no offense. It is just something we as advisors must think about in regards to the royal bloodline."

"Please, my lord," Mesrod said calmly, "royal protocol is different than normal Azrom rules. With the state of our people, surely you understand the concerns."

The claws stopped in midair and Halfar paused his rise off the throne. What they said made sense although it made him feel ill. His father had been adamant about the bloodline during his rule but he, himself, had never paid much attention to the old warrior's rants. Now here he was, the Supreme Ruler, having to deal with all the nastiness it entailed. Retracting his claws, he sat back in the throne.

"I do understand. I just don't want to think about that right now. Let's get through Kur's dilemma first."

He heard sighs of relief escape their lips but he wasn't sure if it was because they skirted death or something else entirely.

⁎⁎☼⁎⁎

"Your presence is requested by Supreme Ruler, Halfar, immediately."

That is what the preening shiny faced royal advisor Prevcan spurted out of his mouth as he walked into Kur's chamber unannounced, disrupting his mating with Rass. With his back still to the entryway, he sat up and turned his head to stare at the man. Every kind of venom he could conjure up in in his mind translated to the look on his face. It worked.

The advisor stepped so far away from the entrance that he bumped into the veranda, nearly falling over backwards into

Azromian air. The drop would have surely kill him. Kur smiled at that.

"What could our lord want at this hour before evening meal?"

"It is urgent, General."

"Should we don our full regalia?" Rass asked, sitting up.

"No. Just you are requested, General Kur."

That sent alarms off in Kur's mind and he looked down to see the same apprehension in Rass. Whatever Halfar wanted with him could not end well, he thought. He reached over the side of the bed and pulled his white tunic back on before stepping onto the floor and retrieving his leggings. Putting them on along with his boots he grabbed his longsword and stood.

"You will not be needing your weapon, general."

"I do not venture anywhere without it."

A nervousness about the advisor made him angry and he became suspicious. For Halfar to summon him and to be told no weapon was unheard of. He turned to Rass who nodded shifting back to male form and reach for his robes.

"It is just a talk and," Prevcan paused, "a precaution."

"Very well," Kur snapped as he tossed his longsword onto the bed. "Proceed."

He gestured the royal guards to march and followed the advisor to Halfar's throne room. Two royal guards with twitchy hands on the hilts of their weapons fell in behind him.

The immediate clearing of the room except for three advisors, two guards and Halfar surprised Kur as he entered, making his way to the foot of the throne ready to bow. Halfar raised a hand when Kur was mid bended knee, signaling Kur to rise back up.

"What urgent matter requires I leave my longsword and not be in uniform?" Kur demanded.

"It is a delicate matter."

Kur frowned.

"There is nothing delicate on Azrom. Even flowers have might here."

"True but I want to tell you something I should have a long time ago."

"And that is?"

"Your origin."

Kur's eyes went wide, his feet rooted to the floor with a storm of emotions going around in his head. *Halfar knows my origin?* Sadness, anger, curiosity, and pain rushed in all at once. He lifted his head up to see if Halfar was joking and saw no such thing.

"Your mother worked in the mines."

Halfar looked at him, anticipating some violent reaction but Kur refused to let him see that. Instead he stood perfectly still and let him resume.

"The mines are inspected on rotation by a delegate of the royal family. Each house makes sure it runs smoothly. One such time, the delegate decided to alleviate his sexual pleasures with a female worker. It was brutal and unbecoming of the royal house. The incident was concealed."

"By who?" Kur asked softly.

"The delegate's royal house. When it became known she was pregnant, a deal was made under the condition that you would be raised in the palace for military training. After I found out, her duties were changed to a position in the royal courts."

"I am a royal," Kur said. "Of your bloodline."

"That is so."

"What house?"

"The third. But your mother serves the first. So, as the son of a handmaiden for the first royal house courts, that is where you belong."

Kur's distant stare changed and his eyes narrowed. A new kind of anger rose up in him as he remembered all the trials and harm Halfar had administered, solidifying his plan to defy him.

"We are cousins," he said through gritted teeth.

"Yes," Halfar sighed heavily. "Your father is the brother of an uncle. An uncle through bonding."

Kur understood why he was not allowed to bring his longsword. They knew he would try to cut them down like the fleas they were. Even Halfar deserved to be skewered for keeping this secret all this time. Not willing to give them what they wanted, Kur turned away from Halfar and strode out into the hall.

He could hear the horrified advisors yelling at his backside.

"You have not shown respect for your lord!"

"You have not been dismissed from the Supreme Ruler's presence!"

"Guards! Seize him at once!"

"Do not obey that order!" Halfar roared.

Kur stopped at the entryway. "Where is she?"

"In the first royal house courtyard. She tends to the children there," Halfar answered.

He left then, heading to his chamber and ran into Rass halfway. His counterpart was in battle armor carrying his longsword in one hand and his own in the other. Rass stepped away from him in dread.

"What? Why are you backing away from me?"

"Do you not know?" Rass breathed. He raised his hands to the sides of Kur's face and let them hover there. "You are shedding tears."

"That is impossible!" Kur snapped.

He felt the wetness course down his face and he tried to fight them back. Rass placed his hands on his cheeks and drew his head to him. They stood foreheads pressed together.

"What has happened, my love?" Rass whispered.

"It is more than I can bare," was Kur's answer.

Together they trekked to the other side of the palace where the royal houses were adjacent to the main. None of the royal guards stopped them so Kur assumed they were ordered to stand down for him. The first royal house sat in the middle of the cluster, bigger than all the other palaces. It was an hour before evening meal yet they could hear children playing in the courtyard. Sand colored structures were decorated on each end by three foot flower beds bursting with Azrom flowers of every color. At the archway leading into the palace, the children were being ushered in by the consorts. One in particular stood out among them.

Her hair was a flowing river of dark forest green down her back, swishing across the shiny green sleeveless dressing robe that was fastened at the waist by a gold metal rope. Her smile was wide and familiar, just like his own. She caught sight of him and Rass out of the corner of her vision and stood straight, motionless.

Kur tilted his head to one side intrigued by her calmness and elegant stance. She was definitely of the royal court. He advanced into the courtyard until he was only a few feet from her.

"So here you are," he spoke.

"Yes, here I am."

Her voice had a creaminess that soothed him.

"You are quite beautiful. If you were not my mother," he didn't finish.

"As are you." She ran her fingers through her hair. "They told you."

"Yes."

"They took you from me when you were only a few months old. You were the only child I was not allowed to take care of."

Kur felt his hands ball into fists and seeing this, she reached over and pried them loose. Her strength stunned him.

"General, that is not becoming behavior for a royal."

"Neither what was done to you," Kur yelled.

Spittle flew from his mouth. Embarrassed, he wiped it off with the sleeve of his robe.

"General Rass, are you here for support?"

"Something of that nature," Rass whispered.

"I heard rumors. Are you mated to him?"

Kur became afraid and felt tension coming from Rass. To stop the line of questions, he answered for Rass.

"WE cannot tell anyone of this!" Kur whispered in fear.

"Why is that?"

"Because that would make Halfar angry," a voice called out from the outside corridor.

Kur turned along with his mother and Rass to see Lord Romnus strolling along with his handmaid.

"Isn't that correct, Generals?" He stopped near them and sized up mother and son. "So, you really are of royal blood. I thought it odd that one of our court maidens looked identical to you." Biandra handed him a small fruit. "The question is," he bit into it and chewed, "why did he tell you this now?"

"I am suspicious as well. It was obviously a decision made by his advisors. They even made me forgo my longsword."

"That was probably the smartest decision they had ever made." Romnus shoved the rest of the fruit in his mouth and when he was done consuming it, said, "Come. Let's give you a proper introduction." He nodded to Kur's mother. "You should get going and catch up before your lord comes searching."

Her mouth formed a devious smile that filled Kur with pride at inheriting such a thing. She caressed the side of his face then turned around, entering the palace. Beside him, Rass stared at her in a state of awe.

The communal hall where the first house royals lounged before evening meal reminded Kur of those rustic styled living room images he had seen on Earth. A large Gruloc beast's head hung mounted high above the hearth and the table was made from a fallen tree, the notches still showing in the wood. Dim lighting made the great hall seem smaller, more personal. All seven of the first royal children were present with Kur now making it eight.

He sat down across from Chastan who glared at him for no reason. Kur took his longsword from his waist and clanked it down on the table in front of him. Chastan flinched and his sister let out a mighty laugh that scared even Kur.

"Oh!" She said after finally catching her breath. "Please, you must do that always. It keeps my brother in his place."

"Chastan," Romnus said, "have you forgotten that he is the general of our great Armada?"

Rass snorted. Kur felt the same amusement but decided not to show it. Instead he surveyed his surroundings. He knew all of them, just never had any reason to converse with them. Now seeing the royals up close in their environment, it dawned on him how isolated they already were before Halfar's new decree. That alone made it more disturbing, the timing of this new revelation. He had intended to seek them out regarding the rations for the villages and this was his chance to finally do so.

As if reading his mind, Romnus sat up from his laid-back position at the head of the table, leaned forward and said, "Your loyalty to his reign is needed."

"He doesn't have it," Kur replied.

"Oh, I know. And what do you think, General Rass?"

Rass clutched the front of his cloak.

"Nor mine. Too much has happened and there is no remedy except…" He left it at that.

Kuhala, also dressed in battle gear, finished it for him.

"Removing him from the throne. You can say it. This is a safe place. His royal guards do not dare tread into our palace unless they want a fight."

"It may come to that in time," Romnus added. "Halfar is losing grip on his reign. I fear his advisors have once again taken control."

Kur's chest tightened as he recalled the previous advisors

devious plan that manipulated him into doing their dirty work. They had the right idea but the wrong agenda. Halfar does need to go but not at the expense of throwing their race into chaos.

"Enough of this depressing talk." Romnus laid back into his cushion. "Let us feast."

Servants arrived with evening meal and Kur thought they must be having a banquet given the amount of food and drink. He saw Chastan grab a drink before it was barely set on the table. Feeling it rude, he removed his longsword and set it underneath so there would be more room in front of him.

"Let's get to know each other better." Romnus smiled.

Kur kept silent for the duration of the meal but when the platters were cleared, he spoke his mind.

"I am aware that this house is distributing the rations for our people outside the great wall."

"That is correct. You do act fast, don't you, general?" Romnus replied.

"It seems the council does not see the caring of our people as a priority, and I need to find a way to circumvent this without putting a target on your house."

"Our house," Keita corrected him. "You are now part of it as well. As for being a target, it is too late for that."

"We are doing the best that we can," Romnus added. "There has been a restriction on the use of transport vehicles. Some of the tracks were blocked in one sector."

"That's…" Rass gripped the edge of the table. "I had not heard of this."

"Nor would you. It is not something the council speaks of freely."

"Does Halfar know of this as well?" Kur asked but wasn't sure he wanted the answer.

"Probably not," Keita answered.

"So it really is like before. The new council and advisors are just as bad as the previous."

"I think they may be worse. The fact being how sneaky they are," she said.

Kur looked around the table at everyone and realized as a member of royal blood he was obligated to keep the reputation of the royal house intact. He had power, even if it was limited. They still had to abide by protocols, the outcome of not doing so detrimental to their plans.

"I will see what I can do on my end," he announced.

"While in the bowels of a rotting beasts?" Romnus asked.

"Absolutely. I have no choice."

"You're curious."

"I want to see just how short a leash they intend to put on me for the success of their agenda. How far will our Supreme Ruler go to gain my unwavering loyalty?"

Rass slammed a fist on the table.

"No! I can't let you do this. It's too dangerous. He could slide off into a new kind of madness."

"Unfortunately, that is a chance we have to take," Romnus said.

Boots stomping against pavement thundered towards the hall and all their eyes widened collective in disbelief at what they were hearing. To confirm the sounds, a group of six royal guards from the main palace came to a halt at the entrance of the hall with obvious harmful intent in their demeanor.

"Generals! Our lord has demanded you return to the main palace, immediately!"

"And if we refuse?" Kur inquired as he grabbed his longsword from under the table.

"You will come as directed if you wish to not cause conflict within the first royal house."

"Have you forgotten who we are?" Rass stood, his arms already formed into claws. "Have you lost all of your senses that you dare demand from your generals?"

"Our orders are from the Supreme Ruler! His word takes precedence over your rank."

"Then you have also forgotten something else," Romnus added. Every royal at the table stood ready for battle. "To come into my house means you are under my reign. If you wish to deny my authority, so be it."

Kur watched as Chastan morphed along with two others, the two sisters drew blades and Romnus came from the head of the table. The royal guards' leader frowned and nodded his head to the side. The other guards drew weapons. A split second later they were all sprawled backwards on the corridor floor.

In front of them stood Romnus, nearly eight feet tall with shiny black pincers the length of a man. His praying mantis like legs were thin yet surrounded by lean muscle.

The leader, still standing at the side, raised his longsword to strike and Romnus caught the blade in a pincer without even looking, snap- ping it in half. More guards came rushing towards the entrance but were stopped by the house's own royal guards.

The ones who got through were met by the royal family. Romnus grabbed the leader with a claw that engulf the guard's entire body. Blood dripped from where it punctured skin. With a slight movement, he tossed the royal guard out of the hall and over the veranda into the evening Azrom sky.

Kur sat motionless at the table. Everything had moved faster than anticipated. He heard that if Romnus had been in the succession battles, Halfar would not be ruler but didn't know why; until now. He turned to Rass, who also stood rooted to his spot by the side of the table with eyes wide and met his gaze. Looking back towards the entrance, he saw Romnus regain his original form and shake the blood from his right hand, spraying it across the floor.

"Tell our Supreme Ruler that if he or any of his royal guards disrespect our palace in any way ever again, it will be a declaration of war."

Romnus said it calmly with no hint of malice, only a statement of fact. The royal guards backed away and left the area of the palace, returning to their posts on the dividing line of the main palace. Only the five on the ground were left and they stood up cautiously. Kur sheathed his longsword and motioned for Rass to follow.

"No need," he said. "I will personally deliver the message myself." Kur stared at the five royal guards and they eventually understood.

Two turned and headed forward as he and Rass exited the hall. The other three fell in line behind them. He took a quick glance at Romnus who smiled ever so slightly. Kur saw what was really in those bright green eyes; rage.

Halfar was not pleased when his generals came into the throne room after evening meal relaying Romnus' message. He turned to his advisors questioning and saw them fidget. This is not what he had planned.

"I requested that my generals be present for a late evening council session with the military advisors and somehow," he paused for effect, "a royal guard is on the brink of death and the First Royal House is ready to engage in battle against their ruler!"

"My lord, I am not sure why the royal guards went into the palace in such a manner," Mesrod said. "That goes against protocol."

"They said the order came from you personally," Kur interjected.

"To bring you back by force if necessary? I would not do that! For them to treat their own generals this way is," Halfar couldn't find the words. It was just too outrageous. He didn't know what was happening. Signals were getting crossed.

"Please send a request to Lord Romnus for an audience tomorrow. A request," he stressed. "I need to apologize for this and try to fix it."

"Of course, my lord," Prevcan bowed.

"Not any of you!" he snapped. Halfar turned to Kur. "Lord Kur, would you please do this as a member of the First Royal House, and a favor to me?"

He saw Kur struggling with an answer and realized he didn't blame him for being wary. To his relief Kur nodded.

"I will relay your request in the morning, my lord." Kur bowed low.

"Thank you. I will be in the battle conference chamber shortly."

As his generals left, he got up from his throne with lightning speed and wrapped one hand around Prevcan's throat. He lifted the Azromian off the floor and looked deep into his eyes.

"If I find that you were behind this, I will snap you in half and feed you to the mongrels outside the wall." He dropped the advisor and headed out of the throne room, four of his royal guards flanking him.

✱✱☼✱✱

Rumors spread across New Lassa about an uprising but Chardon paid it no mind for she was certain that Modas would not launch some hellish assault on his own people. It had been going on for a little over two years and now she was starting to see tiny fractures in the Lassians' trust of one another. Small incidents of aggression between the man- beasts and the sword wielders became numerous. This was not how Lassians behaved.

We have become our own worst enemy.

Chardon walked down the hill to Jaron and Modas' family chamber. Time to get some answers.

Her cousin, Jaron, looked up from her gardening with a scrunched-up face that relaxed when she saw Chardon. She always tried to appear angry or disgusted about everything and it just made her laugh, which infuriated Jaron.

"What brings you down this way?"

"I was searching for you mate."

Jaron made another strange face.

"He is not with you. That is odd."

"Yes, it is. The rumors are spreading. Do you know what this is about?"

"Hmm. Not really, but I did get a hint of it being about something that happened in the past. My guess is the murder of his family."

"But that was by a rival manbeast clan. What does that have to do with all of us?"

"If the system were more stable, maybe it would not have happened."

"Again, that was in the past under my father's leadership, not mine."

"Manbeasts hold grudges."

"All of them are rebelling?" Chardon shouted.

"No!" Jaron snapped back. "They do not all share the same sentiment. Trinon and Und are actually appalled by some of the manbeasts behavior the past few years. I think maybe most of my litter feels that way."

"What do I do, cousin? Why is this happening after everything we have been through?" Chardon plopped down in the dirt next to her.

"Honestly?" Jaron sat back and stared at her.

"Yes."

"Your leadership skills are lacking."

Chardon felt like she had been punched in her midsection. Her cousin was always quite blunt but this was a bit much even for her.

"In the past hundred years and more, you have let others sway your decisions. The ones you do execute are based on emotion, not logic. If you want to fix this, you need to show true leadership. Do not back down."

"I get it!" Chardon grabbed a handful of soil and squeezed it in her fist.

"Do you? I hope so." Jaron stood up and held out a hand to help her up. "About this so-called uprising that may or may not happen in a few years yet, you can't do anything."

"What? Why?"

"It has to run its course and then after the debris settles you can fix it. Because if it does happen, there will be a lot of despair."

"Don't they know this?"

"I don't think it is part of the equation. I think they don't care. But they will when it happens and they will have great regret."

"I need to stop this!"

Chardon pleaded with her but Jaron shook her head.

"And that is why I never trusted manbeasts."

The voice interrupting was all too familiar.

Chardon and Jaron turned to see Ganna walking towards them carrying a large potted plant. She thumped it down on the ground and wiped her brow with the back of her sleeve. The last person she wanted to see was their head scientist. If their race didn't need her, she would have slit the woman's throat a long time ago.

"You do not need to comment on this or anything else," Jaron seethed.

"Yes, yes, you wish to kill me." Ganna waved a hand in the air. "Join the ranks and wait your turn. In the meantime, I created a plant that will spread like fire. It should bring a harvest within months and will span a wide girth in meters."

Ganna turned to walk away then stopped. She gave them a winning smile and added, "If you need me to create something to eradicate the manbeasts, you know where to find me."

As she walked away, Chardon and Jaron held each other at bay.

When she was no longer in sight they let go of each other.

Meetings were in the dark of night for a reason and Modas prohibited any light be brought to them, the moon giving off a sufficient amount. He had to call an emergency gathering because of the increased incidents. Some of his manbeasts were sabotaging the agenda early and he needed to rein them in. They had to exercise patience for a few more years which meant squashing the rumors quickly. Having that kind of mistrust now would be like losing Lassa all over again.

"What are you doing? Have I not explained the reason for this cause?"

A few mumbles could be heard and that infuriated him. He too had been slipping over the years and needed to regain Chardon's trust. Telling them to do what he hasn't would sound like preaching.

"We must be calculated and in sync with our efforts. Yes, we should be angry but this is to establish a new order to ensure this does not hap- pen ever again."

"Will Chardon be our final sacrifice?" A manbeast asked. Others laughed.

Modas felt his eyes burn and he roared. When everyone was silent, stunned out of their thoughts, he made it clear.

"No one harms our leader! Has your core gone dim?"

"I thought we were recreating the actions of the father. Chardon must die."

Four manbeasts nodded in agreement then saw the looks from others in the group. Modas could see them become aware how wrong they were. He had never said anything about recreating the past. That would be disastrous.

"Why would you think that? We are not murderers." Modas snapped.

"We want to be heard. For them to feel our pain. To instill fear of the manbeasts once again so we are not underestimated," Barbon stated. Modas was thankful for him trying to steer them towards the true cause. "Calm yourselves and make this right. Make the rumors go away. If they know we are coming there is no element of surprise." He watched some hang their heads in shame. "That is all for now. Go home and be kind until it is time."

Modas watched them disperse and a nagging feeling tugged at his gut. A few of his manbeast looked dissatisfied with the notion of killing Chardon being off the agenda.

They won't listen.

He immediately got nauseous and dry heaved over the hilltops edge. This kind of sickness had never happened to him before.

Is this a bad omen?

Standing up to his full height, he jumped down from the edge.

Fateful Encounters

Another visit to Azrom without her mother or younger brother made Farin elated because she could roam the palace, under Trinon's watchful eye of course. But lately he was letting her go off on her own. She felt better being in female form and relished it. A quick overview of her body finally filled out in all the right places made her wish for better attire to accentuate her assets.

She ran around the corner of a veranda on the palace's far side, where she had never been and noticed the sun was blocked. Up ahead she saw royal guards at the entrance of a chamber and smiled.

I wonder whose it is.

Curiosity piqued, she headed straight for it.

As she neared the entrance, the two guards turned their heads towards her with eyes bulging out of their sockets at the sight of her. They both gripped their weapons, ready to bar the entrance when Lord Chastan came out.

He was straightening his top robe over one shoulder and looked over at the guards. They removed their hands from their weapons and resumed watch. Farin grinned as she caught a glimpse of the inside be- fore Chastan blocked her view, an obvious move to stop her from seeing.

So it's true.

Feigning ignorance, she stepped back from the entrance a bit and exclaimed, "Lord Chastan! What are you doing? Were you visiting?" Lord Chastan let out a small laugh and hooked his arm in hers, steering her from the chamber.

"My beautiful Farin, this is no place for you to be."

They walked back down the outer corridor.

"Why?"

"Because there are those who would gladly desecrate you with no regard for their lives. And if you are harmed within our palace, Halfar would kill us all."

"Oh. So you would protect me?"

Lord Chastan smiled.

"Of course. You shouldn't be here with me."

"Everyone says that."

"Your father will be searching for you."

"Where are you going now?"

His pace slowed and a sinister look came on his face. She could tell he was thinking something unclean.

"Would you take a bath with me? Being scrubbed by an attendant is so impersonal."

"Really? Like in the communal basins I heard about?"

"Not quite, this one is for royals only."

"I haven't had one since I got back on Azrom."

"Then let's get clean together."

They walked arm in arm to a bath chamber further in the palace than she had ever been and admired the large basin set deep into the floor. Lord Chastan nodded to the attendant who hurriedly ran the water and added the solvents. The washing cloths and sponges were set on the edge and the attendant fled the chamber.

Turning around to walk backwards into the chamber, Lord Chastan took her hand and guided her to the changing station to the right of the entrance. He reached over to push her hair from her shoulder then gently pulled her robe down until it fell on its own to the floor. He knelt down and did the same with her leggings and boots.

Farin giggled, startling him to stand back up.

"Your turn."

She pulled off his robes, tearing at them, each layer flying into the air haphazardly. She adored the look on his face at her boldness.

The attendant returned to fold their clothing in a neat square pile and left again. Farin got the impression that Lord Chastan was not very nice to the attendants and probably harassed them brutally; sexually. It didn't matter if they were male or female.

He held her hand as she stepped down into the basin and settled on the ledge. Expecting a drunken splash, she was surprised by how grace- fully he slid into the water. With smooth precision, he gently pulled her by the hips to him, not disturbing the water. His hands came up dripping wet, soaking her hair as he brushed his fingers in it.

"You are quite beautiful," he whispered in her ear.

His breath was hot and she could feel him getting aroused. She smiled, tilting her head back and pushed away from him.

"Lord Chastan, that's dirty."

"Well, we are here to bathe." He reached behind him and removed the sponge from the ledge. "May I?"

Farin turned around and let him move her hair to one side so he could wash her back. His touch was very soft and again she wondered how he could be so crude in public. Even when his hands roamed to the front of her and ran the sponge down her breasts, one side at a time. She turned back around to face him.

"My turn?" He asked.

She grinned then used both her arms to scoop up water and splash him. At first, he was stunned but recovered quickly and did the same to her. They laughed like children as they wrestled with each other, not caring about their nakedness. Farin was having fun.

Out of breath, they went back to washing each other, Farin making sure to wash every part of him she deemed unclean. She watched his eyes close in ecstasy as she ran the cloth around his genitals, scrubbing gently. He's so easy. When she was done, he grabbed her by the waist and set her on the inside ledge. He spread her legs wide and let them rest on his shoulders while he used one hand to wash between her thighs.

"Ahh, that tickles!" Farin laughed, throwing her head back. It didn't tickle, it felt heavenly. He stopped and pulled her legs down around his waist. "Why did you stop?" Farin asked searching for an explanation on his face.

"Because," he replied, tangling his fingers in her hair, "if your father found out, my demise would be imminent."

"But I'll never tell."

"No," he sighed, "you wouldn't"

He kissed her then, hard, blocking off her air supply. She stared at him as he disengaged and saw fear in his eyes. Smiling to change his mood, she wrapped her arms around his neck and blew warm air in his face.

"What are you doing?" He laughed.

"Making you feel better."

"You already have."

"With just a kiss?"

"Ummm, maybe more than that." He swatted the side of her buttocks and pushed away from her. "We need to go."

"Why?" Before he could answer, she said, "My father."

"Correct."

He got out of the basin and pulled her by the underarms onto the ledge. The attendant appeared with large drying towels but Chastan only took one and dried them both off with it. They laughed the entire time while the attendant took care of the basin, as they dressed.

"Come on, if I'm going to get caught at least it won't be in a bathing chamber."

She let him lead her by the hand to another part of the royal palace and was taken aback by the golden colored inner corridors. Handmaids traveled along with purpose, moving out of their way and bowing low at the same time. Lord Chastan stopped at the entrance of a personal chamber and found it to be his.

Entering his chamber, he went to a shelf and removed a large tablet. She came closer and he set it on the bed. A virtual board game appeared on the display.

"Let's play."

"I've never played this game. What is it called?"

"It's called Konterra and it's a game of strategy."

"So, you'll let me win?"

"No." Farin pouted and he laughed at her. "You can't learn if I do that."

"Fine." She crawled on the bed across from him and he set it up. "What do I get if I win?"

"What do you want?"

Farin blushed, her pale skin turning the lightest shade of pink.

"I want to have more fun in the palace. Will you show me?"

"I would do anything for the beautiful Farin," Chastan replied.

Of course, you would.

Farin giggled again and settled further onto the bed.

Boots striking hard on the lacquered halls of the First Royal house caused panicked handmaids to usher their masters into random available rooms out of harm's way. A small group of Halfar's royal guard was marching with purpose, faces scrunched up as if something smelled rotten. They formed a perfect diamond, one in the front and rear with two of them in the middle side by side. Chastan's handmaid, Ponnae, paled and hurried ahead of them towards her master's chamber. She knew who they had come for. Gathering the edges of her robes, she broke into a near run.

As the sound of the guards' advance began to disappear she rounded the corner at the end of the corridor and deeper into the palace. Directly in her path, Lord Romnus and his entourage were headed towards her. His face frowned as he looked at her. She had no choice now, she had to tell him.

"Lord Romnus," she greeted him. She bowed deep and tried to catch her breath.

"Why are you in such a hurry?" He seemed angry.

"I must warn my Lord to send off Lady Farin."

"Oh?" Lord Romnus replied playfully.

"Halfar's royal guards are in the family palace."

Something dark and unholy spread across his expression and she could tell he was going to address it. That was not ideal but he was royalty and could probably get away with doing so. To her surprise, they all turned around and Romnus gestured her forward.

"Come, let's get Lady Farin safely away."

Grateful for the back up in case the royal guard did catch up, she obeyed and continued her fast-paced stride to Lord Chastan. Not two corridors away she heard the boots get louder. She broke into a full run ahead of Lord Romnus' group and made it to the chamber entrance.

Lord Chastan and Lady Farin were playing a board game on the bed, laughing and tagging each other. She exhaled and blurted out, "My Lord!" They both turned to her, smiling. "Lady Farin must be escorted out, now."

Her master gave her a warning look. She knew her tone bordered on insubordination but there was no time. He could punish her later. In her defense, Lord Romnus came up behind her.

"It really is imperative that you go, Lady Farin," Lord Romnus commanded lightly.

Lady Farin began to pout. "But I just learned how to play! I'm having fun."

"Yes, well your father has sent his royal guards into our palace looking for you."

Lord Chastan's eyes went wider. She saw fear on her master's face. It was a rare thing to see since he feared almost nothing. He started shut- ting down the game.

"Fine, I'll go," Lady Farin huffed. She leaned over to Lord Chastan, her face dangerously close to his. "But I can come back, right? You'll play with me again?"

"As much as we love having you come to visit us, we are trying to not be slaughtered because of it," Lord Romnus answered for her master.

Lady Farin stood up with her hands balled into fists.

"I know."

Lord Chastan nodded to her and she held out a hand to Lady Farin who took it.

"Make sure you find Trinon, Lady Farin. This could become messy," Lord Romnus said to her.

With a nod, Lady Farin followed her out of the chamber and down a private corridor hidden in the walls. She kept a good grip on the Lady's hand, not in the mood to fall for her childish games of running off on her own. This was a serious matter and her first priority was the safety of her master.

Lord Romnus waited patiently for the royal guards as they came around the corner of the corridor breeding intent to harm if the situation necessitated it-again. He forced his mouth into a smile as they marched up to him at Lord Chastan's chamber entryway.

"Where is she?" The leader roared. "We know she was sighted in this palace with Lord Chastan!"

"Lord Chastan has had many females in his presence. You have to clarify..." he was not allowed to finished.

"Do not kolbrec me, royal!"

Royals watching from their doorways gasped at the term only uttered by mothers to unruly children.

Lord Romnus held out an arm to his side, stopping what he knew was his own guards grabbing the hilts of their longswords. His eyes narrowed and locked on the leader's, who flinched slightly, looking sideways without moving his head to make sure no one saw it. Romnus didn't let his stare waver as he spoke.

"You have entered the palace of the First Royal house without my consent. Here, I am Supreme Ruler and you will tell Halfar this is not acceptable." He did not raise his voice and knew there was no need.

"You may rule here but Halfar is the Supreme Ruler of our race. You would do well to remind this palace of that. We will find that halfbreed in due time," the leader spat as he spun a finger in the air. The royal guards made their way back from which they came.

"Halfbreed?" Romnus asked no one. "Now, that is telling."

"I think I have a fear for her," Lord Chastan said.

"I think you should." Romnus eyed him. "What, exactly, were you doing with the beautiful Farin?"

"You saw, we were playing a game." Lord Chastan smiled sweetly.

"And before that?"

"What are you implying?"

"They said you were sighted with her, Chastan."

"We bathed together. That is all."

Romnus was well aware of Chastan's ideas regarding baths and felt his stomach cringe. Then he thought about it logically and came to the conclusion that the beautiful Farin would not have allowed such debauchery be administered on her. She was feral and ripe for mating but not reckless.

"I hope so, for your sake," Lord Romnus turned away, "and ours."

He and his entourage left to resume their walk to his original destination. His rage against Halfar combined with the image of Chastan touching Farin made him force back a sudden surge of bile that filled his throat. The latter should be of no concern. Farin ending up with another after Chastan before he got her was fine. That way she would be well seasoned in mating.

It was the first that infuriated him more. Since the forced segregation, it was explicit that no royal house would be invaded in such a manner. Halfar was breaking his own rules for his own agenda.

Halfbreed?

For Halfar to allow his inner circle to define his first born as such meant the council was pushing harder.

He decided to let Chastan and Farin's relationship flourish a bit. It would put her under the protection of the First Royal house. If even her father tried to harm her, he could retaliate on her behalf. Plucking the round fruit from Biandra's upstretched hand, he took a bite, engulfing half of it. The juice dripped down his neck and he wipe his face with the back of his robe's sleeve, he felt his eyes burning. The end of Halfar's reign was near.

It didn't take long for Trinon to reattach himself to Farin. Even though he let her roam, she was always in his sights. He was testing the waters to see how bad Azrom was becoming for the young royal. Halfar was putting a shorter leash on his child as each year passed. The encounter he just witnessed with Lord Romnus and Halfar's royal guard confirmed his fears. Farin was in danger from her own father. That one term he heard the leader spit out is what gave him cause for alarm.

Seeing Lord Chastan's handmaid lead Farin down the stone paved ramp that ended back on the side of the main palace, Trinon jumped off the steeple above and landed soundlessly behind them. He smiled at how well it went and decided he had now perfected it.

"Trinon, are you upset with me?" Farin asked.

That startled the handmaid who nearly stumbled backwards as she turned and saw him so close behind them. Her look of terror was almost comical. He set a hand on Farin's head and shook it.

"How? Where did you…?" The handmaid stuttered.

"It's okay now. You can go back to Lord Chastan. I'm sure you're worried about leaving him with my father's royal guards," Farin said. Her smile faltered a bit.

"I am, thank you."

With a low bow, the handmaid ran back up the ramp. He felt bad for her. It was obvious to him that she would end up in the middle of all this and not come out unscathed. His hand still on Farin's head, he gripped harder, forcing her to turn around and face him.

"I cannot protect you if you do reckless things."

He made sure his voice was low enough for only her to hear. Royal guards were everywhere in the main palace. Her mouth trembled and he folded her tight in his arms. He had been with Farin since infancy and if he was of mating age when she was born he could be her father. Years of watching, training, protecting. He was not going to let her own father destroy her, let alone anyone else.

"I'm sorry." His robes muffled her whimper.

"You're not stupid and you're not weak. Acting like it is one thing, being is another."

Farin pulled away from him and smiled for real this time.

"Manbeast!" A royal guard yelled at him. "You are lacking in your duties!"

He turned to the four royal guards from earlier and the disrespect they exuded rubbed him the wrong way. With a grin, he instantly grew claws from his left hand and swiped across all four at chest level. Their breast plates split in two, the lower halves falling to the ground in loud clanks. Other royal guards looked over and Trinon saw them itching for a fight, but hesitating.

"Let's play nice, shall we? I have been watching Farin all day, as usual," he laughed.

"You lie! She was seen with Lord Chastan!"

"She is never alone," Trinon replied.

This time he didn't smile, letting his voice drop an octave lower along with his stare. He watched it strike fear in the royal guards around him. At nearly seven feet tall like most of his family, he towered over the guards. Out of the corner of his vision he saw two royal advisors and their guards come towards them in what may become a brawl if the royal guards decided to strike back. The other three were still in awe of their breast plates on the ground. Retracting his claws and resuming his goofy demeanor, he waited for the reprimand.

"What is going on?" Mesrod, Halfar's first advisor, demanded. He noticed the half-cut uniforms and stared at him in anger. "Did you do this?"

"Yep!" He replied in Earth slang he learned from Kelin. His understanding the improper dialect conveyed a kind of disrespect. "I sure did!"

"Why would you do such a thing?"

Prevcan, the second advisor, asked.

"Simple. They weren't being nice," Trinon said. He reached back and ruffled the back of his mane. "I don't like that."

Mesrod pursed his lips and his brow furrowed.

"Return to your posts," he commanded the royal guards, including the four in front of him.

They picked up the other half of their breast plates and marched off back into the main palace. Prevcan tsked at him.

"Halfar will not be pleased with your idea of watching, manbeast."

Trinon cocked his head to one side at the last word the advisor uttered and waited. He saw the realization enter the man.

"My apologies, Trinon," the advisor cooed.

"Can I rip your throat out?" Trinon asked playfully.

"What?" The two advisors asked, horrified.

"Kidding," Trinon laughed.

"Please see that Lady Farin," he said it with obvious disdain, "is confined to her chamber for now."

"Of course."

Trinon watched them wait for his bow and he gave them no indication that he would. After a few moments he guessed they realized it as well and walked off in a state of anger. He did like that.

****☼****

Talas stretched the fingerless leather glove over one hand, pulling it tight. In female form she was not much different with the exception of the barely there breasts and slight curve of her hips. Her body was all lean muscle so it didn't surprise anyone that she wasn't more endowed. The deep rust colored leather jacket strained slightly across the chest making it impossible to close all the way. Even her leather leggings hugged a bit too much, but not enough to restrict her movements.

She felt moody. Raising one hand to inspect the glove's fit, it occurred to her that this feeling was due to her female form. It caused a shift in her psyche. Movement from behind made her turn and she saw Kelin setting up the weapons table for training. She let out a soft sigh watching him be meticulous with the arrangement.

A finger was poking at her breasts and she heard a giggle. On instinct, she slapped the finger away and turned her attention to the culprit; Trinon.

"Cushy," he laughed. His nearly seven-foot frame was bent towards her but she still had to look up at him.

"Don't do that!"

"It's fun sparring when you're in female form. You get all ferocious."

"Is that so?" Talas frowned at him.

He smiled that big goofy grin.

"Can I join in?"

"As long as your father doesn't intervene, again."

This time Trinon made a sour face. The childlike grin gone. A serious look surfaced.

"My father is stuck in the past." His natural tenor emerged and Talas thought about how shocking it would be for anyone else to hear. Only three people knew what he truly sounded like.

"And you're not?"

"Not in the same way."

Trinon, along with Talas, watched Kelin approaching and his childlike demeanor returned. He placed one hand high above his mane, rubbing the back of his head and let out a loud laugh. His eyes squeezed shut and mouth went wide open.

Don't overdo it. Talas silently chided him.

Seeing his transitions, and knowing why he had to do it, hurt her. For years she watched the young manbeast struggle all by himself. Having his litter brother, Und, to confide in didn't give him much solace. She wanted to embrace him like a small child but that was his mother's duty.

"Feel better?" Trinon exclaimed.

"What?" Talas snapped out of her reverie.

"You were being all moody."

Trinon walked away backwards and turned as he neared the combat training arena.

"Observant little," Talas started to curse but was stopped by laughter behind her.

Kelin rested an arm on her shoulder and kissed the side of her head. Blonde strands stuck to his face and formed a web before falling back in place as he disengaged.

"I swear the two of you are like twin stars on opposite axis. It's kind of cute, how he teases you."

Talas eyed her mate and felt a sense of guilt. She didn't like hiding things from him after all the chaos they had been through but it was not her tale to tell. Now she knew why she was moody. It wasn't just her female hormones, it was the date. What a terrible anniversary. She grabbed the hilt of her longsword and headed for the arena. At least she would get to release some of her frustrations for a while.

⁎⁎☼⁎⁎

Rass stood perfectly still as Halfar marched into the conference chamber, his stride full of purpose. For the Supreme Ruler to roam the palace unguarded meant nothing good would come from this visit. He also knew that Halfar was the only one aware of his location at this hour of the day. Taking a quick scan of his face, he tried to decipher his ruler's mood. When Halfar did look up to meet his gaze, something like icy liquid ran through his body.

"Are we alone?" Halfar asked. His tone was brisk.

Rass blinked then noted his surroundings.

"Yes, my lord."

"Good. I have decided that the council is correct in their assessment of a pure-blooded heir."

"Have you spoken with Chardon about this?"

"Chardon has nothing to do with this matter! She is not of Azrom."

Rass reared back as fear began to form in him. The way Halfar spoke bordered on madness.

"That being so," Rass tried to quash the heat, "she is your mate."

"She won't be the only one. I can have as many as needed." Halfar stepped closer. "After having offspring, I felt like I had wasted so many decades by not solidifying my bloodline. The first to bear my seed should have been you."

Alarms went off in his head and the rest of the color drained from his already pale complexion as he tried to step away. Halfar grabbed hold of his forearms, stopping him.

"I am already mated to Kur, my lord."

"He can have you," Halfar's grip tightened, "when I'm done."

"I cannot…"

Halfar's eyes burned with an intensity he had only witnessed during battle.

"You belong to me," he seethed. Rass felt his own eyes start to widen and fought the urge. He knew Halfar could already smell his fear. "If I had not dragged you out of the brothel and wanted you, this junction in your life would not be possible. You will submit to me!" He leaned in and sniffed at his hair, inhaling deep. Rass stiffened.

In that moment, he knew how far his ruler had come unhinged. Halfar let him go and walked backwards to the doors, his eyes never leaving Rass'. At the entrance he turned and exited the chamber.

The doors slid shut, a loud swishing sound he had never noticed before emitted from the sealing mechanism, and his legs buckled. He reached out to the viewing platform and used it to keep himself from falling. It had been a long time since he had felt so defenseless. Not since his early years in the brothel. It reminded him how much he feared Halfar and chided himself for forgetting that fact. He had grown arrogant over the past century and was now paying the price.

Afraid Halfar might return, Rass quickly came to his senses and fled the chamber. The only place he could think to go was the First Royal House palace, where Kur was.

Rass finally made it to the communal hall by using every tactic he could think of to sneak out of the main palace. Kur sat at the table end closest to the entrance. He halted for a moment at the archway and watched Kur sip his drink while listening to Romnus speak. There was no sound. Rass felt panic.

When his eyes refocused, he saw everyone getting up from the table staring at him with great concern. Kur was right in front of him, yelling. When did he get there?

"What's happened?" Kur yelled again.

"Halfar," Rass managed to whisper. Then he noticed the room. "Not here, please." Rass took hold of Kur's tunic.

Kur turned to the royals. "I must go."

They found an empty chamber along the outer corridor and stepped inside. Kur placed his hands around Rass' neck. So warm. Rass leaned forward until his forehead touched Kur's.

"What is it?" Kur demanded. "What madness has he spouted now?"

"He wants pure blooded offspring."

"Yes, the council has poisoned his mind with that."

Rass began to shake and used Kur to hold himself steady. "He is going to force me to bear his seed." He felt Kur's hands tighten as they slid away, his fingers digging into flesh.

"You are mine," Kur said through gritted teeth.

"He does not care. His claim to rights is that he owned me first."

Kur pushed himself away and began to leave the chamber. Rass knew that look on his face and hurried after him, pulling him back.

"No!"

"He's gone too far!"

"I won't let him have me!" Rass snapped back.

"And how are you going to stop him?"

Now there was fear in Kur's eyes and Rass began to understand their predicament.

"I don't know," Rass replied softly.

Kur wrapped his arms around him and they remained that way for a while.

Servants bustled around the communal hall replenishing empty platters and drinks. Romnus clapped loudly, once, getting them to stop moving, then waved them away. Once they were gone he brought his attention to the other royals. Although they tried to hide it, all of them were shaken by the young general's appearance earlier. Invoking that one name sent them into a frenzy as of late. He, on the other hand, kept his composure. In truth, it didn't surprise him that his cousin had done something bordering on insanity. The royal houses were in a state of heightened security these past few years.

"What should we do about this, Romnus?" Reita asked.

He leaned back against the wall and contemplated for a moment.

"First, we need to know what he's done."

"Does it matter? He needs to be stopped!" Chastan yelled.

Romnus looked around at his family members' faces and saw tension on the verge of snapping.

"I understand your concerns, I do. But you know we cannot move against Halfar unless we have a solid plan in place."

Kuhala began playing with her short blade, swirling it between her nimble fingers. "And no, we cannot kill him." She stopped the motion of her blade and laid it flat on the table. "Kur has an idea, I just don't want to do it." They all stared at him, their anger evident. "You know how I feel about being next in succession."

"How you feel is of no concern to us, brother. This is for the glory of Azrom," his sister chided him.

"What glory we have left," Chastan snorted.

"Enough!" Romnus was tired but more than anything, he was disgusted. This was not how he envisioned Azrom under Halfar's rule. If he had known, seen some hint of this, he would never had withdrawn from the succession battle.

Farin clung tight against the wall as a group of royal guards marched across the platform a mere five hundred feet from her. She took a peek around the corner as they disappeared down the adjacent stairway. The first royal house palace side was less than a third of a kilometer away. If her speed was constant like Trinon had taught her, it would be a cinch to get there in under two seconds. Crunching down into a launch position, she exhaled slowly then pushed off.

Her ability to stop was lacking so she ended up slamming into the wall of the courtyard to the dismay of the three consorts and the children. In an attempt to not damage her face, she had turned away from the wall. She pushed herself off and stepped back holding the left side of her face. When she turned around, Kur's mother, Emalli, stood in front of her.

"Hurry before they see you." Her tone was firm.

"I know."

Farin ran through the archway and into the corridor of the palace. She found the golden hallways and ran into Chastan's handmaid. The woman gasped loudly at seeing her and something like fear passed over her face.

"Please?" Farin said.

The handmaid sighed and turned around to escort her to Chastan's chamber. Of course, he was there lounging on his bed playing that game of strategy like he always did in the mid afternoon. He looked up from it and she smiled at him.

"The beautiful Farin," he exclaimed.

He patted the top of the bed.

"Lord Chastan," Farin answered.

With a giggle as she hopped up beside him.

"You play a dangerous game," he said.

Farin didn't like talking about this again. It was always brought up every time she showed up. She knew what was going on and refused to live in a cage. As everyone kept pointing out, she was a royal too.

"I want to play! This time, I know I can beat you."

"Is that so?" Chastan swiped a hand across the virtual board and reset it.

"Mmm hmm."

"And, what do you get if you win?"

"Whatever I want."

"And, if I win?"

"Whatever I want."

"Isn't that wrong?"

Farin smiled. "Do you not want the same thing?"

She saw him understand what she was implying.

"You're trying to get me killed."

"No, just trying to have fun." She felt her mood darken for a second. As if noticing it, he caressed her cheek.

"Let's have some fun then."

Midway through the game, when she figured it was a called game, she tackled him down on the bed and kissed him. At first, he seemed surprised then his body relaxed and he let her do what she wanted. Straddling him, she sat up and stared down at him. He was very pretty and did have a sweet side to him, although she wasn't sure if it was a ruse or not, just to get her.

He reached up with one hand and ran it down from her neck to her breasts. She pulled her robes off from the shoulders and let him tug them the rest of the way down. He undid the sash and tossed the robes on the floor. She removed his tunic and pulled his leggings off in one motion, his expression full of amazement.

"Why are you always so impatient?" he asked.

Farin leaned over and planted her hands on both sides of his chest and slid them under his armpits. She brushed her lips against his, teasing him before kissing him full on. His hands grabbed hold of her hips and he slid her down until she could feel the hardness of him force its way into her roughly.

It hurts! Why couldn't he learn to be gentle?

His hips thrust upwards into her with powerful force, the pace faster than she liked and she kept her hands under him, gripping the bed covers beneath. She could hear herself crying out. He liked the sound of it and wouldn't cease his rhythm. Her back arched sending her hair around her like a spider's web.

She could feel the sweat coming off her, making contact with his and their bodies slid across each other as if oiled. She became lightheaded, the muscles in her womb contracting and her arms started to shake.

Chastan grabbed her by the hair with one hand and he let out a loud grunt that turned into a growl and she felt his seed spew into her as they let out a final cry. Pain, ecstasy and euphoria claimed her all at once and she fell atop him with a resounding smack.

Covered in each other's juices, they lay like that for what seemed hours though only moments had past. Shaky, she lifted her head and kissed him. It stopped his heavy breathing for a second and he just looked at her. Then, she burst out laughing.

"Oh, you are so very dangerous," Chastan said. He cupped her but- tocks and slid her off of his now soft member. "Really, Farin. You will get us all killed."

"Don't say that!" Farin swatted his head and climbed off him.

She found her robes on the floor and redressed. Chastan sat up and did the same. The game was still counting down when they both looked at it and she laughed again.

"Shall I deliver the finishing blow?"

"You haven't won yet."

"Oh?"

Farin laid on her stomach and observed the last moves of the game while Chastan sat propped up on one elbow with his head resting on it. He was just being arrogant and a sore loser, she thought to herself.

She vowed to come back whenever she wanted and did so for weeks on end knowing her luck was bound to run out eventually.

Just not the way it did.

Halfar couldn't believe where his child had gone yet again. He had repeatedly confined her to the main palace but somehow, she managed to sneak out and end up back in the First Royal House palace. This time, he decided to fetch her himself along with four of his royal guards. Romnus brought this down on himself. He had asked his cousin numerous times to restrict Farin from entering his palace.

Deep into the first royal house palace he turned down the inner corridors, passing through the golden halls, watching royals and their servants scurry away in fear. It was probably the look on his face, he thought, for he was indeed incensed.

Within minutes he saw Romnus coming down the corridor from the opposite side and between them, a female servant standing in the entryway of a chamber glancing back at him in terror as she talked to whoever was inside. Then she ran in.

"Lord Chastan!" Ponnae came to the entrance of her lord's chamber out of breath and scared to death. Alarmed, she saw Lady Farin naked on top of her master and knew they had just finished mating. Lady Farin had her back to the entrance so had to turn to look at her.

"Lady Farin! You must go, now!"

Lord Chastan's face went ashen and he quickly lifted Lady Farin off him so he could get dressed. Lady Farin halfheartedly moved to find her robes and Ponnae snapped. She rushed into the chamber and hurriedly helped Lady Farin into her robes, stepping back towards the entrance as the two readjusted themselves on the bed, now fully clothed. Ponnae turned around cautiously, feeling a presence behind her and breathed a sigh of relief when she found Lord Romnus standing there. His gaze fell on Lady Farin and Chastan.

Not a second passed before Lord Halfar also appeared next to him, royal guards in tow. Her master sat frozen on the bed, not sure what to do and she couldn't think either. Lady Farin just looked up with a smile on her face.

"I hope you are having fun," Halfar yelled.

"I was," Farin laughed. "Lord Chastan was teaching me how to play this strategy game." The game was indeed still counting down on the edge of the bed.

"Did he now? Get up!" He commanded.

Lady Farin flinched and slid off the bed.

"I just wanted a companion, father."

"You can't blame her for that. She has no one to engage with in the palace," Romnus added.

"Don't!" Lord Halfar warned him.

"It was just a game, cousin."

The moment Farin got to the entrance, two of the royal guards snatched her roughly and headed down the corridor. Lord Halfar stared at her master briefly then said.

"I will publicly execute you if I find you near her again."

Lord Halfar turned to leave but to her shock and amazement, Lord Romnus blocked him. She had never seen them side by side and noticed Lord Romnus was taller and bulkier.

"You will not threaten my family in my palace, cousin."

Lord Halfar's and Lord Romnus' guards unsheathed their longswords. She raised her hands to her mouth then her master grabbed her by the shoulders and into the furthest part of the room. Lord Halfar took a quick glance at her then back to Lord Romnus. That look scared her more than anything. After what seemed like an eternity, the stalemate was broken by Lord Halfar. He made a gesture and his royal guards sheathed their weapons. Lord Romnus stepped to the side to let him through, his guards still battle ready.

Her legs buckled and she slid to the ground in her master's arms. She had forfeited her life to protect Lady Farin and her master's relationship. And she knew, Halfar knew it.

Two days.

Farin stared at the walls of her chamber and tried to think of something to do by herself. She was not allowed outside, her meals brought to her and four guards escorted her to the bath. Trinon was always near but kept hidden from them. He said it was to make them feel more comfortable but she knew it was to see if they would harm her or not. The guards would sometimes 'accidentally' come into the bath thinking she was done and find her still in the water, naked. One of them would unconsciously fondle his crotch while he stared at her hungrily. He was the most dangerous.

She winced at the pain in her abdomen and did a few breathing techniques. They came off and on since the start of the new moon and she wasn't sure if it was anxiety or she was being poisoned. She put nothing past her father's advisors. This time it blossomed like fire and it lifted her off the bed as she cried out. Tears sprung from her eyes and she couldn't shake it.

Trinon emerged and held her down until it passed. He looked at her then placed a hand on her belly. At first her mind went blank, confused by his action, then she understood. Clasping her hands over her mouth she cried and screamed. When her hands weren't enough to muffle the sound, Trinon brought her to his broad chest and stifled it.

"We have to go. Right now," Trinon said. She nodded.

He lifted her up and walked out onto the veranda. With one leap he landed on the gate platform on the other side of the palace. The guardian stared at them in puzzlement. Trinon set her down and knocked him out before he could question their reason for being there. Then he opened the gateway to New Lassa. Right before it closed shut royal guards came running down the corridor towards the gate.

Safe.

Safe Advantage

Sunlight started to wane, casting shadows along the hilltop where Farin sat with her legs extended out. The breeze made her close her eyes and smile. Beside her, wrapped in soft cloths, was her newly born son gurgling happily. Her sudden unauthorized flight back to Lassa after realizing she was with child had her father angry, demanding she return soon. Something blocked the breeze so she opened her eyes and saw her mother towering over her.

"You need to get inside and rest."

"I'm fine."

She saw the look her mother gave and decided not to have a verbal fight. There was a sadness in her mother and she could guess where it stemmed from. Rolling over on her side, she picked up her baby then sat up to a kneeling position. A wave of weakness came over her but her mother was right there to steady her.

"It takes a lot out of you. Come," her mother said.

"I'm sorry," she whispered.

Her mother frowned.

"What for? You did nothing wrong."

"He has to stay hidden here on New Lassa and you'll end up having to care for him while I'm away."

"If it keeps him safe, I'd gladly do it. I just need you to be more careful. Your father has…changed."

Farin laughed. It was much more than that. Her father was being manipulated like a puppet and had gone insane with power. She couldn't tell her mother that, she still loved him. There was a chance he might see reason and stop his madness. She looked down at her tiny son of three days. He looked more like her than Chastan but there was a hint of him in those tiny features. Such a beautiful lifeform who could not know his father until it was deemed safe.

"I'm so sorry." This she said for Chastan.

Farin held him close to her bosom as she slowly rose from the ground with the help of her mother.

"When does your father want you back on Azrom?"

"Four moons."

"And how long does he expect you to stay?"

"About the same. Mother," she met her gaze, "I'm afraid."

Her mother enclosed her and the baby in her arms. Farin relaxed her body and breathed in the scent of her mother's hair. When she let go, there was a wet stain on her mother's robe.

"Thank you, I needed that."

"I know," her mother replied. "Now stop stalling."

On the way down, Farin caught a glimpse of Trinon watching from a higher hill. She felt guilty for putting him in such a position but it was too late for that now.

✦ ☼ ✦

Romnus knew he wasn't being delusional when he saw Farin strolling along the outer corridor of the First Royal House's palace. He just couldn't fathom how no one else noticed it. He watched her breasts nearly strain against her robes as they heaved up and down with every step she made. The slight color in her usually pale skin also gave it away. He decided to feign ignorance.

Her stride slowed as she spotted him and he gave her a broad smile as he opened his arms, waiting for her. It was something he always did lately whenever he saw her. Any excuse to lay his hands on her was a good tactic in his book. She slammed into him giggling, her hair covering his face and he inhaled deep. She smelled of open air after a rainfall. He dug his fingers into her hair to hold her closer to him and let the other hand trail down her spine to rest just above the curve of her buttocks. Her body relaxed and he could feel how soft she had become.

"Did you miss me?" she asked, looking up at him.

"Tremendously." Romnus reluctantly let her go and stepped back a bit. "I see you're defying your father's demands yet again."

Her face scrunched up and her stance stiffened.

"I am not a prisoner. He can't keep me locked away like that!"

"He shouldn't, but he will and can. Be careful, beautiful Farin." He brushed her cheek with the back of his hand and her head tilted into it.

"I will."

"Promise me." He gave her a serious look.

"I swear it." Farin smiled up at him again.

"Good. I believe Chastan will be glad to see you."

"Really?" She cocked her head.

He laughed, forgetting how observant she was assuming that Chastan took to the brothel more than most.

"Walk with me, Farin. Chastan can wait."

Her smile sent a shiver right down to his groin, forcing it to tighten.

Fortunately, patience was a trait he had an abundance of.

✶✶☼✶✶

Even on the holoscreen hovering above in the newly constructed war room, the Dreridians' appeared made of rough rocks bond together, forming crags. Halfar stood glaring at Lord Pondur's smiling image. It had taken days for the connection to be established because he felt there was no rush to speak with them. As far as he was concerned, the Dreridians were also the enemy.

His two generals did not agree which infuriated him. The entire race should embrace his agenda and mirror his views. Something about the way Lord Pondur grinned made him wonder if the greedy trade merchant sensed it. Kur and Rass stood silent by his side.

"Lord Halfar, good to see you are well."

Pondur bowed forward ever so slightly.

"Despite your part in the attempt to cripple my planet and my people, I am always victorious."

He purposely left out addressing the Dreridian ruler.

"Til death!" every soldier in the room resounded.

A craggy brow lifted on Lord Pondur's face and he seemed amused by the outburst.

"Oh, Lord Halfar. We have no intention of letting you meet your demise. We simply helped out a desperate race who continued on a flawed plan."

"You gave those reptiles an advantage over us!"

"Did we?" Lord Pondur raised a delicate chalice to his stone cracked lips and took a small sip from it. "I am baffled by this. Did you not raze Razzna's surface, leaving them no choice but to flee?"

Halfar clenched his fists at his sides. He had no response to that so gritted his teeth to remain silent for a moment. The minute infiltration team that consisted of twelve Razznians was just a slight hiccup and he had to confess that yes, he overreacted to a small fleet entering Azrom space that his generals could, and did, handle.

"What do you want?" he finally asked.

"A meeting of course."

Pondur took another small sip and set his chalice down beside him. In the background Halfar could see a lean figure bent over a handheld holoscreen, oblivious to the conversation.

"For what purpose?"

"Payment."

Pondur leaned back and folded his hands in his lap.

Halfar could feel the rage building up inside him as he watched the Dreridian sit patiently waiting for his reply. Before he could, Pondur continued.

"Of course, we shall meet here on our home world. I fear my envoy would be in jeopardy if I were to arrive at Azrom."

"You would be correct," Halfar seethed.

"The Lassians must be in attendance as well."

"What?" Halfar jerked his head up to meet Pondur's gaze.

"This entire plan originated from the Lassians."

"Chardon had nothing to do with that plan!"

"Is Chardon not the leader of Lassa and responsible for any decisions made on behalf of his race, regardless of who made it? Sestis was his mate and also leader. Do the same rules not apply to Azrom?"

"When?"

"Let's say in three moons. I am sure you can prepare within that timeframe."

"And what of the Razznians?"

"Oh, they will be there as well." Pondur smiled again.

"How? You said they left Razzna."

"We were able to establish communication." Pondur waved a hand at the screen. "That is of no concern right now. You should bring any delegates necessary for the negotiations." Pondur tilted his head forward, not even attempting a bow. The holoscreen went black.

"That..."

Halfar found he couldn't utter a single profanity. Too many phrases could be used and his mind didn't know which one to pick. He had a sour taste in his mouth.

Turning to his generals, he was about to ask their opinion when three of his royal advisors spoke ahead of him. They were here as observers only and Halfar was taken aback by their audacity.

"I believe this would be a great platform to reeducate them on Azrom ideals, my lord," Mesrod stated.

"Take Lord Romnus with you as a show of force," Prevcan suggested. "His brute demeanor would put them on edge."

Halfar saw Kur and Rass' jaws clinch tight and they remained silent.

Seeming to pick up on this, Dondar, his third advisor interjected.

"As revered as they are in battle, my lord, your generals are not schooled in the ways of commerce and politics."

In his mind, that made sense. He knew how devoted to Azrom his generals were but it was also true that they had little dealings with this side of rulership. Having his cousin there would show that he was not the only one with Azrom's future in mind.

"So be it," he announced. He returned his gaze back to Kur and Rass. "Make the preparations for a hostile encounter, just in case."

"As you wish, my lord," they replied in unison, bowing low.

Leaving the war room, he tried to figure out how much strength he could muster while in the same room as Razznians. He would not initiate a fight but would engage if they did. Now Lassa was to come to the table as well. He went to his chamber to talk with Chardon on his private commwave.

⁕⁕☼⁕⁕

Chardon did a final check on his list of talking points as he headed towards the gate to meet up with Halfar on Azrom. From there, they would both journey to the Dreridian solar system. It was no mystery what they wanted and Chardon found Halfar's stubbornness to negotiate frustrating. He was starting to see a big change in his lover's demeanor and he didn't like it. He also noticed Halfar's harsher treatment of Farin and their youngest child, Chafar. At one point, Chardon heard rumors of royal guards mistreating Farin and hoped, for Halfar's sake, that it was just that; rumors.

Behind him, Modas trudged along silently. There was some un- spoken agreement to not speak for the duration of the journey. Tension drifted off the manbeast. Farin was already on Azrom from the time be- fore and, Halfar assured him, under careful watch. Trinon was there so he didn't worry too much. The decision to go in male form was his own much to Halfar's dislike. Chardon had taken to hearing his own councils' suggestions and it was unanimous. Going as Halfar's mate would make it seem they had conceded New Lassa to Azrom. He didn't dare tell him that, knowing the ruler's tendency to lash out in anger, more so these past few years.

"Modas!" Chardon turned around and halted. The manbeast, startled out of his brooding, stopped in his tracks and looked up at him. "If conflict breaks out."

"We are prepared for that," said Modas with a raised a hand.

"Good. Let's get this over with."

Chardon eyed the entourage he had picked for the meeting. Talas, Modas, Mara and Ganna, the latter only as a necessity. He couldn't stand being in the same vicinity as the chief scientist yet he agreed with his choices; a Lassian warrior, a manbeast, an energy user and a mad scientist.

Let's see how they perform for the Dreridians.

⁎⁎☼⁎⁎

Two vortices opened up side by side, their gaping mouths ready to eject what they had swallowed previously. From the first came a gleaming white monstrosity nearly a mile in its diameter, its massive body decelerating as it cleared the vortex. Halfar's Armada ship was the only one of its kind. The other vortex brought forth a ship blood red, nearly black in color, its red lights giving it the appearance of a giant insect. Though half the size of Azrom's, it appeared deadlier. The Razznians had arrived.

On what seemed like a timed maneuver, both ships sent out carriers towards the surface of the solar system's conquering planet. A guidance system locked on and brought them to the main docking hub of the commonwealth. The two ships weren't the only ones landing and the hub was bustling with activity.

An urge to vomit came over Chardon as the Azrom carrier settled into the designated slot before being clamped down. He had forgotten how much he hated traveling to other worlds for that reason. Out of the corner of his vision, he saw Lord Romnus raise an eyebrow at him with a grin on his face. In the face of possible humiliation, Chardon held back the nausea and rose from his seat.

He could see the Razznian ship docked catty corner from theirs on the right and rage came creeping in. *Not now!* Chardon forced it down. Halfar turned to him and a knowing look transpired between them. In the corridor leading out of the carrier, he noticed the size of their combined entourage. There were seven royal guards, four of them Halfar's, the two generals, his group and Lord Romnus'. They appeared to be coming for a fight indeed.

When he was visiting other worlds with Sestis, they had come to meet Lord Pondur once at an interstellar meeting in the Huun system. His mate at the time was quite comfortable making conversation with the diplomats but he stayed focused and only asked what was needed. He felt disappointment and guilt for not ceasing her downward spiral sooner.

On the platform below a Dreridian convoy waited for both ships' passengers to disembark. Chardon took a good look at the craggy skinned species in tailored wardrobes made of the finest textiles. They stood in a pyramid formation, a tall, portly male at the front. He wondered how different a diet this one had than the others.

To the right of their group came the Razznians and Chardon got his first look at their ruler. It was shocking to see the massive reptile lumber down his ship's ramp onto the platform, Commander Sars following close behind with his own men and six Razznian soldiers. Sars made eye contact with him and again that look of pity was on his face. It angered Chardon because he had no idea why the Razznian would feel that way towards him.

"Honored guests, I am Lord Greggor. Such a pleasure to welcome you to our fair home world." He made a slight bow with one arm across his chest, hand laid flat.

"Lord Greggor. To finally meet the creator of such fine machines is our honor."

The Razznian ruler stopped his advance.

"The pleasure was mine, Lord Kraznan."

"Are we done with the stroking of ego?" Halfar spat.

"You are on their home world, Lord Halfar," Lord Kraznan retorted. "You should show respect. Or do you not require it of your own guests on Azrom?"

Halfar looked as if he had been physically assaulted into silence and Chardon feared there would be bloodshed. A hand brushed his shoulder and he saw Lord Romnus approach the Dreridians.

"My apologies, Lord Greggor. I am Lord Romnus of the First Royal House of Azrom." He bowed deep, as did his entourage, then turned to the Razznians and did the same. "Greetings, Lord Kraznan." Romnus stepped back behind Halfar's group.

Not knowing what to make of the situation as Halfar stood dumbfounded, Chardon made a bold decision and introduced himself as well.

"I am Chardon, the leader of New Lassa. We are grateful for your welcome, Lord Greggor. Greetings to you, Lord Kraznan."

He tilted his head slightly. Deep enough to show some respect but just enough to show his place in all this.

Halfar was clenching and unclenching his fists several times until finally he too made a sweeping gesture, bowing nearly to his knees while keeping his eyes on the Razznians and Dreridians.

"Apologies. Lord Greggor, Lord Kraznan."

As he stood back up his overdramatic greeting cemented his obvious disdain.

Kur and Rass stayed back, glancing at each other. Chardon's skin crawled and he felt tiny raised bumps form as if the temperature had dropped. This meeting was not going to go well in his mind. He remembered his first interstellar campaign, where he met Halfar, and the lack of obedience amongst the different leaders.

"Come, this way," Lord Greggor commanded.

The conference chamber was larger than Chardon had expected and also unexpected was the other world leaders already present around the table. He recognized a few from his previous visits on their planets. The Yaos leader grimaced at him and he gave him an equal look back. All the guards were required to either stand against the walls or along the corridor outside. Chardon was glad to have just four people so they were able to sit at the table together. Halfar sat across from him along with his generals and only Lord Kraznan and Sars were seated near the edge.

A few minutes later, Lord Pondur entered the chamber and sat at the head of the table with Lord Greggor and a thin male not quite of the same height seating themselves on either side of him. Servants came carrying trays of beverages made to each representative's tastes. Chardon wondered how they would know and Lord Greggor answered his unspoken question.

"Please enjoy. I have done extensive research on your species and I'm sure you will find them quite accurate.

Ganna snorted as she stared at the chalice set in front of the Lassians.

"Extensive research, hmm? So how many of these species did you consume, Lord Greggor?"

Silence fell over the room and some halted their chalices inches from their lips. Lord Greggor laughed.

"I assure you, this comes strictly from chemistry."

The smile on his face told Chardon otherwise but he knew it would be rude to not par- take. He watched the faces of the other diplomats come to the same conclusion and they all took a tiny sip. From his view above the chalice as he tilted it up, he saw Lord Greggor and Ganna engaged in a staring contest, a mutual understanding passing between them that made Chardon shudder.

Across from him, Halfar had the chalice in his hand, slowly swishing the liquid around. His gaze was on Lord Pondur who sat straight in his seat, legs crossed, and sipping his drink. Chardon turned to Mara who shook her head.

Lord Pondur set his chalice down and placed both hands on the table.

"Let's begin, shall we?" He scanned the room, making sure he had everyone's attention. Chardon found it unnecessary. They were all here to pay heed. "As you know, a small outbreak occurred between Azrom, Razzna and New Lassa. This tantrum was brought about by the Lassian female leader, Sestis who commissioned the Razznians to go up against Azrom."

"Such stupidity!" The Yaos leader exclaimed.

He sought approval from the other world leaders and received nods.

"Yes, I would agree. Because of all this, Azrom thought it necessary to send a hyper dimensional beam to Razzna, thus destroying much of the surface and collapsing the mines. Some of you at this table rely on Razznian ore for its many attributes and now it has become a rare commodity, driving the amount of barter to new levels. So now we have a dilemma."

"Who pays for the disruption in commerce and damage to trade?" Lord Greggor piped in.

Chardon sat upright in his seat. New Lassa had nothing to offer in exchange for such a barter. Halfar seemed unfazed by this and the Razznians looked like they were prepared for it. Modas was frowning next to him with arms crossed over his chest.

"You look frightened Lord Chardon," Lord Pondur said.

All eyes fell on him. He wanted to leave the room but held fast. He was the leader of an entire race and would not show any more weakness.

"Frightened? No. I am just surprised you would involve us when you know we are just starting to adjust to a new planet."

"Yes, also because of Azrom's ill balanced judgement."

"What are the terms?" Halfar asked impatiently.

"My treasurer will explain." Lord Pondur gestured to the lanky Dreridian hovered over his handheld holoscreen.

The treasurer stood and cleared his throat.

"For exchange of natural resources to alleviate the debt, a rulership pact will be negotiated for each planet. Razzna will share joint ruling for one half century and we will install a new automated mining system. After the duration is complete, the system will have made up for the demand."

Lord Kraznan's lidless eyes narrowed into slits. He obviously didn't like the idea and Chardon didn't blame him, then he realized this may be New Lassa's fate as well. Anger welled back up.

"Since New Lassa is not on our trade client roster, we will have to establish what can be produced from the planet that is of value. An ambassador will be assigned to oversee production for one century."

"On Lassa's head you will not!" Ganna yelled as her fist slammed on the table.

Halfar turned sideways in his seat and leaned towards the Dreridians.

"This plan, it does not pertain to Azrom. I am supreme ruler, no one else."

His eyes had that burning glow Chardon had witnessed only once and it signaled combat.

"Azrom will ramp up production of their mines and have an ambassador for fifty years due to its level of stability in contrast with Razzna and New Lassa," the treasurer continued, paying Halfar no mind.

"There will be nothing of the kind!" Halfar yelled.

"Your juvenile confrontations have caused strife in our trade networks!" another leader roared. "This will ensure profits!"

"Maybe there is another alternative?" Romnus asked politely.

Lord Pondur cocked his head to one side and smiled.

"Ah, Lord Romnus. The next in line of succession who conceded his position for his younger family members."

Halfar whirled on his cousin.

"What do you think you're doing? WE are not negotiating!" He turned his attention back to Pondur. "If anyone should be compensated, it is Azrom for your poor judgement in assisting Razzna to harm us!"

Arguments broke out all around the table and the yelling formed a cacophony of sound that hurt Chardon's hearing. He tried to block it out, squeezing his eyes shut as he did so. It didn't work. Lord Romnus was sitting at the table calmly eating a fruit Biandra had plucked from her robes. His gaze was locked on Lord Pondur. Chardon watched some strange communication transpire between the two

"You know what I find interesting about your races?" Lord Pondur spoke, his voice cutting through the sound. Everyone stopped arguing and turned to face him. "You only have an interest in technology when it applies to transport. To this day, you all insist on getting your own hands dirty in battle."

"It's called honor. We like to look our enemy in the eyes when we bring them to death's embrace," Halfar said through gritted teeth. "We don't mow them down behind their backs, unlike your kind."

"Of course we do, it is an element of war. Eliminate your enemy."

Lord Pondur picked up his chalice and took another sip of his drink.

"You will not set foot on Azrom and take from us as you wish!"

"If Azrom does not agree to the terms, then all commerce from the Dreridian system will be blocked from Azrom. No new shipments will flow."

"Then so be it!" Halfar stood.

"Tread carefully, Lord Halfar. Your people need resources."

"If any of them cannot show strength for Azrom then they do not deserve my compassion!"

Chardon cringed in his seat as if he had been struck. The look and tone coming from Halfar was not the mate he knew. Catching a glance at Sars, he saw pity and finally realized what it was for. Halfar had always been known as a ruthless, cunning ruler but because he was in love with him didn't see how deep it went. Halfar had just condemned his people to an existence of strife. Lord Romnus had dropped his half-eaten fruit on the table and sat in a state of what could only be shock.

"We are leaving!" Halfar turned to the door and when no one followed him, he turned back around. A crazed wide-eyed stare formed on his face. Kur and Rass jumped up and went to his side. He looked over at Chardon. "Did you hear me?"

Chardon snapped out of his haze and their eyes locked.

"What is right for Azrom is not necessarily right for New Lassa. You can leave, but I am going to stay and negotiate for MY race."

The crazed look worsened. "Do as you wish," Halfar spat and left the room.

"Good for you, leader!" Ganna exclaimed. "I knew you had it in you."

"I believe we should do separate negotiations from this point forward," Lord Pondur stated. He turned to the end of the table to his right. "Lord Romnus, are you staying on behalf of Azrom?"

Chardon didn't even realize he hadn't gone with Halfar. What was the royal thinking? He hoped it wasn't a tactic to go against his own ruler.

"I am just observing, Lord Pondur. Since Lord Chardon and Lord Halfar are mated I find it my duty to make sure New Lassa is not being raped by your greed." He looked at the other diplomats in the room. "Or theirs."

"And Azrom?"

"As I have asked, is there no alternative?"

"Are you negotiating, Lord Romnus?"

Chardon gave the royal a look that he hoped said 'don't do it'. Lord Romnus seemed to have noticed but there was something else.

"Is that not what you do?" Lord Romnus replied.

Lord Pondur smiled at that and sipped some more of his drink. Chardon felt a large boulder plummet into his gut. Things were not going so well. And throughout the entire session, Talas remained unnaturally silent. That alone frightened him.

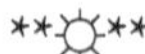

A great divide had formed on the Azrom carrier when Chardon returned with Lord Romnus. No one spoke during the ride back to the Armada ship still orbiting the Dreridian home world. It was worse than any funeral march yet no one had died; not yet. Passing through the vortex, Chardon noticed the route was different and before he could ask, the ship came out on the other side into familiar territory. Halfar had brought them to New Lassa.

"Are we going to continue talks with my council?" He asked Halfar.

"I assume you are. I will not be joining." His level tone held contempt.

"So, you are just going to drop us down and go back to Azrom with- out at least seeing your offspring?"

"I will see them as I see fit. Do you really want me to come now?"

Chardon stood up in anger about to yell at him, finding Halfar's behavior unacceptable, when Talas clamped a hand around his wrist. Looking down at the warrior he saw Talas stare at him for a brief moment then let go.

"No. I suppose not."

"Escort them to the carrier and New Lassa," Halfar commanded his guards.

On the way to the hangar, Chardon felt uneasy in the presence of the royal guards. It seemed as though they harbored ill will against them. Talas walked in dead silence, keeping his fingers on the hilt of his long- sword as they headed out.

The journey down to the surface was no better with communication nonexistent. Once the carrier landed, Halfar's guards remained seated and the hatch was opened remotely for his people. The lack of respect for his title and his race made Chardon wonder if it was by Halfar's decree or of their own doing. Within minutes after the last Lassian stepped onto the planet, the carrier was ascending back up towards the Armada ship.

"Well, that was eye opening, don't you agree, Ganna?" Talas finally spoke.

"I believe that is an understatement. The audacity."

"They are more advanced than us and the others, for that matter."

"That does not give them the right to dictate those kinds of terms."

"But, you did not back down," Talas remarked. "And neither did you, Chardon. I'm glad."

"Yes, for one particular moment I thought we were going to have to have you removed as leader. Well done keeping our best interests at the forefront."

"Why do I feel like a child being praise for good behaving?" Chardon snapped.

"Don't take it as such," Talas said.

"Look, the council is waiting," Mara exclaimed, pointing ahead.

A large tent had been erected in the middle of a field and all the council leaders were assembled. With it being such a beautiful day out, he couldn't blame them for conducting the meeting outdoors. He turned to Ganna and for the first time, appreciated her presence. If it weren't for her knowledge and quick mind, they might be under Dreridian rule or at war.

"So, what did the Dreridians propose?" Jaron came strolling out from the crowd.

Chardon had that feeling of being chastised again. It never ceased to amaze him how Jaron kept up such a ruse, knowing she was more caring than anyone.

"Let's get it over with," he declared.

Modas stood outside the tent along with three other manbeasts, guarding all four corners. Chardon sat in the middle at the table while field workers came with bowls of produce and carafes of drinks.

"Ganna will explain. I am too exhausted and angry to do so." The council gave Ganna a wary look, an unease filling the room and Chardon sighed. Baby steps. "She was able to negotiate a deal better than any of us," he continues as he waved a finger at Talas, Modas and Mara.

"Well then," Ganna started, "I will tell you their proposal." She made herself more comfortable on her cushion. "They propose we let them research then harvest any valuable resources New Lassa may have for commercial trade under the supervision of a Dreridian ambassador for one half century."

Accusatory glances immediately came Chardon's way and his defenses went up. He could tell what they were thinking; that he caved in the face of the enemy. Ganna came to his rescue.

"Our leader refused their proposal and did not falter." Wide eyed shock was the response which offended Chardon even more. "We came to a compromise. I will offer my services in conjunction with their scientists to build clientele for New Lassa and release ten percent of any valuable resources we find to them as barter payment."

"No ambassadors?" the head of military asked.

"No dictatorship?" the head of agriculture asked.

"None of that," Ganna replied proudly.

"Then what are these services for? What do the Dreridians want?"

This time Ganna frowned. "Weapons."

"For them to use on other races, including ours?" the head of military cried out.

"Make no mistake! Whatever new weapons we jointly create, I will make sure is also in our possession as well. We will not be so far behind in technology as we once were."

"Once again, you have saved us from doom," Chardon said softly.

"It's what I do, leader. My only goal has always been to make Lassa capable of holding her own in the face of conflict."

"And we owe you gratitude for that. Though, we are still quite angry with you, I will concede to that."

The nods around the table confirmed it.

"Now if you'll excuse me. Ganna can take it from here?"

Chardon rose from the table and left the meeting, heading straight to Farin's personal chamber. Inside she found Farin on the bed playing with her child, making the little one let out an infectious giggle. He went and sat down on the bed next to her and used his fingers to join in tickling the baby's belly.

"How was the meeting?" Farin asked.

"Everything went well."

"And father?"

Chardon stopped tickling the baby for a second.

"It's worse than I could have imagined."

"He didn't come planet side to see me or Chafar." Farin looked over in the corner of the room and Chardon noticed her younger child slumped against the wall sleeping. He was covered in dirt and had a look of content on his face. "Why is father so angry? What happened at the meeting?"

"I stayed to negotiate for New Lassa after he refused to do so for Azrom. I told him what was good for his race did not mean it was for mine."

"Oh!" Farin's beautiful face scrunched up with worry. He hated seeing that. She should be happy but had to live like a prisoner. "His council is probably happy about it."

"I have no doubt. If his manic behavior causes harm to my people, especially you, I will show no mercy."

"Even though you love him?"

"More so because I do." He turned back to Chafar. "Why is he covered in dirt asleep on your floor?"

Farin giggled. "He's been training with the warriors."

"But he's an energy user."

"That doesn't mean he can't learn to fight in combat like a warrior, mother." The way Farin said it made Chardon feel like he had been restricting not only his children, but his race. "That's what's wrong with our people right now. No one is willing to cross share their knowledge."

Chardon sat up straight, her words hitting like a boulder to the chest. Farin was right. He always knew how observant she was but this was a whole new level on par with Talas or Trinon.

"You're correct, my child, and I am going to try and fix that."

⁂

When the carrier touched down on the roof of Azrom's main palace, Lord Romnus immediately exited the opened hatch. His entourage kept in tight formation behind him and they swiftly made their way to his own palace, disregarding Halfar's royal guards' demanding they halt. The faster he distanced himself from his cousin, the better. His blood felt like it was boiling beneath his skin and he had no idea what would happen if he were to engage them at that moment.

The group nearly ran down the staircase adjacent to the palaces' dividing line then across the courtyard into his own. He steered them towards the communal hall and as he set foot over the threshold, let out a roar that turned into a high-pitched trill, lowering to a deep tone. The servants in the room became visibly shaken and some had covered their ears in vain as they passed out from the frequency.

Seated at the table, the heads of the first royal house family halted what they were doing, now staring at him in fear. He brushed his hair back from his face and stood tall. Biandra brought out a fruit from her robe's sleeve, handing it to him. His family members' stares, still wide with wonder, followed him as he sat at the head of the table and settled into the cushions.

"Halfar," Reita breathed.

"Halfar," he said.

"What happened? What was this meeting for?" Chastan asked.

"Apparently, the Dreridians wanted compensation."

"For what?" Kuhala yelled. "They helped the Razznians attack us!"

"Actually, no, they didn't." He saw the shock on their faces. "This was something set in motion long ago by Chardon's former mate. The Dreridians do not want compensation for anything regarding that."

"Then what?"

"By our retaliation against Razzna, we have essentially destroyed commerce for the ore they mine, which was already a high valued commodity. Azrom is being held responsible for that."

"But we were in the midst of a battle!" Chastan cried out.

"That did not warrant our cannon be fired to razed the surface of Razzna," Romnus shot back.

"I do agree, it was overly aggressive," Kuhala said.

"Halfar refused to negotiate and left the meeting."

"But, that also affects our trade."

"Exactly. A blockade has been placed on Azrom."

Reita leaned forward, terror on her face.

"Our people need many of those outside resources! We have not recovered from the last great war over a century ago!"

"Our people will starve and live in worse conditions than they already are. The battle with Razzna did us no favors," Lord Aloni, who hardly ever spoke, added.

He had recovered from the initial shock of Romnus' entry and was now engaged. Romnus felt relief, worried that Aloni would remain quiet.

"I know."

Romnus took a bite of the fruit in his hand and felt the effect of its nectar course through his body. A normal Azromian would be put down like a death blow, the sedative juices being so strong but it only managed to calm him down.

"What do we do?" Chastan asked.

"Nothing."

"What?" Reita and Chastan yelled at once.

"We have to wait and see," Aloni replied. "If it becomes clear Azrom is indeed going to be crippled, we will act. Until then," he tapered off.

"Out!" Halfar roared.

He had made it to the throne room and his two advisors went to brief their colleagues while he settled himself on his throne. For what seemed like an hour, he had sat fuming before deciding he wanted to be alone. The decibel of his command made everyone flinch and they fled from the room. Now alone, he went over the meeting in his mind, unable to forgive Chardon for going against his demand to leave.

His advisors slowly crept back into his throne room some time later and bowed deep at his feet. The mock fear gleaming in their eyes was a joke. They were not afraid of him by any means because their job was to help him rule.

"My lord, I truly understand your anger. That was a blatant defiance on your mate's part." Prevcan began.

"Which is why we are so adamant in finding a true Azromian

to be at your side. Only one of our own can relate to Azrom's needs." Mesrod's lips curved up.

"You must also find a way to keep Farin in check when she is here." Dondar added his opinion.

"I propose you have her visit only twice a cycle for no more than four moons until she is mated." Mesrod suggested.

"Her manbeast is not efficient in watching her and should be left on New Lassa. Our royal guards are quite capable of doing the task, maybe even better." Prevcan stated.

Halfar nodded in agreement at the bombardment of ideas. He would not monopolize Farin's time on Azrom but he did see reason to get rid of the manbeast. Countless times he had to send guards out to find her when she snuck out of her chamber. Chardon would be angry but he didn't care anymore. This was for the sake of his race, not Lassa's as it was told to him.

"Agreed. I will discuss this matter with them on their next visit."

"Very well, my lord," Mesrod said. He bowed deep along with the others and he was alone once again.

The five advisors walked slowly down the outer corridor enjoying the midafternoon air. Royal guards bowed to them as they passed.

"This is coming to fruition better than we had planned," Prevcan remarked.

"Yes, we can get rid of the manbeast, give that halfbreed to some high ranked soldier or lower royal and have the people of Azrom in the palms of our hands," Jabarz piped up.

"There will be dissent," Dondar warned.

"Of course, but it can be easily squelched with the right discipline. Fear is always a great motivation to stay obedient," Mesrod answered.

"What of the first royal house? They are helping the destitute," Calba asked.

"Let them. That is of no concern and they are no threat. We have an entire royal army at our disposal and no matter how strong they are, cannot fight such might."

Mesrod waved a hand as if brushing it off.

They all smiled, bowing in greeting to some of the royals visiting by appointment only.

Yes, it's all going well, Mesrod thought to himself.

☀

The gate opened and the rooftop of Azrom's main palace came into view. Chardon, back in female form for Halfar's sake, stepped onto the platform with Farin, Chafar and Trinon beside her. Modas had become unbearable so she commanded him to stay on New Lassa. She could defend herself if need be but had never come into harm's way on Azrom since the battle.

In front of her stood two advisors and four royal guards. Not a good sign. Halfar always greeted them when they visited. She turned to Trinon who also seemed disturbed by this.

What is happening?

"Lady Chardon, Lady Farin and," Mesrod paused, "Young Lord Chafar. How wonderful to see you again. "Our Lord has been so busy lately. I am sure he would appreciate some personal time."

"Is he well?"

"Of course. He's just in the middle of restructuring some logistics. Come, let's get you settled." The way he waited for them to move gave Chardon the impression that it was an order, not a request. "A small banquet for just the family is being prepared." He smiled.

Chardon nodded to his group and they followed with two guards ahead and two positioned behind them like prisoners led to the dungeon. A hand brushed against hers and clasped it. Farin was shaking. Chafar's full lips went thin seeing that. She knew he hated being on Azrom and this situation was only going to make it worse.

They first led Chafar to his chamber, leaving two guards at the entrance, then Farin and Trinon, doing the same. At her own personal chamber, Chardon sighed.

So I am not staying with Halfar.

Two guards were position at her entrance as well.

"We will come to escort you to evening meal later. Please, rest until then."

"I wanted to take a walk in the gardens," Chardon said.

"Oh? I think you should rest for the day. We will discuss a trip to the gardens tomorrow, perhaps?"

"There will be no perhaps. What is going on?"

"Nothing, I assure you. If you insist, I will have the guards escort you."

"They never have before."

"Things are different now, aren't they?" Mesrod gave her a look that said she was to blame for this.

"Fine, bring my children and Trinon so we can go on a family stroll before mealtime."

Chardon watched the advisor's eyes narrow even as he smiled in acknowledgement.

"As you wish."

He left with his partner and the royal guards.

⭒

Evening meal was fraught with such tension that Chardon almost couldn't eat. An awkward silence set heavy above them like a veil of smoke. Having had enough, she slammed her fist down on the table, the bowls jumping up off the surface and landing with a melody of clanks. Halfar looked up from his platter and stared at her with such contempt that she reared back away from him. Trinon's claws came out as he stood in the vicinity behind her.

An advisor came over to Halfar and whispered in his ear. His face changed and he sighed heavily.

"What is it, my love? Is the food not to your liking?"

"No! You will not be cordial to me because your advisors think you should! If we are not welcome here then we leave!"

Chardon stood up and gestured for her children to do the same. A mortified look fell on Halfar's face.

"Wait!" He stood and held a hand out in front of him. "Don't go. I'm sorry. It has been a stressful time and not my intention to take it out on all of you."

His advisors seemed displeased with his outburst and Chardon claimed victory.

"Is that so?" she asked.

"Yes. Chafar, come. I am sorry to have neglected you lately."

Chafar slowly got up from his seat and went to his father. Where Halfar's embraces was tight, Chafar's was lackluster. When he let go, he gestured for Farin who also reluctantly went to him. They sat back down and Trinon retracted his claws.

"Please, let's finish our meal," Halfar suggested.

Conversation was light and Chardon could hear nothing. Her mind had turned the volume down to nearly white noise as she continued to eat while watching everyone else's mouths move. It should not be this way.

"Shall we retire to bed? It is later than we thought." Halfar's voice cut through the deafening static.

"I have not finished arranging my chamber so I will be up regardless."

"What do you mean? My chamber is always prepared."

She saw his advisors squirm.

So it's not Halfar's doing.

He looked around the table and then at his advisors before returning her gaze.

"I am in a personal chamber of your advisor's choosing."

"What?" Halfar's soft tone peppered with malice sent shivers down her spine.

"You have been so busy, my lord. I felt some rest alone would do you good until tomorrow, at least." Prevcan stumbled over his words.

"You made a decision FOR me?"

"My apologies, my lord," he said, bowing deep.

"I am sorry," Halfar said to her. "We do have things to discuss, but that can come later." He stood up from the table and came around to her with his hand held out. "Please, come with me."

Chardon glanced over at her children who nodded. She took his hand and let him lead her out of the banquet hall. He had that familiar mischievous grin she loved on his face and for a second, she forgot that he was on the verge of losing his mind.

It didn't take long for her to be reminded when they reached his chamber. He literally tossed her onto the bed then climbed on top of her, tearing at her robes. She heard the fabric rip as he grabbed hold of them at the collar and pulled. They splayed open all the down, the sash torn in half, and he laid the tattered edges at her side.

Hunger. Rage. Those were what she saw in his eyes.

He stripped naked and wrapped his hands around her knees, pulling her to him violently. She tried to get loose from him even as he plunged into her like some wild beast. When she was able to get leverage and attempted to turn from underneath him, he surprised her by partially morphing one arm and bringing the pincer a hair from her neck. They opened and embedded themselves into the pillows beneath her head, holding her neck down. She didn't dare move as the tiny teeth of the pincer made contact with her skin.

Each thrust was more painful than the one before and she thought right before passing out that he was going to kill her.

The pain came back fiercely along with a garbled sound. She forced her eyes open and found Halfar looming over her in a state of panic. His hands were gripping the sides of her face and he seemed to be yelling. A look of relief came over him and his hands slid down to her shoulders.

"I'm sorry," he cried in a weak voice.

That brought her out of the blurry space she was in. She had never seen Halfar cry. The tears were big and dripped down onto her breasts like rain. Then everything changed. He looked up at her and the tears stopped. Sitting up, he wiped his face and climbed off her. That expression was the same as that advisor's; this was her fault.

Halfar dressed quickly and headed out the chamber. Before he disappeared around the corner she heard the orders he gave the guards.

"See that she is escorted to her own chamber before I return at sunrise."

****☼****

By morning, Chardon had recovered and rounded up her children with the help of Trinon to make way towards the gate. She would not stay on Azrom any longer nor her children. Halfar had changed into a being she didn't know. Their psychic bond so strong before was nowhere to be found, the severed link between them painful. In her plan to escape, she and Trinon had to knock out their guards in order to buy time and they had made it to the gate.

Halfar and his royal guards were not a minute behind them. There he stood ever the supreme ruler. Two of his advisors were with him as well and Chardon cast an evil stare at them. They just smiled.

"Where are you going?" Halfar demanded.

"Home."

"I never asked you to leave," he yelled.

"You didn't have to," Chardon snapped.

Halfar made a nod and four guards came at Farin, grabbing her by the arms. Trinon drew claws and Chardon let energy grow in her hands. As they both prepared to strike the guards, Halfar stood between them and his guards.

"Stop!"

"Let go of my child!" Chardon yelled back.

"Farin stays here with me." He looked over at Trinon as he signaled ten more guards to cover him. "Without the manbeast. We have no need for him. We can protect her on our own."

"Why would she need protection?" Chafar asked loudly.

Halfar was taken aback by his son's question and Chardon felt ill.

Yes, why?

She watched the rough way the guards handled her child and unleashed a ball of energy on them. Farin got herself out of the way in time.

"What are you doing?" Halfar roared. "She will be back in four moons!"

"If I ever see or hear of you or any of your so called royal guards treat my child this way again I will never forgive you. And I will come back and kill every last one."

The gate was activated, forming the vortex that would send her back to New Lassa. In that moment, as she turned away from Halfar, she vowed to keep that promise.

Halfar turned away from the gate and looked down on the two half dead guards on the ground. Farin was unharmed but shaken. This is not what he wanted. It was only to keep Farin safe while on Azrom, nothing more. The way Chardon looked at him as she left felt like he had been run through with a longsword. Realizing he had an audience, Halfar regained his demeanor and started giving orders.

"Take these guards to the medical bay. I want a meeting with the councils before evening meal. Bring my child to the throne room."

He looked down on her then and the endless disobedience filled his mind.

Two other guards picked her up after Halfar walked away.

He didn't look back because he might witness them manhandling her again. As long as he didn't see it, he could feign ignorance. A pain stabbed him at the thought yet he decided to dismiss it.

In the throne room, he sat letting his gaze bear down on Farin as he took a good look at her. She was indeed beautiful and well-rounded for mating. He could see the four guards he had assigned to her leer in the corridor. A certainty that they would never touch her for he would surely kill them was his reassurance.

"You are to stay in your chamber unless otherwise requested," he spoke to her sharply. "You will only stay four moons and only twice a cycle. That is until I find an appropriate mate for you. Do you understand me?"

Farin just stood there unmoving with her head down.

"Do you understand?" He yelled.

She looked up then, tears in her eyes. "Yes."

"Yes, what?"

"Yes, father."

"Yes," Halfar rose up from his throne, "what?"

"Yes, my lord," she cried out softly between sobs.

"Good." Halfar sat back down. "Take her to her chamber," he ordered the guards.

He turned his head away as they came and dragged her out of the throne room. Even with his eyes averted he could still see the way they held her. *It's for her own good.* Halfar felt that pain again and forced it away. He had no time for pity.

****☼****

The bonding ceremony for Kur and Rass was getting closer by the hour. Servants ran to and fro setting up the banquet hall and arranging flowers. In their chamber were six tailors doing last moment alterations of the ceremonial robes. Kur glanced over at the one he was to wear and frowned. It looked heavy and gaudy. The fabric was pearl with gold and silver accents, the inside a light shimmering green. White leggings and a gold tunic were picked for his undergarment.

"Such beautiful work, isn't it?" The master tailor beamed.

"Of course it is," Kur replied.

Rass had been sent off to a stylist for her hair. He was angry about that. Rass' hair was just fine the way it was. The idea of them doing un- natural things to it gave him pause. Lord Romnus came into the chamber, took one look at his wardrobe and raised an eyebrow.

"Not my choosing," Kur explained.

"No."

Kur peeked around. "No entourage this afternoon?"

"They are further down the corridor making sure no one disturbs us."

Kur clapped his hands and gestured towards the entrance. Everyone set down their work and left the chamber. He turned to Romnus.

"What has happened now?"

"I want you to get Lady Farin out of her chamber."

"She is to attend the ceremony. Her guards have escorted her to the bath already is what I was told."

"Then I will fetch her from there."

"Romnus, this is a dangerous plan. Halfar keeps her on a short tether."

"All the more reason to snatch her, even for a day and make him relent."

"Don't ruin my bonding ceremony, Romnus," Kur warned.

"I would do no such thing. Oh," he said as he went to the corridor, "don't worry about Rass. Your mother is quite capable."

"My mother?"

"She has many talents. One of them just happens to be a stylist. Congratulations, General."

Romnus led his entourage down the bathing corridor in a near run. He had a sinking feeling in the pit of his stomach and couldn't squelch it. As they neared the royal sector, he held up a hand for his entourage to hold while he continued on. He found the bath chamber she was in by the two guards at the entrance in relax formation looking in laughing. From his distance he could also see inside and the blood drained from his face.

One of the guards had walked in just as she was reaching for the towel held by the attendant to dry herself. The attendant was pushed away and the guard slammed Farin into the wall, the side of her face planted firmly against it. He grabbed her wrists and held them up above her head with one hand while he inserted the other between her buttocks and squeezed her flesh before gliding it up her back.

"You should really dry yourself off, Lady Farin before you become prone to illness," he sneered in her ear.

Letting go, he smacked her ass and threw the towel at her. The attendant moved to leave the room but the other guard stopped him.

"Do your job properly next time or our lord will hear about it."

All four guards positioned themselves at the entrance, proud of their little stint. Romnus approached them then and they looked up at him with contempt. He smiled and morphed both his arms into giant pincers. The guards went pale and moved out of his way.

"Thank you." Romnus returned his arms back to normal and entered the bath.

The attendant was shaking from fright so he placed a hand on the man's shoulder and nodded for him to step away. Farin too was shaking but a look of defiance set on her fair facial features. He carefully knelt down and wrapped his arms around her from behind. Her body went limp and fell into him.

"I will save you from this, my beautiful Farin. I promise. Just hold on a little while longer."

"Okay," she whispered.

Romnus turned his head back to the entrance. The guard who had assaulted Farin stared at them then smirked. Batis. Recalling the guard's name, he gripped Farin tighter, a hopelessness engulfing him.

****☼****

The main palace hall was nearly bursting at the seams close to over capacity. Representatives from all four royal houses were in attendance for the bonding ceremony of their new-found royal brethren who just happened to also be one of the Armada Generals. That he was bonding with the other General made the occasion even more significant. Halfar didn't find it all that joyous and he was put off by the number of royals in his main palace.

His advisors told him this was a necessity, a show of good faith. They also insisted that Farin be let out for the festivities as well. After much thought, he agreed. Not having Farin attend would stir up questions he had no intention of answering. He had even granted Romnus' request to have her stay in the first house palace for a few days after the ceremony.

Being a guest in his own domain infuriated him but he knew he had to endure. The supreme ruler did officiate bonding ceremonies, yet he felt the council should have made an exception considering the strife Azrom was currently in. Of course, if he had been asked to do it, he would have denied the request for union. It was so much better when his generals hated each other. He remembered the hesitation in Rass to kill Kur on Earth.

Was there ever really hate?

The head of the council for domestic affairs entered the hall from the left entrance and walked up to stand on the platform overlooking the guests. Two of his councilmen came to stand on either side of him and a hush fell over the hall. Halfar turned his head to watch. His table was near the platform where the newly bonded couple would sit after the ceremony. As supreme ruler he demanded that they not sit side by side. He would be between them, his advisors noting that he must always be the center of attention even in events such as this one.

"Greetings, my lord," the official said, bowing low, "and honored guests. Let us rejoice in the bonding of our two finest warriors, Kur, General and Lord and General Rass."

Ethereal music combined with the tinging of chimes echoed through the hall and at the entrance appeared Kur and Rass. Halfar had never seen them in royal attire, and was awestruck by the sheer sparkling of their dress but mostly how enticing Rass looked in female form draped in royal fabric.

Her hair had been manipulated and styled into large bouncing coils that shined as if lacquered. The gown was the same shiny green color as the inside of Kur's robe and it complemented her skin. Each stitch of embroidery matched the other's attire. Jealousy and lust consumed him and it took every fiber of his being not to jump up and cancel the ceremony.

Kur and Rass made their slow secession down the aisle created by the masses who preened and whispered well wishes as they passed. Kur assisted Rass up the narrow stairs to the platform and there they halted side by side in front of the official.

"Do you swear devotion to each other even in death?"

"I swear this," they both said together.

"You will demonstrate your proof."

He nodded to the councilman on his right.

A knife was produced and the couple held out their wrists. With one swift cut, the councilman sliced both at the same time without blood splatter. The thin cuts stayed fused for a moment then opened up, spilling blood that dripped down into chalices placed directly beneath each arm.

When the chalices were half full, the second councilman came with fabric folded in his arms. He unraveled it and bringing the two wrists together, bound them with it, stopping the blood flow.

The councilmen each picked up a chalice and handed Kur's to Rass and Rass' to Kur. Halfar had seen a few bonding ceremonies and it al- ways fascinated him when the couples stared at the chalice of each other's blood for a moment before tentatively drinking it, taking forever. To his shock, that didn't happen. Kur and Rass stared at each other without averting their eyes as they downed the contents of the chalices in one gulp then handing them back.

Small cheers and sounds of astonishment went softly around the hall. The official nodded in approval and placed his hand on the wad of fabric covering their wrists.

"By Azrom's decree, you are now Lord and Lady of the first royal house. Present yourselves."

He removed his hand and let them turn to the guests. They bowed deeply and the thunderous clapping began mixed with more cheers. The fabric was removed, the councilmen checking to make sure the wounds were sealed, then replaced it with shiny green ribbon on each.

"The bonding is complete!"

"Not until their mating after evening meal," Halfar heard Chastan chuckle.

He looked over at the table next to his where his first cousins sat. Chastan had been drinking already and he assumed it was before the ceremony because his servants wouldn't dare sneak the young lord a drink in his presence.

The bonded couple was escorted down the platform and to

their seats at Halfar's table. Kur was to his right and Rass to his left. A strained kind of atmosphere occurred and he smiled. To separate the newly bonded was in bad taste.

"Let the festivities commence!" Halfar shouted gleefully. At his command, the food and drink began to flow.

On Rass' left sat Farin in a royal blue gown and he saw the two clasp hands under the table. He wondered what that was for. Farin did not smile and picked at her meal when it was placed in front of her. It angered him. So much so that he leaned close to Rass' ear and whispered.

"Tell my child to enjoy your special occasion or I will rescind my blessing."

Rass' eyes went wide and she turned to him. He smiled back at her and she in turn did what she was told. Farin struggled with her facial expression until the corners of her mouth peaked upwards into a small smile, yet her eyes were dull. He felt eyes on him and looked to his right. Kur and the rest of the first royal house were assessing him like he was some kind of pariah. Smirking, he went back to his meal.

One by one, the royal house representatives came to the table to greet Halfar and congratulate the bonded couple. Romnus sat back in his seat and observed his cousin relishing in the fact that he was wedged between the two. In the far corner he could see the advisors delighted with the outcome. A clanking sound from his side made him avert his stare to see Chastan had knocked over a chalice.

"If you cannot keep Farin safe this night or any other these next few days, I will gladly find someone else who can," he whispered to Chastan. Startled, Chastan's head popped up and he looked around his table, then at Farin on the far end of Halfar's. He glanced down at his spilled chalice and frowned. A servant came to right it and was about to refill it when he clamped his hand over the mouth. The servant bowed and walked away.

"You are letting Chastan be responsible for Farin?" Kuhala laughed softly. "Please, let me handle this. He is of no use."

Chastan slammed his fist on the table. "I won't let anyone harm her! Ever!"

Romnus grimaced. It was safe to say that Chastan will have sobered up by the end of the banquet and there would be no issue. For added assurance, he had Farin drink a concoction earlier that, unbeknownst to her, destroyed the male seed should it find itself in her womb. He was certain of her fertility and the last thing they needed was her impregnated, again.

✺*

The opening vortex added strength to the wind on the platform atop the main palace. Chardon hesitantly stepped onto its surface and felt the gate close behind her. Standing next to her was Und in place of Trinon. She didn't want to be here but had to make sure Farin was okay before taking her home to New Lassa for a while until the next visit per Halfar's insistence. Hearing about Kur and Rass' ceremony and not being invited made her fume.

Ahead of her were four royal guards and Dondar. He had a grin on his face so she conjured a ball of energy for him. His grin faded, replaced with a look of fear.

"That is not necessary, Lady Chardon!"

"Is it not? I am under the impression that I was to fight my way to my child by any means."

"I assure you, Lady Farin is well," he glanced at the guards who refused to engage him. "I will take you to her first."

"That is what I want, thank you."

She turned to Und. He took a quick look back at her. This was hostile territory. The quicker they grabbed Farin and left the better they would both feel.

At the entrance to Farin's chamber, Chardon saw the four royal guards stationed there and the rage returned. There was no reason for Halfar to set that many on his child for the sole purpose of confinement. The leader of the guards, Batis, caught sight of her and frowned. She wanted nothing more than to have Und slice him apart. His look let her know he underestimated her. Big mistake.

Chardon went up to him and holding back her full might, backhanded him across the face, sending him flat on the ground. Blood trickled from his mouth and his comrades went to unsheathing their weapons while Und grew claws. The advisor clasped his hands together.

"Do not engage!" he ordered the guards. "Lady Chardon, I am not sure why you insist on," he was not allowed to finish.

"You think I don't know how my child has been treated

here? As her mother, I want to remind them that she is not just Halfar's and I will not tolerate it in my presence. I thought I made myself clear before. I will administer punishment every time I am here until treatment of my child is resolved." She looked down at Batis as he moved to get up.

Chardon went into the chamber and climbed on the bed. Farin was in a deep sleep, one filled with struggle as she watched her child tremor, small sounds of terror emitting from her lips. She stroked Farin's forehead damp with sweat.

"Und," she called. The manbeast came further into the chamber and stood by the bed's side. "Wet me a cloth." As he did so, she turned to the advisor and the now six guards at the entrance. "You can leave."

"Lady Chardon, these guards are assigned," again she did not let him finish.

"They are not needed here. My kind can protect her at this juncture," she sneered throwing Halfar's words back at the advisor.

"Very well. I will have you escorted to the throne room when it is time for departure. I am sure our lord would want to see you off."

"Good, I will relish in the three days of peace."

She watched them leave, Batis giving her a look of vengeance. He was of no concern to her and the last person she wanted to see was Halfar. As much as she still loved him, she knew there was no reasoning with him. It may be his death that stops his madness this time.

****☼****

The corridor was mostly empty during early afternoon and Halfar took advantage of this by roaming it without guards to his destination. He did request they position themselves moments after reaching his goal to ensure no one disrupted him. The sun was at its brightest making the outer corridor gleam like white pearl. His palace was such a beautiful structure, he laughed inwardly.

He stopped at the entrance of the chamber he wanted and stood looking inside it. The room was much bigger than the previous chamber the residents had occupied and allowed more light in. Cream walls, light colored floor coverings and sheer green and white fabric covered the tops of the bed. The bedding was the same cream as the walls with green undercovers peeking out.

On the bed lay Rass sleeping on her side in a white robe, her hair in disarray. It had been two moons since the bonding ceremony and both his generals were present less and less in the war room. No matter. He could easily strip them of their positions if he wanted, although his advisors warned him against such a move. Right now, all he wanted was to impregnate Rass for the glory of Azrom and his own ego.

He walked further in to stand at the foot of the bed and waited for Rass to feel his presence. It didn't take long. Rass slowly raised her head from the pillow and wiped sleep from her eyes. They stared at each other and Halfar saw the panic in her even though she tried to remain calm. He could tell from the way she was sleeping that she had been mating with Kur only this morning. So, she's weak from exhaustion.

"Stay away from me," she said.

"You dare order your lord?" Halfar yelled. He climbed onto the bed and yanked the covers from her body.

"Don't do this!"

"You will submit to me." He growled in her ear as he leaned down onto her.

"I will fight you," she cried out.

"That won't stop me. I don't need you conscious to accomplish my goal."

Rass's eyes widened and he knew what she saw in him. Deep seeded lust. His guards were already at the entrance to wave away anyone who neared the chamber. To his surprise, Rass morphed an arm and moved to strike. He dodged it and landed a blow to her side but that only angered her and she was able to counter with a direct hit to the back of his shoulder blade. He moved forward to lessen the impact, knowing it could have easily cracked the bone.

Grabbing hold of her ankle, he was able to pull her fully off the bed and into the air, smacking her against the headboard. It cracked into pieces as she landed back on the bed. Upset from the time being wasted, he ripped the robe off her and held her down by a pincer, removing his leggings while she still lay disoriented.

Kur hurried along the corridor to his chamber with Aloni and Kuhala. Romnus had suggested at his bonding ceremony that he invest in a private intel to watch his chamber from the satellite castle across the way. He thought it would be useful and so he was stricken with fear when the report came in that Halfar and two of his royal guards were at his chamber. Rass had been sleeping when he left this morning. Supreme Ruler or not, he would strike him down if Rass was desecrated in any- way. He knew Rass would fight and there would be blood, but if Halfar somehow got his seed in her, the next round of bloodshed would be his.

He wasted no time and struck down the first guard as he came up to his chamber entrance. Kuhala took down the other and they all advanced into the room. Halfar was straddling a naked, half-conscious Rass. Kur noticed the torn beddings, the destroyed headboard and blood splatter. Halfar stopped his penetration and sat still. Then he turned and met eyes with him.

Three against one. Kur made his decision. Halfar was stronger than him but if the other two backed him up, there could be a chance. He was about to strike when Aloni stopped him and nodded to the entrance. Royal guards, six of them, were blocking it and he felt his heart sink. Halfar's face scrunched into a frown and Kur was confused until he looked back again and saw behind them, Romnus' royal guards.

"You will leave this quadrant of the first royal house, my lord," the captain of Romnus' royal guard demanded.

"What did you say?" Halfar replied. His eyes went red.

The unsheathing of longswords was like a hurricane ripping out trees. Kur lifted his own and went into a battle stance.

"Get off my beloved," he said calmly.

Halfar disengaged himself from Rass and pulled his leggings back up. He slowly slid off the bed and stood in front of Kur. They didn't move for a long time. Halfar stepped around him and went to his royal guards.

"Sheath your swords. We're leaving." He turned back to Kur. "I get what I want."

Kur didn't drop his sword.

"No, you won't. She belongs to me."

As they left, leaving Romnus' guards in the corridor, Kur

dropped his sword with a loud clank and crawled onto the bed, gathering Rass in his arms. Her eyes were glazed over and blood seeped from the back of her head. A high pitched raspy cry came out of him in short succession and he couldn't stop it.

****☼****

Halfar sat on his throne seething, his urges not satiated. He couldn't figure out how Kur knew to come and interrupt his fun. For a few brief moments he felt the familiar warmth of being inside his former slave despite her being only half conscious. That Kur was going to fight him head on was laughable.

An echo of boots forced him out of his reverie and three of his advisors came into the room. They bowed deep at the bottom of his throne.

"My lord, it is time for Lady Farin to depart with her mother to New Lassa. I informed her that you would like to see them off."

"What? Chardon is here?"

Halfar brought up the date in his mind and realized it was indeed time for Farin to leave.

On cue, Farin's four royal guards came escorting her along with Chardon and Und. He reared back in his throne. Chardon did not look up at him. Her expression was that of disinterest.

"Chardon, my love," he said sweetly, "I was not informed of your arrival. When did you?"

"Three days ago, my lord," his advisor answered for her.
She won't speak to me.

Halfar felt that pain creep in and this time it lingered. He realized that no matter how good Rass felt, it was nothing compared to Chardon. But, this was all her fault. If she had just been loyal to him, he wouldn't have to hurt her, alienate her. She was not of Azrom, as his advisors constantly pointed out. He came down from his throne and went to stand before them.

"I should have been informed of your arrival. Come, we can talk on our way to the platform."

He was leading them to the side exit by the throne when a loud ruckus traveled down the corridor and into the room.

"Dear cousin, I have warned you on so many occasions and I feel we are not communicating well."

Lord Romnus stood in his throne room with a full battle-ready unit of royal guards behind him as well as Kur and three other royals. He had a smile that conveyed disappointment, and malice.

"Lord Romnus, what brings you here unannounced into my throne room?" Halfar motioned with his head and twenty royal guards surrounded them.

He glanced at Chardon who halted and turned to see what was going on.

"When your advisors suggested you find a vessel for your pure-blooded offspring, I was amused by it. But the fact that you went after the mate of a lord in the first royal house, namely Lord Kur's mate, I find it disrespectful and unbecoming of a supreme ruler."

"Halfar," Chardon whispered, "tried to impregnate General Rass? For a pure blood?"

"Oh yes, in the most violent way. Lucky for you, cousin, she recovers quickly." Romnus moved closer. "Make no mistake that any other incident such as this will be a declaration of war."

"Let's not move too hastily," Prevan cried out. "I am sure there has been some misunderstanding, as you've stated.

"I was not mistaken when I decided to strike him down if he did not climb off of my beloved," Kur replied.

Silence. Halfar felt panic.

Chardon glanced at him then Kur, her eyes hooded.

"I am so sorry, you had to endure such a thing," she said to Kur. "Please tell Rass I offer the love of Lassa up to her." She placed a hand on Farin's back. "Let's go home."

Romnus turned away, his entire entourage following. Kur gave him one last look before leaving the throne room. Halfar clenched his fists and went after Chardon. She was already ahead of him at the elevator that ascended to the gate's platform. He made it just as the pod activated to go up. They all rode up without saying word. The pain inside him was almost unbearable.

The gate was already in flux when they arrived on the platform, a vortex forming as they reached the threshold.

"Chardon," he called to her. She stopped but didn't turn around. "It was for the sake of Azrom," he snapped. "You would do the same for your race!"

Farin held a hand to her mouth, tears streaking down her cheeks. Und glared at him from a sideways glanced.

"Goodbye Halfar. Farin will be back as promised."

The trio walked off into the vortex and disappeared. Halfar found himself alone with the exception of the gate operator. Hate filled him. He just wasn't sure if it was towards her or himself.

An atmosphere of tension and heat engulfed the entourage of the first royal house stemming from Romnus but mostly General Kur. It put Biandra on edge and she deliberated with herself on whether to hand her master the small fruit that would calm him down or give it to General Kur. She had waited in the corridor as instructed to ensure safe distance in case a battle erupted in the throne room. Deep within her soul she knew there would be a declaration of war between the royal houses and the supreme ruler in short time. From what she witnessed, Lord Halfar was not in control of the palace or himself.

Despite her misgiving, she reached into her robe and pulled out one of the small fruits. She barely got it held up to his shoulder when he smacked her hand away. The intake of air from his soldiers made him halt. Her skin became clammy and she braced herself for whatever verbal onslaught he was about to unleash.

Nothing.

She peeked up and saw Lord Romnus staring at them all with a wildness only seen in beasts. Then it softened replaced by shame. He inhaled, holding it in, then exhaled slowly before holding his hand out to her. She set the fruit in his hand and quickly hid her own. There was a bruise forming and he didn't need to see that. Lord Romnus prided himself on never hurting his own.

Lord Kur had also stopped, seemingly puzzled by the display and she couldn't help but smile from embarrassment.

"Are you as angry as I?" Lord Kur asked her master.

"More than you know," Lord Romnus replied. He took half the fruit in one bite.

"I remember saying he had gone too far once."

"And?"

"It is much more than that. He just made an enemy of his two generals. What is he thinking?"

"He's not," Lord Romnus answered.

Lord Kur eyed her for a moment then pointed at the fruit in her master's hand.

"What is that you are always feeding him?"

She looked up at her master and their eyes met. A mischievous smile spread across his face and he nodded. Dismayed, she tried to dissuade him with her own look but he just smiled wider. Going into her inner pouch, she pulled out a fruit and handing it to Lord Kur, tried to stop her hand from shaking.

"It's quite sweet," her master said. "It calms the soul." That awful smile remained.

"Hmm?" Lord Kur twisted the fruit in his hand, getting a better look at it.

He began to walk and took a bite as he went. The entourage was moving again. A few minutes later, Lord Kur faltered, his eyes wide with terror. She watched him try to force his body to stand and then he went face forward down on the cold pavement of the outer corridor. His eyes rolled around in their sockets as the eyelids fluttered shut.

"Pick him up," Lord Romnus ordered. "That actually solved my dilemma on how to get him back to reason."

"My Lord," she whispered, "That was," she stopped.

"Cruel? Irresponsible?" She nodded. "My apologies. I should not have put you in that position."

He laid a hand on the top of her head for a brief moment then continued on towards his palace. Lord Kur was draped across the shoulder of a royal guard ahead of them. Things were going to get worse, she could feel it, and handmaids like her were going to get caught in the middle. She was frightened.

****☼****

Modas watched the sunset from atop a hill while waiting for the other manbeasts to show up. After the meeting with the Dreridians, he came upon the decision to set his plan in motion ahead of schedule. The negotiations left him feeling sour and he didn't trust anyone in that conference room. New Lassa needed a stronger leader and warriors more fitting to the task of defending her. He would get vengeance and create a new order in one movement.

Tonight, he had to make sure every manbeast participating knew their roles to play and reiterate to the ones veering off course to stay on point. He didn't want any deaths on his hands. Just because the previous leader was a monster didn't mean they had to be.

The last spark of sunlight disappeared in the horizon and he felt the presence of a large number of manbeasts signaling it was time to finish what he had started over a century ago.

Jaron was waiting for him when he returned home and he could tell by her expression that she was not happy to see him so late. He figured she suspected what he was up to but this time he wouldn't deny it.

"How did your vengeance meeting go?"

"That's not what it is!" He calmed himself. "I am trying to fix things. You weren't in that meeting. We are in danger and we cannot defend this world as we are now."

"As we are now is because YOU have divided us."

"This is not my doing! Don't you dare," he stopped.

"You are going to let manbeasts tear this planet apart over something that happened when you were a young manbeast and possibly get our leader killed in the process. Who will lead us then?" she snapped.

"I would never let anything happened to Chardon!" he yelled back.

Jaron's eyes narrowed. "No, of course not. Because Chardon was who you wanted in the first place. I just happened to be in the same line of vision."

Modas backed away from her. The tone of her voice dripped with malice. It may have been true in the beginning but he loved her more than he ever did Chardon. Hurt he made her feel that way all this time, he turned away and left.

"This will end badly for you and all of Lassa!" she called out to him.

He never glanced back. The crack in her voice told him she was crying.

"We must set up a defense, NOW!" Jaron yelled as she burst into Chardon's chamber.

She ran as fast as she could, knowing there wasn't much time. On her way over outbreaks of battles were already being reported. Modas worked fast.

Chardon just stood there staring at her with a look of surprise.

"He couldn't. He told me he was not going to do this," Chardon said.

"He was lying! How could you believe him?" Jaron grabbed Chardon by the front of his robe. "What are you going to do, leader?"

A dark look fell over Chardon's face.

"If he really wants war, then so be it. Dispatch groups to each quadrant."

"Understood."

"And make sure no one is killed."

Jaron stopped mid step and turned to him.

"Really?"

Chardon stared down at her.

"Yes. I will not have murdering my own race on my hands!" He sighed, slumping his shoulders. "Thank Lassa Farin is on Azrom."

THREE: ALLIANCES

Simple Plans

Homes were burning. Screams of terror and rage mingled in the night air. It took him back in time to the day his entire family was slaughtered. From his vantage point atop a cliff Modas scanned the surface below. For nearly a century he wanted the non manbeast Lassians to know how it felt but something was wrong. He didn't feel avenged, this didn't satisfy him. Instead he felt fear; dread, with it a sense of guilt.

The manbeasts who helped him initiate his cause assured him there would be no deaths. Too much had transpired and although he held animosity towards the Lassian warriors, they were still his people. The race's population had suffered enough. But, there would be bloodshed. Ganna's medical team was going to be busy.

Again. That sense of knowing his agenda was now being tainted; unjustified and dismantled. Adjusting his vision he focused on the village Chardon and his own family lived. At first he was satisfied with the fights erupting and already in full swing.

He could see Talas and Kelin barely holding off four manbeasts as they made their way back to their home, one side caved in exposing its innards. They seemed overly desperate and he almost smiled until Modas' gaze shifted and he saw why they ran so franticly. With shock, he watched his daughter, Una, raise her claws. Below her on the broken floor were Talas and Kelin's children. The two infants were in striking range and the oldest was already on the ground bleeding. He could hear the infants' cries and his legs moved on their own as he leapt off the cliff.

Even pushing his body to tremendous speed he knew he wouldn't make it but he too became desperate and kept going. Still focused on his destination, he saw Talas and Kelin stop cold, a scream emitting from Talas worse than anything he had ever heard as Una's claws entered the first infant. Ribbons of blood flew upwards with her claws as she pulled them out in one quick motion.

Modas could feel the stinging of tears in his eyes, blurring his vision but he strained them, forcing his eyes to readjust.

This is not what I wanted!

He was almost 500 feet away when a flash of fabric came from the opposite side in front of him, halting his advance. His son, Und, flew into Una and punched her into the ground, forming a small crater beneath her. The look on his face spoke volumes. Modas didn't dare speak as he turned to see Talas in despair on his knees moving forward, shakily, towards his home. A wildness in his eyes.

Not bearing to watch, he averted his gaze and it landed on the four manbeasts behind Kelin. They too had halted at the sight of Una striking the infant, their claws retracted. Modas' vision seemed to waver as if he were tilting and his eyes locked with Kelin's.

Murderous intent. That is what he found staring back at him and seeing it in Kelin terrified him. Never had he, or anyone else, seen such malice in the warrior. Even in battles, Kelin was passionate and driven, not overtly aggression. He feared Kelin may not even know what was happening to him, having been pushed to the edge.

Ganna herself came running to the scene with three medical assistants behind her. She scooped up the bloody infant while her aides retrieved and took care of the other two children. Modas stood rooted to the ground where he stood. In an attempt to remove himself from Kelin's stare, he caught Ganna's pause in her stride as she cast a glare at him. In her eyes he saw something else. There was no surprise in what had just occurred. It was like she expected as much, saying 'I knew it'. And that is when he realized this attack confirmed for her and the late Sestis what they had concluded all along. Manbeasts were just genetically made monsters with no sense of gratitude or belonging.

Und stood towering over his sister's unconscious body also staring at him. He could see the rage boiling in his son. Modas mindlessly pivoted to his right and went towards Talas who had stopped mid crawl. In his mind he had to get Talas away from here but as he got within a few feet of the fallen warrior he heard crackling and the air buzzed. Dark blue light cascaded on the ground.

"Get away from him!"

Kelin had formed large energy orbs in each hand, ready to unleash them. Modas halted. The Manbeasts behind Kelin shook their heads in unison at him. A stalemate ensued for what seemed like eternity until Kelin rescinded the orbs and went over to Talas' side. He gently lifted his mate off the ground and carried him away.

"Are you satisfied, father?" Und spat.

Modas turned back to his son. Und grabbed his sister by an arm and dragged her out of the dilapidated home, then disappeared into the night.

One of the manbeasts came over to him and rested a hand on his shoulder.

"We knew there were discontent factions within our ranks. We can try all we want but we can't control everyone."

"Not this," Modas spoke softly.

"Yes, it has all gone terribly wrong."

A sudden thought crossed Modas' mind and his eyes widened. He remembered the meeting a few years ago where a small group was intent on eliminating their leader.

"Chardon!"

"It would take more than a few manbeasts to take our leader down."

"No, only one, if their lucky." Modas knew all too well.

"Then we must hurry."

Modas nodded and they headed towards the communal building where Chardon would surely be in full battle mode.

What have I done?

Chardon didn't want to harm the angry, misguided Manbeasts surrounding him. He searched their faces for some sense of hesitation or regret, finding neither. Six in all, they bared teeth and claws already caked with the dried blood of their fellow Lassians.

It really has come to this.

Standing beside him was Mara, breathing heavy from the fight. They were both determined to shield Jaron who lay behind them on the ground bleeding from four deep punctures in her left shoulder down to her abdomen. Claws had gone right through her front to back. Seeing her struggle to stay conscious through excruciating pain gave Chardon more resolve to stop them.

"Don't force my hand," he pleaded with the manbeasts. "If I must…I will use it…again."

This made them hesitate in their advance, giving him and Mara a window of opportunity. But, they weren't able to take it. From out of the dark came a blur of motion and the six Manbeasts were knocked back a few hundred feet flying in the air like leaves in the wind before crashing down with loud thuds. In their place was Modas accompanied by three manbeasts. Chardon flinched when he turned a wild eyed stare at him, mouth twitching. Modas was in a sea of sadness, regret and madness. It was as if the great manbeast had come unhinged and it worsened as his gaze fell on Jaron.

Chardon knew why Modas had come so quickly; to save his leader. But Jaron was his mate and for the first time, Chardon felt relief that he had finally realized who was more important.

"You don't touch her!"

Mara rushed over to her mother and cradled her in her arms. Her stare burned into Modas, causing him to back away. Jaron had finally given in to her injuries and was unconscious.

⁂

Azrom

The royal advisors stood around in a huddle off to the side of the throne while Halfar sat watching them. Everything in him said they were corrupt yet their words resonated with him. He had given Farin some leeway in visiting the first royal house palace to alleviate conflict because he was tired of having to keep tabs on her every waking hour each day.

Sometime earlier in the new season he noticed how developed she had become and how her guards often leered at her. His advisors suggested many times to find a lower royal to mate with her and now he understood. He wasn't ready to mate her to anyone but knew it was only a matter of time before someone snatched her. If they did manage to somehow take her, he would tear them apart, publicly.

Tapping a finger on the armrest of his throne, he asked, "Are you done plotting so we can commence our meeting?" All five turned towards him and bowed.

"Our apologies, my lord," Mesrod replied. "We tend to congregate so often that it is part of our making."

"Yes, well the council is waiting. We need to put an end to these incidents of rebellion."

"Our people are upset about the blockade the Dreridians have placed on us," Prevcan stated.

"We have endured worse than this."

Halfar stepped down from his platform and walked towards the corridor to the left of him.

"What of Lady Farin?" Dondar inquired. "It would be wise to have her confined when you are away for these meetings."

"She is residing in the first royal house palace for the next moon phase." He saw the frown appear on three of his advisors' faces. "I do not have time for such constant supervision!"

"Of course, my lord."

Four royal guards followed Halfar into the corridor. He felt bothered by his advisors' reaction to Farin not being in the main palace and couldn't figure out what the issue was aside from her safety.

Dark grey sky hung over the region of the palace due to the cold weather making its way across Azrom. Most of the red flowers had closed their buds turning a pale violet to give a hint of life in the gloom. The landscape mirrored Farin's disposition as of late these past few weeks, wishing she could immerse herself in its dark embrace. Romnus had advised her to keep up the gleeful façade, a task she found harder to complete each day.

She leaned over the veranda just outside the banquet hall of the first royal palace and looked down. Far below she could see Batis lounging around the palace's boundary line along with his men while they waited for her to return. From her view they were tiny monsters. Batis turned around to look up, meeting her gaze, then smiled. She flinched, backing away and returned to the hall where the rest of the royal members waited.

"Come sit with us out of the cold, beautiful Farin!" Chastan sang, holding a hand out to her.

"The air felt nice." Farin sat down beside him

"Yes, the season is changing."

He took hold of her sleeve and tugged.

"Time for heavier wear."

Romnus glanced over at her.

"It's getting late, we should disperse for the evening."

"What about my guards?"

"Batis will be fine where he is." She could hear and see the darkness fill him. From the moment he had come to get her for General Kur's bonding ceremony only to find Batis abusing her, he despised the soldier.

"No need for them," Chastan waved a hand, "I will escort you to your chamber."

He had volunteered as she knew he would. They had been spending more time together since her father started to allow visits. Their mating used to be fun but now as she tried to keep him focused on her she began to realize he could not be tamed. Romnus had warned her about his attention span waning after a while and of course, she knew soon after giving birth to their son on Lassa that he was not what she thought. Their son, a child he still could not know about.

"One last drink before we go?" Romnus gestured to a servant who turned and picked up a tray that had already been prepared. The servant carried it over and waited. "The elegant azure colored chalice is for you, beautiful Farin."

"How fitting," Reita cooed.

Farin reached over and carefully lifted the chalice off the tray. She inspected the delicate curves of its structure, marveling at how it sparkled like a gem.

"You had this made for me?"

She almost couldn't contain her joy. He always knew how to make her smile, unlike Chastan.

"Of course. Anything for you."

Lord Aloni and Reita made a stern face and she wondered for the thousandth times how they really felt about her. Romnus raised his drink once the servant had finished serving everyone.

"To blood that binds."

They all raised their chalices and quickly downed the contents. Farin was never good at that so it took longer to consume her own. When she set her empty chalice on the table, Chastan stood, grabbing her hand to pull her up.

"Shall we, Lady Farin?"

Farin made a small bow to the royal family members. "May you rest well." She turned and left side by side with Chastan.

In her chamber, Farin crawled on the bed and laid flat on her back to stare at the ceiling. Immediately after, Chastan blocked her view with his flushed angelic face. He let one hand caress her breasts as he smiled down on her.

"You really are quite beautiful," he whispered.

She found no comfort in that since he frequented the brothel every chance he could. It was apparent to her that she was never going to be enough for him. Lowering onto her, his lips brushed hers. Farin felt exhausted from the stress her father had created and her body would not respond the way she wanted it to.

"Will you just hold me?"

"Only if you're unrobed," he laughed as he proceeded to undress her then himself.

He was groping her with fervor but it began to lessen until she saw his eyes flutter. In moments he was asleep, his nude body wrapped around her like a reptile. She was surprisingly relieved. Pulling him closer into her arms, she felt sleep take her as well.

Dondar stood stunned at the entrance of Farin's chamber along with Batis. He had donned on leather footings as suggested by Batis to eliminate the sound of their advance. The guard had told him of the recent rendezvous' between Lady Farin and Lord Chastan but he had not expected this. She was tainted, he was sure of it. And as Batis had reported on his observations, possibly by Lord Romnus as well. It solidified his advice to keep her confined. Now she was going through the royal palaces spreading her thighs for anyone who would want it.

It dawned on him that his lord would never believe him. He turned to Batis.

"Leave them be until morning before they wake. Do you have a reconnaissance device?" Batis nodded. "Record this. I will tell our ruler there is a problem in this palace that needs his direct attention and then show him. Be ready to escort that half breed to the throne room when he requests her."

The smile on Batis face made the advisor cringe. He never liked the soldier and his men. Their methods for just about everything in life were barbaric. Pushing that aside from his mind, he focused on his new task. He had to report this to his colleagues. They would be just as thrilled as he was right then. Together, he and Batis crept slowly away back to the main palace border.

Halfar did not like being tested so early in the morning even if he had not slept during the night. His advisors had sour expressions and he almost feared what they were up to now. Sitting on his throne in casual attire, he threw one leg over the side of the armrest out of habit and leaned an elbow on the other.

"What is it?"

His first advisor moved cautiously forward and bowed deeper than usual. "My lord, there has been a development in the first royal house that needs to be addressed."

"And?" Halfar was getting irritated. They had a flare for the dramatic sometimes and it tried his patience.

"We will show you." He waved Dondar up and a recon device was produced.

Halfar watched it flicker to life and then the image cleared to perfect resolution. He felt his blood turn to ice water in his veins and a stabbing pain erupt in his chest as he stared at the image of his child wrapped in the arms of Lord Chastan. Of all the royal members of the first house, he was the worst. Halfar was well versed in Chastan's perversions and knowing his child was one of his conquest made bile rise up in his throat. He found that his body was now sitting upright and his hands were gripping the armrests so hard, the stone began to fracture.

"We are sorry, my lord. We did try to warn you. She is not fit to be in your presence and now tainted beyond finding a suitable mate. Putting her in the brothel would have been better than this."

Halfar wasn't listening anymore after that. He could see the advisor was still speaking but there was no sound. A flash of memory came to him and he remembered Chastan's handmaid scared as he marched down the corridor to her master's chamber. If she knew then so did Romnus who appeared at the right moment that time.

"Bring me Chastan's handmaid and Romnus' pet."

It took all he had not to yell.

His advisors looked confused then two of them left with a set of royal guards accompanying each. He sat back in his throne and waited patiently. They would be gathering essentials for their masters and unguarded. He was going to teach them a lesson in true reign.

Within an hour, he heard the crying and yelling of Chastan's handmaid, Ponnae. He knew it was her because Romnus' personal servant, Biandra, would never show fear in the face of his guards. The two females were dragged roughly into the throne room and thrown at his feet.

"Show them," he commanded Dondar.

Ponnae's eyes grew wide with terror while Biandra just stared unmoved while they watched. It told him his hunch was right. They both knew what was going on in their masters' palace. He felt stupid for lifting the ban and allowing her to visit.

"You were accomplices to this. For that, you will be punished," he seethed.

The indignation on Biandra's face angered him further.

"Since you like to observe, maybe it's time you participated," he said to Ponnae. "Take her to the lower guards. Let them determine her fate."

He liked the fear that oozed from her very being.

For Biandra he stepped down and backhanded her with the claw he had morphed his hand into. She went into the air and skidded across the floor as she landed. "Bring the Gruloc tamer."

His advisors pursed their lips simultaneously as they watched his royal guards oblige. He was amused by their reaction, so sure it was what they expected of him. Smiling, Halfar stood in the middle of his throne room listening to the handmaids cries fade as she was carried off.

Two of his royal guards came into the room carrying what he had requested. The Gruloc tamer was a giant whip, the fattest part nearly four inches in diameter and the end coming to a needle point. It stretched fifteen feet, weighing approximately forty kilos.

Grulocs were large beasts that stood eight feet in height and could push an entire structure down with its solid muscle giving the massive frame extraordinary weight to accomplish the task. Many of their kind had been made to submit using the taming whip.

He went over to Biandra and using his claw, ripped her robes open to expose her flesh. Two columns were moved to stand side by side and tethers were secured on them. With a finger, he gestured to her then the columns. Guards dragged her to her feet and tied her wrists together before attaching the tether. From the opposite sides, they pulled the ends until she was three feet off the floor her body dangling.

Standing twenty feet away from her he let his eyes linger on her for a moment. Everyone in the throne room stepped far away, not wanting to get accidentally hit by the tamer. Halfar wound it up into the air several times then let it go. The sound when it made contact to her skin was that of bones crushing but Azromians were tougher than that.

He wanted to break her. Her face contorted but she didn't scream. No. She was not going to give him that satisfaction. No matter. She was going to suffer for as long as he deemed it. He wound it up again unleashing another blow. By the fifth time, there was blood dripping on his throne room floor but she still refused to scream for him. He expected nothing less from one of Romnus' pets.

There were six of them surrounding her as she lay face down on the chamber floor being beaten. Ponnae bit her tongue to stop herself from screaming and they seemed to like that. When she was sure they might have had enough since they ceased the beatings, she let her tongue go, tasting her own blood. She was mistaken. Two of them held her down while one from behind used his sword to slice open her robe. Out of fear, she screamed and they laughed.

They took their time having a turn, always two holding her in position for whoever was next, another slamming her head into the floor after each time. When all six had finished, they left her there, bloody, in pain. She felt like dying then. A separate set of guards came in and lifted her off the floor. She saw the ceiling move as they carried her off down stone stairs and into a dark chamber she knew well; the dungeon.

Tired, yet still angry, Halfar dropped the tamer and ordered it away. He stared at the mess in his throne room then his clothes. Even at a distance, the blood splatter reached him.

"Clean this up! I have to change."

He left the throne room and marched to his chamber alone. His guard knew better than to follow him when he was in this state. In his chamber, he whipped off his once white tunic and brown leggings, now stained with blood. Standing naked he examined the lean muscle taunt with unfulfilled rage in the mirror. Grabbing a towel from the wet basin he meticulously wiped away every drop of blood from his flesh.

Halfar returned to his throne room wearing clean garments, the rage slightly subsided but his blood still boiled within him. The throne room was spotless as if nothing had ever happened and he decided to reward the cleaning servants later. His advisors kept their distance from the throne as he slowly sat down.

"Bring her to me."

He knew he didn't have to specify who. Batis and his men bowed low to him then rushed off down the corridor. Halfar thought he saw the soldier smile and was certain Farin would be brought in non-too gently. It was her own fault. Morning was in full swing meaning Chastan would have fled her chamber by now and Romnus would notice he was missing a member of his entourage.

The sound of claws scraping against stone screeched into his ears. From around the corner of the entrance came Farin fighting against her four guards, mainly Batis who finally gripped her wrist and flung her into the throne room. She landed halfway inside, bruised and bloody, in front of him. He held on to the armrests and leaned forward.

"Did you sleep well, my child? Was Chastan's flesh keeping you warm?"

Her face drained of color, her eyes widened and tears formed. She was in a dressing robe so he assumed Batis had dragged her out of bed naked and put it on her. There was silence in the room. His advisors had looks of approval.

"You have made a mockery of my kindness and disrespected my will on every occasion. Was that amusing for you?" She still did not answer him.

"My lord," Mesrod interrupted. The five had turned from their deliberations and stood side by side to face the throne. "It is a shame that she is no longer fit to be formally mated."

"Then what am I to do with this filthy thing?" Halfar asked. His voice was close to yelling but he had restrained himself. "She no longer has value in my court."

"That is true, my lord. No one in the royal houses would want her now, save for maybe Lord Chastan. And he would tire of her soon enough."

"See what you have done?" He finally yelled at her. She was crying softly still sitting with her legs sprawled awkwardly apart. "Even with royal blood coursing through your veins, you are nothing but trash!"

Batis advanced further into the throne room and bowed to him. There was a grin on his face. One even Halfar could see held nothing nice.

"If she is no longer fit for royalty, I would gladly take her. She could still at least be of use mated to a royal guard. That would keep her in the palace under your watch. She is of royal blood, as you've said."

"Yes," Prevcan said. "Half breed she is but of your seed. We can't have the people or the royal houses against us. She is beloved by them."

Halfar sat back in his throne and thought for a moment. It did make sense to keep her in his circle. This time he would make sure to have a tighter rein on her. He met Batis' stare.

"Take her, if you want her." He waved her away.

"Thank you, my lord." Batis made another deep bow. "If you don't mind, I would like to seal the bond, with your permission."

"She's yours now. You can do as you please with her."

Farin screamed as Batis came and grabbing her by hair, forcibly removed her from the middle of the throne room with his three subordinates behind him. Halfar cringed at the sound, but endured it. They were just outside the entrance and he could see what was about to occur.

Farin fought with everything in her being even though she knew Batis was much stronger. She was barely past twenty and he was a seasoned war soldier of a hundred and forty years, maybe more. When they arrived just outside the threshold, she was at the point of defeat. Her body was too damaged for any longer of a fight along with blood loss. She could see it streaked across the throne room floor behind her. Batis threw her down on the floor, keeping hold of her dressing gown which tore partially from her body. Ringing filled her head as it landed hard on the surface bouncing slightly.

"Do not fret, lovely Farin," Batis laughed, removing his breast plate and cloak. They fell beside him in a clank. He bent over and grabbed one of her ankles, pulling her to him. "I will make sure my men get to taste royal flesh as well when I'm done. You will be thoroughly satiated before long."

A longsword with a hint of green in the blade went through the guard to Batis' right. It ran down in a diagonal path from shoulder to abdomen before disappearing back out from where it entered. The guards opposite Batis on the left protecting the advisors were collectively cut down in the same moment. Halfar sat up in his throne, eyes bulging. From behind the advisors came Romnus. He went to Batis and yanked the soldier by his hair into the air and threw him into the throne room.

Halfar counted twenty or more royal guards loyal only to Romnus invade his throne room. General Kur appeared from the right, having dispatched the other two of Batis' unit. Blood was everywhere, even on his attire and he seemed to not care. There was nothing aesthetically pleasing about the bloodshed he just caused.

"I have warned you cousin," Romnus stated.

His left arm now a pincer was driven down into Batis who lay flat on his back. Romnus stood up and kicked his body further in but to the side away from him.

Halfar, still angry, stood up as well. He walked down the steps of his throne and onto the floor.

"You dare come to my palace after the deceit you perpetuated? Passing my child along your royal court? Was she to your liking, cousin?" he spat.

"I have never mated with Farin. If that is what your advisors have reported, they are mistaken. You do not listen to reason. I warned you that harming anyone of my royal house would be a declaration of war."

"Farin is not of your house! She is my child to do with as I see fit!"

"She is mated to Chastan and the mother of his child," Romnus replied calmly, "therefore part of MY royal house."

Loud gasps echoed through the room and Halfar sat stunned.

He looked over to Farin lying half naked in a bloody heap, then to his advisors who were suddenly frightened. Romnus glanced in the same direction.

"Once again, you have been manipulated by a corrupt council instead of ruling on your own. How much lack of judgement do you now possess to do this?"

"I am the supreme ruler of Azrom! You dare judge me?"

Halfar morphed his entire body, rising to nearly seven feet tall. A hint of dark red glinted along the armored shell of his body and the pincers opened. Romnus tilted his head slightly then morphed as well. It had been a long time since Halfar had seen his cousin's full form and had forgotten how enormous and truly menacing Romnus was, easily over eight feet in height. His black lacquered body and pincers dwarfed his own.

For the first time, Halfar was caught off guard and it cost him. As large as Romnus was, his speed defied reason. Before Halfar could think of moving, his cousin was in the same breathing space and a pincer made contact with his chest. His body was slammed into the stairs at the base of his throne. All the air left through his mouth as he tasted his own blood and knew the damage was bad. With one blow, Romnus had taken him down.

His cousin turned and walked away, morphing back to normal as he did so. Kur, Aloni and Kuhala stood waiting for him in the middle of the room. He turned to face Halfar again and sighed.

"You have brought this upon both our houses. I want mine and Chastan's handmaid returned. I know that in your madness, you have done something foul to them but let me make it clear. If they are near death or harmed in such a way that it is deemed worse than death, your reign ends."

The royal entourage exited the throne room. He watched Romnus carefully lift Farin off the ground and cradle her in his arms. She seemed so small against his broadness. Batis lay broken, covered in blood by a column and his advisors were visibly shaken. Two of them had slumped to the floor in fear. Azrom might apparently had its limits, Halfar thought silently.

A medical servant came rushing in and injected healing gel directly into his chest while he remained unmoved on the steps. He didn't dare try to rise, the pain excruciating and not sure if Romnus would return to deliver another blow which would probably kill him.

It all began to sink is as his wound healed.

Farin had already found a mate and birthed a child? Have I been so blinded by my advisors that I did not see?

Another revelation popped in his head. Chardon knew. There was no way Farin would have a child and her mother not know. More importantly, it was obvious that the child was not born on Azrom. He took one look at the advisors again and immediately felt nauseous.

What have I done?

Feeling the tissue fuse back together in his chest, was not a moment too soon as his body pitched forward from the power of bile coming up to vacate. A second wave sent him to his hands and knees, the ends of his hair dragging in the pool of vomit.

What have I done?

The tears stinging his eyes felt like hot embers were being pressed into them. He could feel the tension in the air. His royal court had just witnessed the downfall of their supreme ruler and he had no idea how to transition from this.

Blood Ties

Romnus marched straight to his chamber. There he laid Farin down on his bed. Within moments, his personal medical team swarmed into the room and he stepped back to let them perform their work. He wanted to go back and dismantle Batis piece by piece then move on to the advisors. Halfar would be last to deal with. Behind him, General Kur stood silent. A new dilemma must have been brewing in his head.

Aloni went to retrieve Chastan from the royal bath. That he didn't bother to inquire his handmaid's whereabouts when he went back to his own chamber this morning was testament to his lack of leadership. It was why Romnus never gave him any real assignments for the royal house. Chastan's priorities were not in line with his or the other family members.

"This will end badly, won't it?" Kur asked.

"That depends on what Halfar will do after this. If he does not submit, there will be war between two royal houses. If he accepts his newfound situation, then I will be lenient."

"The royal advisors?"

"The same. If they defy me, they die."

Kur snorted. "That is not the same, Lord Romnus."

"She will need to rest for a while. Let's leave her be." Romnus walked out of the chamber.

"You love her," Kur said.

Romnus stopped at the veranda and wrapped his hands around the stone railing. He looked out into the horizon and let the morning breeze sweep over him. Then he turned back to Kur.

"Yes, I do."

"Yet, you're willing to let Chastan have her?"

"He doesn't have her. But, for now, we can let Halfar and the rest of Azrom think he does."

"She's so young!" Kur exclaimed, slamming a fist into his own thigh. "One usually doesn't mate until the age of fifty."

Romnus smiled. "Farin never saw it that way. She likes to define her own destiny, even when it turns out to be wrong." Darkness filled him as he was about to call on his entourage. "You will search for our handmaids?"

"No need to search. He would have thrown them in the dungeon to rot. I'll go get them. Medical treatment should be ready and waiting."

"I will bring them with me."

Kur stared at him incredulous.

"You can't be serious? Why would you want to come?"

"To bear witness to Halfar's madness. I want to know just how far he has gone."

"What if it's worse than death, as you stated?"

"Then there will be nothing for Halfar to redeem."

Romnus contemplated the real possibility that Halfar had indeed gone to a depths so foul he may have to put both handmaids out of their suffering. Losing part of his entourage was like losing part of his family and Chastan's handmaid was loyal to a fault. Pushing his rage to the side, he was glad Biandra had left a fruit by his bedside the night before. Eating it was the first thing he did when he awakened. It was only an hour later that the guards he had posted to watch the main palace came bursting in past his chamber guards to deliver the report. By that time, the effects of the fruit had kicked in so he was able to remain calm. Halfar should thank her for saving his life for without it, he would have easily torn his cousin apart.

The dungeon had been newly enforced after the Razznian attack but it remained cold and barren with stale air. Romnus and the rest of the family leaders were led by Kur down into the deepest part of the palace. Guards watching the corridor did not engage them, instead moving away in fear as they passed. News traveled fast this day. Romnus saw the tremors in Chastan's hands, knowing what the young lord was thinking. Unlike Biandra, Ponnae was a timid creature.

Kur halted in front of two cells across from each other and went pale. Romnus stepped around him to take a look. In one sat Biandra, slumped against the wall, her body bloody, swollen, tattered, yet her eyes still shone with defiance. She squinted her one good eye and seeing him forced a tight grin.

That's my loyal servant.

He smiled back. A burning rage like nothing he had ever felt rose in him, negating the effects of the fruit but he kept his sanity by sheer will. Then he turned to the other cell.

The strangled cry that came out of Chastan was nothing compared to what Romnus thought he felt. Aloni raise a hand to his mouth, the sleeve covering the lower part of his face. Kur just stood, head reared back in awe. Chastan fell to his knees, hands extended in front of him. This was worse than death.

Even from his distance, he could see the shredded tissue between her thighs. They had literally destroyed her womb. The abrasions and bruising told where the bones had been broken. She lay on her stomach, head turned to one side, and her eyes void of everything. A soft puff of dust by her lips meant she was still alive, barely.

"We kill them now!" Kuhala shouted. He knew she was referencing whoever did this, but now was not the time.

"Have patience," he stated. "We will find who did this."

"Patience?" Chastan whispered. He dropped his hands down to the floor. "I want them torn apart." He raised his shaking hands again. "I want to tear them apart."

Romnus motioned to the medical team and they dispersed into two groups. He figured it would take weeks, maybe months, for the healing gels to repair such damage. A tremor went through his body, forcing him to turn back down the corridor and make his way out the dungeon. He couldn't bear another second of the tragic scene. Halfar had lost his mind. That was his final conclusion.

Reaching above ground, his legs faltered and he gripped the stone walls of the dungeon's entrance. His vision blurred until he saw everything in shades of red.

I'm losing control!

He raised a closed fist to hit the wall but it morphed on its own and the giant pincer punched through. His legs formed into lean muscled praying mantis legs and before he lost his senses completely, launched into the fields on the other side of the palace where his beloved fruit grew.

Field workers cried out in terror as he tore through the orchard, flattening the tall stalks, making a path to his prize. Barely of his own mind, he snatched a handful, shoving them into his gaping mouth and began to devour. With so much of its juices coursing into him all at once, his body froze from the shock. He immediately came to his own mind but too late as his vision cleared briefly before his entire system shut down. Romnus went face down into the dirt like a dying Gruloc beast, shaking the ground beneath him.

⁎⁎☼⁎⁎

New Lassa was left in a state of anger and chaos in the aftermath of the manbeasts' insurgence. When the wounded count was announced, there was enough shame and blame to go around. Chardon made the decision to remain in male form as way to convey his seriousness. It didn't matter much to others but for some reason he felt it was the best course. As much as he despised Ganna, she had come through on all fronts. Her swift actions were unprecedented because she had expected it.

That angered him more. She and Sestis knew this would happen centuries ago and waited for the event with baited breath. It never occurred to him how wide the division in the three species of their race was. Manbeasts were created so many millennia ago that he assumed it was a non-issue. They were Lassians, plain and simple, just like the energy users and the warriors and everyone else. Everything had been fine until his father's leadership. He wasn't told all the circumstances but just finding out about them was no excuse for his poor judgement in leading his race.

In a bunker nearby, he sat on a concave bench along the wall of the large healing chamber, watching over the wounded as medical pods repaired their bodies. The chamber was full to capacity as well as another bunker in the east. He had chosen the bench closest to the little ones section. The tiny pod before him held Talas' infant boy. Thin tendrils of light ran back and forth inside the wounds, slowly closing them while reconnecting any blood vessels.

"You don't have to stay and watch," a female voice chimed.

Chardon looked up, coming face to face with Ganna. She too was tired, he could see it in her demeanor. The scientist went about checking each pod's data, making adjustments as needed.

"Yes, I do."

"It's not your fault, really."

"How can you say that?" He snapped. "I."

"Are you a terrible leader? Of course. But this was set long before you became one. The reason I dislike manbeasts is because they are generally prideful and overly aggressive."

"That's not true! Modas was not like that and neither are his children." He stopped as he looked at Talas' child who was nearly killed by one of Modas' own.

"There are exceptions to the rule like all races," Ganna continued. "But we were not concerned with them."

"You mean Sestis and yourself?"

Ganna let out a loud sigh.

"As a scientist I am always fascinated with the evolution of species, especially my own. Since we had closed off our access to other worlds there was no reason to keep such a large force of manbeasts. Sestis was just weeding out the bad from the good and finding a remedy that benefitted our race."

"No she wasn't!"

"Ah, yes. Her ambition did get in the way of the original plan and I tried to justify so much of it. Now, I just want to make our race better. Not a super power like she wanted, but as I said before, capable of holding our own against any enemy."

Chardon actually welcomed Ganna's blunt honesty. It dawned on him that it was not loyalty to Sestis or anything else. Ganna was always trying to find a way to make their lives better, just her execution lacked finesse.

"You will help me?"

"No," she replied turning to look at him. "I will help our race, in the name of Lassa."

A loud beep interrupted them and she ran over to the origin of the sound. Chardon stood up and went over to see what was going on. In the pod lay, Jaron, her skin not quite back to normal color. A few strands of pale red hair were visible, a sign of premature aging. Lassians didn't get those until they were at least four or five hundred years old.

"Oh my," Ganna commented, noticing the strands. "I think it makes her look more distinguished, don't you?"

He stepped away from the pod and leaned on the one behind him. Tears streamed down his cheeks and he tried to fight them back.

The second beep sounded and the pod was purging the dry liquid from its chamber.

"I better contact her family," Ganna said. She moved to the commlink.

Chardon grabbed her wrist and stopped it midway.

"Don't."

He knew Modas would be there in seconds and he was the last person Jaron needed to see when she woke up. Leader and scientist locked eyes and they silently concurred.

The pod's locking mechanism disengaged with another beep and the hatch receded exposing Jaron's naked body to bunker's open air. Ganna went to a cabinet and retrieved a robe, tossing it to him. He caught it and waited.

Jaron's eyes fluttered sporadically until finally they slowly opened to slits. The light hit them and she winced in pain. Chardon knew that feeling from when he had just awakened from a healing pod before. Forcing her eyes to open wider, Jaron stared up at the ceiling for a long time. Tears ran down both sides of her face then her hands cover it. Gently, he lifted her up and arranged the robe around her. She bent over all the way and continued to cry.

Ganna gave him a nod and exited the healing chamber. He couldn't bear it; not understanding the heartache and rage Jaron must be feeling. The doors opened again and he thought Ganna had forgot something until he heard a loud gasp. Mara stood in the entryway with tears forming. She sniffed hard, not letting a drop fall. He envied her strength.

"Mother?"

Jaron removed her hands from her face and looked up. Mara went to her, wrapping her arms tight around her. Chardon watched her stare at the red strands in her mother's hair, knowing what it meant and squeezed her tighter.

"Don't bruise her, Mara. She just woke up."

"I don't care," Mara sobbed.

"I do," Jaron said. "Let go of me, you foolish girl."

They both laughed at her usual disdain for affection. She reciprocated with a look that matched it. Chardon tried to help her out of the chamber and was shocked when she smacked his hand away.

"Don't touch me!"

"Mother!" Mara gave her a rueful stare.

"Don't! You should have stopped this!"

"You can't blame him for this, mother! It was father who started this!"

"You are the leader of our race!" She ignored her daughter's outcry. "I warned you. Now look what we have." Chardon hung his head and backed away from her. Her eyes softened then and she smiled a little. "I'm sorry," she too hung her head and resumed crying.

"What do we do, leader? Everyone is so angry," Mara asked.

"I don't know, but I have to fix this somehow."

"Where is he?" Jaron suddenly blurted out. She amazingly had stopped crying and now had a look of poison.

"I think," he replied, "we should wait on that."

"Chardon!"

"No!"

"I'm going to have to agree, mother. None of us have spoken to him and he is not around. He may be hiding in a cave meditating."

"That won't help him this time," she snapped.

"No, it won't. But, he needs to stay away for now. He knows that, at least." Chardon held out his hand. "Come on, let's get you out of here."

"Are you going to fill me in on why so many healing pods are in use?"

He exchanged a look with Mara. It was going to have to be done sooner than later and he knew the first person she would want to speak to about strategy was Talas. That was not a viable option and won't be for a little while longer. Right on cue she asked.

"Where is Talas? I would have thought he would come running to see me back."

"This way," Mara spoke softly. She helped her mother out of the pod.

"What's wrong? Why are you both quiet?" Jaron's eyes bulged. "Is he…?"

"Just come," Mara nudged.

He led her to the little ones section on the other side of the healing chamber and stopped at the farthest pod. Jaron's hands went to her mouth as she saw the wounds being repaired on the infant boy. Her look of horror turned to rage.

"Who did this?" She demanded.

Mara didn't turn to her but responded.

"Una."

Jaron's' hands clenched tight, all the color drained back out of her skin and her eyes went blank. There was nothing anyone could say to her now.

The chamber was dark. Jaron peered in to decipher a presence as she crept on unsteady legs towards the bed sitting against the far wall. Her eyes adjusted and finally a lump became visible on top of it. Light strands of hair hung over the edge. She went to the side and pulled the nearby chair closer so she could speak softly. On the other side of the bed lay Kelin, in deep slumber. Jaron didn't want to wake him with any talk above a whisper.

She sat on the chair, easing herself down slowly and jolted with fright midway. Talas lay on the bed, eyes opened staring into the abyss. There was no life in them. One arm crooked under her, the hand limp. When Talas didn't register her being there, Jaron continued her descent into the chair. She brushed some of the strands from Talas' face and a whimper followed.

All these decades she had never truly despised Talas, although there had been moments of disappointment and even envy, but not hatred. Looking back she realized how much energy she had wasted being angry and cruel to the warrior. And not just Talas. When she learned about Modas' feelings for Chardon from long ago it explained her own feelings of distrust towards him. Her unconscious decision to ration out affection spread onto everyone around her.

Now here she was showing affection to the one person who everyone deemed her rival. She snorted softly. Talas had the one thing she envied most of all; conviction.

"Why have you come?"

It was barely a whisper, like it had been breathed out and startled her out of her thoughts. She looked over and saw Talas focused on her. Those words of air came from Talas' lips.

"Shh," Jaron answered. "Don't speak. Just sleep."

Talas balled her hand into a fist and her eyes narrowed.

"Why?" she demanded more forcefully, yet still barely audible. "Did you come for entertainment?"

Talas choked a little and coughed. Tears brimmed.

"Of course not," Jaron seethed, trying not to yell.

"I would never do such a thing."

"You have no love for my sake," Talas sputtered, "so why?"

Sobbing quietly with eyes squeezed tight, Talas started to curl further into a ball. Jaron had enough. She grabbed the edge of the bed cover and yanked it off just Talas. The room has chilly and she watched the shocked reaction from Talas.

"Get up!" She didn't care anymore if Kelin woke up as well. Seeing them both in such a pitiful state angered her more than Modas' unjust coup. "Your children need you! Get up and go take care of them!"

Talas stared up at her in awe, then rage crossed her face. Jaron smirked.

That's right, get angry at me.

She waited for Talas to get up, ready for a scuffle then remembered she wasn't in any condition to fight any more than Talas was.

Before Talas could plummet to the floor, Kelin reached over and stopped her fall.

"Let me go!" Talas' voice croaked slightly. She took in too much air and had trouble regulating her breathing for a moment.

"You too!" Jaron addressed Kelin. He gave her a look she didn't like but let it slide.

Kelin activated the glow orbs in the corners of the chamber and Talas leapt at her. She stumbled backwards, having no intention of letting the grieving warrior land a blow and lost her footing.

Oh, for the love of Lassa, this is going to hurt.

As she got closer to the floor, a hand grabbed her arm, stopping her fall. She used it as leverage to right herself and came in the direct gaze of Talas with a stunned expression. Kelin stood not far behind on the end of the bed with the same look.

Hands shaking, Talas reached over and pulled a few strands of her hair. In the now brightly lit room her red streaks shined like fire. Jaron gently took her hair out of Talas' hand and backed away.

"Good, you're up. Let's go."

"Jaron," Kelin called out.

But she was not going to hear what either of them had to say.

She knew that tone; pity.

"I know I haven't been very nice to you in our lifetime together but you need to know this. I have never hated you." She felt the tears well up then stream down her face so she sniffed loudly while wiping her nose with the back of her hand. "Now come on."

Jaron walked out of the chamber to give them time to get dressed properly. Her body gave out and she slid to the corridor's floor. She felt so weak, drained of everything, but there was no time for that. The person she had to face, the one who needed to tell HER why, was still missing.

You can't hide forever, Modas.

Shivering from the waterfall rushing down on him, the pressure almost too much for him to bear, Modas focused on stillness. The reason he had sought out the waterfall was due to insects becoming attracted to his increasingly pungent body scent. His mane had grown tangled from neglect as he wandered the planet in a state of despair. He had stripped down to his leggings and was attempting to meditate while being cleansed.

He sat akimbo on a large rock beneath it, hands folded in his lap as he tried to focus on nothingness. It failed. He remembered when Jaron was pregnant with their first litter after returning from Earth and he told her that she meant everything to him. The strength of the water bent him over further and he let out a loud cry that was drowned out by its rushing roar. Modas planted both hands on the wet stone and let the water beat down on him.

There was no more vengeance, no hatred, left inside of him. All that remained was guilt and sadness. Jaron should have been the one person he protected in all of this. She would despise him for this, he knew, and it would take a miracle for her to forgive him. Again, he saw his daughter's face full of hate as she ran her claws through a helpless infant. Bile tried to make its way up his throat and he forced it down. No good. It came back up with brute force, sending him to his knees.

Using all the strength he could muster in his arms, he pushed himself up off the stone and stepped down into the shallow creek. Drenched, he stood staring up at the horizon and a pain crept in him. This was not their home world, this was not Lassa which made what he had done more heartbreaking.

Apologies were not going to be accepted.

What am I supposed to do?

The person he feared most was Jaron. She had warned him over and over that his agenda was nothing but a petty tantrum. After he had finally convinced Mara to let him take Jaron to the medical chamber, she was taken away from him by force. No one wanted him near her let alone in the same room. Stricken with grief he started his trek.

Movement from one of the cliffs above him put him on alert and he quickly spit out the last of his vomit, wiping his mouth with the back of his hand. His claws slowly extended.

"So this is where you came to hide from your sins," his son, Mota, called down. He leapt along the ridges of the cliff until he landed on the ground and walked towards him.

Modas tried to gauge his son's mood and determined it was neutral. He rescinded his claws and turned to him, Mota stopping a few feet away to look him over.

"You look like a dead hoisen beast left out in the hot sun, father."

Modas grimaced at his joke. It was in bad taste even for him. He saw Mota spot the pool of vomit spreading thin in the water.

"How did you find me?"

Modas was surprised how cracked his voice sounded.

"You sound like one on its last light too."

Modas felt tired. So very tired. Even at the death of his family, he did not have this feeling of utter defeat. Back then, he was filled with fire.

"You need to come back."

Modas just stared at him. He knew that but wasn't ready. As if reading his mind, his son sighed.

"Whether you're ready or not, it is imperative that you explain your actions to the council," he paused, "and my mother."

"I know," Modas whispered.

Mota went to his pile of robes and tossed them at him. Modas caught them, holding them to his chest. He raised his gaze up at his son and could feel the tears stinging his eyes.

"I can't," he replied.

"I can't explain this. It wasn't supposed to happen this way."

"What did you think would happen, father?" Mota yelled. "You turned our clans against our own people and fueled dissent for over a century!"

Modas flinched violently from his son's words as if he had been physically assaulted. He never knew how only words could hurt so much. Seeing Mota waiting patiently, he finally let his robes hang long from his hands before donning them.

"I guess it's going to take a while to get back. You don't look strong enough to go at any speed other than walking."

"That is true," Modas replied softly.

His son paused mid stride and turned back to look at him.

"If you need to know, the infant is doing well. Talas not so much, but everyone is getting back on track."

Relief nearly took him back to his knees. If Una had killed the child, he would not be going back to explain. He would be going back for her memorial.

Trinon

Madness.

The arguments in the council chamber grew louder and more heated as the session went on. Trinon sat in a corner of the room disgusted and angry, not understanding how it had come to this. When claws and swords were brandished, he had enough. Knocking everyone and everything in his path out of the way, he exited the chamber. Halfway down the corrido he heard footsteps running after him but didn't turn around to see who they belonged to.

In the open air outside the temple, he inhaled deep then let it out. He proceeded up the hill on the opposite side and could still sense his pursuers. At the top, he sat down on the grassy knoll and stretched his legs out a bit, keeping them bent at the knees. His hands were planted flat on the ground and he threw his head back, letting his mane cascade down like a waterfall.

"Trinon!" His mother called to him. He kept his eyes closed. "Answer me!"

He opened his eyes and glanced up at her. She was furious but he could also see the inevitable fear on her face. Trailing behind her was Talas and Kelin along with Und who looked worried. Infuriated, he frowned, not wanting to be soothed like some baby beast.

"I can hear you." That stopped her mid stride and he regretted his tone.

"What is wrong with you? You haven't been yourself in years and I don't understand! Why won't you talk to me?"

His hands turned into fists and grabbed chunks of grass, his fingers embedded deep in the soil. A surge of panic gripped him. Talas came over and laid a hand on his shoulder.

"Be still, she has a right to know. I told you that before."

"Know what?" His mother snapped. He could hear the fear in her voice. "Trinon?"

Talas squeezed his shoulder and Trinon just nodded.

"You know that after the battle with the Razznians we reached out to other planets for resources until our planet recovered?"

"Of course I do."

"There was one planet that we visited where the natives were more than happy to assist us."

Trinon fell into a lull and he could see the lush green forests of that planet. The exotic foliage and how the air smelled slightly sweet. There was laughter all around him and even adults played in the trees with the young ones.

"We made negotiations and were sending what we could back through the gate."

"You mean the vegetation?"

"Correct."

"They were amazing. I wished we could have gotten more."

"So do I," Talas said sadly. His mother frowned.

The taste of the fruit fed to him by her small fingertips, the juice running down his chin and her laughing at his lack of manners. He could smell her deep brown hair as it brushed against his forearms.

"There was another race who inhabited a neighboring planet that also traded goods for their vegetation and they did not like sharing. Their leader came and made threats but they had never raised a battle with them."

"Oh Lassa's love," Jaron whispered.

"They attacked the planet and targeted us." Talas paused for a moment. "The leader of the planet assisting us had a daughter. She took a liking to Trinon and they spent each day together for the three years we were there."

Yes, she thought he was quite funny and beautiful. She told him so many times while they lay on the beach or atop a hill overlooking the forests. Her hair always adorned on one side with a single giant flower of vibrant color in contrast to her bronze skin.

"She was only a few months from giving birth when the attack happened."

Fire raining down on the forests. The smell of burnt timber and flesh. Dark clouds the color of charcoal as they churned from the heat and smoke. Her hand clasped tight in his as they ran for shelter. The enemy fighters descending onto the surface like spores.

"The fight was brutal and unjustified. Many of us were hurt but the planet and its people suffered more."

"They just destroyed the resource they craved so much," Kelin balked.

"Truly disgraceful." Talas looked down on Trinon but he did not acknowledge him. The quicker the story was told and over with, the better. "In their rampage, Trinon's mate was hit by a barrage of laser fire from their weapons."

Fighting back tears he could see vividly her hands holding her swollen belly as he turned to help over a fallen tree trunk. The look of surprise as stray laser fire from behind tore through her, creating three holes that opened up like screams. Her belly torn to shreds, spilling out onto the ground, her shoulder and thigh like chopped raw meat. Him catching her in his arms in a state of shock.

"Trinon became something…else."

The time of darkness he couldn't recall for so long revealed itself to him. He could see enemy fighters being torn apart in a haze of red and realized it was he who was delivering the death rites. At some point he was grabbed from behind and restrained. He remembered howling and screaming to the sky above.

"Containing him took nearly all of us. He went insane. Seeing the carnage caused by his decree, the leader ceased the fighting and helped with the wounded. But it was too late for apologies. They were allowed to stay for repairs, but the leader of the planet made a decision to banish them from setting foot on theirs again."

The long trek into their humble gathering space, still wounded but able to walk, barely. Rows of their people along the aisle letting him pass. Seeing her grief stricken father on his seat at the end staring down on him in pity. His stumble to the floor on his knees as he bowed low in front of him, forehead to the ground, and saying, "I am sorry for not protecting your child." No one moving for a long time and then feeling a thin hand set on top his mane. Knowing it was her mother who adored him.

"He was badly wounded and didn't know it. When he was able to somehow walk he went to apologize to her parents and her people. We had to literally drag him up off the floor. Once our group was healed, we returned to the ship with a few gifts from the people despite the devastation of many forests."

He remembered being basically dragged onto the ship and left slumped against the inner hull of the corridor in a daze. Talas looking down on him full of worry, watching his catatonic stare into nothingness. Und picking him up like a grain satchel and tossing him over his shoulder. Carrying him to an empty bunk in the crew quarters.

"We kept his relationship with her a secret so for our group only Und and I knew about it."

They traveled halfway in the ship, deciding to use the gate at the last moment. Trinon felt numb, his vision blurry all the time and his hearing muted. The final leg of the journey, Talas and Und cornered him in the control room. He was sitting on the floor leaning against the wall, one knee drawn up, when they towered over him.

"Trinon is always smiling," Und said.

"Trinon loves to be playful and take things as they come," Talas added.

"You must return to Lassa as the Trinon we know."

Then it hit him; they were right. How could he explain his current state? Could he pull it off? He didn't have to worry because the moment his feet planted on New Lassa's soil his body reacted on its own. The corners of his mouth twitched upwards until he had a big smile on his face. He looked out to his family and the other Lassians who came to greet them and exclaimed, "We sure had a lot of fun! You should have been there!" He saw Talas and Und's face take on horrified expressions before they dissolved. Inside, his core felt broken and dimmed.

"It took everything in me to keep this secret, but I told him, he should tell you at least." Talas turned to Kelin. "I'm sorry to have kept this from you."

Trinon swerved his body towards them and in his tenor voice, a bit lower than usual, "You cannot tell father!"

His command startled them.

No regrets for that, he was serious. His mother's eyes filled with tears and her hand covered her mouth, stifling whatever sound would erupt. He could tell she wanted to hug him, knowing not to. To his surprise, she took a chance and threw her arms around him. He then surprised himself by not pushing her away but burying his face in her bosom and began crying.

"If father knew, he may understand," Und said after Trinon had stopped sobbing.

He gave his litter brother a look that he hoped would signal his anger but Und just stared back at him in defiance. Their mother, sensing the tension stood and whacked them both in the back of the head.

"Stop that! What is wrong with you?" She wiped her face. "We will not tell your father because I don't think he understands anything right now. What he's done has essentially ruined our race."

"Do you still love him?" Trinon asked.

"I don't know." His mother hung her head.

To his and everyone else's shock, his father's voice rang in the air.

"You're right. I probably wouldn't have understood."

Modas came out from behind the curve of the hill and stepped forward so that he was face to face with Trinon.

"But I do now. You need not have gone through that alone. I've failed you."

"You understand now? Good! Do you see now how trivial your vengeance was? How I wanted no part of your madness?"

He felt a new kind of disappointment in his father and litter sister, Una. Nothing could fix this quickly. Wishing he were back on that lush planet full of forests, he stood up and looked out at the horizon.

Jaron walked back down the hill towards the council chamber, leaving Trinon to some alone time. The way he had left the session, it would have caused an uproar. She was sure Modas was confused at his son's outburst but he shouldn't have been. From the beginning, most of their children did not approve of the uprising and now he was full of regret. She and Talas knew it would come to that.

Do you still love him?

Those words haunted her and the answer she gave made it worse. The lies and deceit he had spun for so long were large and deep.

How could she forgive him so easily?

The answer; she couldn't. It was too much. Nearly a century of hatred and this is what he ends with.

She entered the council chamber to a hushed silence. Everyone had frowns on their faces and knew why. They were ashamed of their own behavior as they should be. Trinon held on longer than expected but she had been on the verge of sending a ball of energy into the middle of the fray herself. A few heads turned to acknowledge her return and she went to take her seat.

Modas went to stand by the window and leaned against it with his arms folded. He seemed less ferocious now. Jaron almost pitied him until the reason they were in the chamber came back to her. He turned to her.

"Will Trinon be alright?"

Her eyes bulged out of their sockets in disbelief, as did a few councilmen. "No, Modas! He is not well!" His eyes grew wide and he backed away from her with nowhere to go, hitting the wall with a thud. "Do you think anyone in this room is well after the heartache you caused?"

"I..."

"Don't you dare speak!" She roared.

In the midst of the silence she caught a glimpse of Chardon sitting at the table shell shocked. This was going to be a difficult task for her cousin and she hoped the unskilled leader would take the reins and soar.

How Far

There was no light.

Romnus felt like he was enveloped inside a deep black hole, his body heavy, as if it had been filled with ore then hardened. He tried to lift his hands and nothing happened. Stillness. It had a calming effect and he decided to let his mind sink deeper.

A tiny prick in his neck made Romnus rear up from his position gasping for air, instantly grabbing his chest. His vision returned and he found himself in his own chamber with servants silently milling around. Reita stood at the foot of his bed staring down at him disapprovingly.

"You weigh more than a Gruloc, did you know that? It took an entire unit to remove you from the grove. What were you thinking, eating so many of them?"

At first he didn't understand what she was talking about, then all the events that transpired before he made the mad dash into the fields came flooding back. Anger rose but was immediately shut down by a massive headache. He tried to use pressure with the palm of his hand to ease the pain.

"Don't go rolling around too much."

Reita pointed to the area beside him.

Romnus looked over. The beautiful Farin was lying next to him in what he assumed was a heavily drug induced sleep. Most of her wounds had healed but the damage obviously left her drained of energy. He had been in enough battles and seen enough wounded to deduct that much.

"How long?" His own voice sounded cracked and broken to his ears.

"Only a few days."

"Halfar?"

"In hiding at his palace. It seems he has confined himself to his chamber."

"The royal advisors?"

"Scared." Reita smiled when she said it.

"And," he began.

"Biandra is already lucid and quite angry at you for the recent episode."

"I'm sure she is."

Romnus motioned to a servant.

"My garments."

"Going somewhere?"

"Are you here to stop me?" He asked as he reached over to retrieve his robes from the servant. "I am not going to the main palace. Chastan needs to be told."

His sister frowned.

"He will be shocked, then devastated."

"Then, won't care."

"Yes, this won't be his first offspring and I am sure, not his last."

"It will be the last with her," Romnus replied.

He slid off the bed, the robes falling into place as he stood. Walking to the other side of the bed, he leaned over and lightly kissed Farin on the lips. When he turned to the entrance, Reita had a smirk on her face, staring at his bare feet.

"Come, lover, we have much to discuss." Reita got to the corridor then stopped. "Oh, and Chardon is returning to retrieve Farin."

"That will not be an option now."

Are you not going to even negotiate with her?"

"I believe once she understands the situation, she will agree with me."

He took another look at Farin before following Reita down the corridor. She was just as beautiful broken and scarred.

"I have a child, with Farin?"

Chastan sat dumbfounded at the table in the communal hall. The rest of the royal house members waited for the information to sink in. None of them had known except Romnus somehow. He glanced over at Kur who shook his head. Not even he knew about this? First there was elation of having a child with the beautiful Farin, then a twinge of anger.

She kept it from me!

As though he had been reading his mind, Romnus spoke.

"She had to hide the child for the obvious reason. She could not gauge how Halfar would react to such news."

"That is no consolation! We would have protected her!"

Chastan made eye contact with each member of his family and saw something in them that he didn't like. It was as if they disagreed or was it disappointment?

I am wrong to assume that?

"Farin is young and headstrong, you are not. It was a dangerous game you played. You should have known better than to engage." His sister lowered her gaze from his.

"The palaces are in an uproar and this news has added to it," Romnus stated.

"The houses know I have fathered a child with Farin?" Chastan could feel a ball of tension form in his gut. "Then I am mated to Farin?"

"It appears to be so," Kuhala answered.

Mated.

He did not like that term. He adored Farin, but not enough to bond with her for eternity. There were others who had birthed his offspring, none of royal blood of course. If they wanted him to play the part to keep her safe, then so be it. His sister was right. He should have known better. Farin was nearly thirty years too young to be mating yet he let himself indulge.

"When can I meet my child?"

"That we cannot know. It still may not be safe here. Chardon will be arriving shortly and it can be discussed then."

Reita stood after that and headed out the hall.

"Halfar is the root cause of this. If he hadn't restricted her, she wouldn't have venture into my arms."

He too stood and left. As he walked out into the corridor, the ball of tension tightened. The last thing he wanted to be was responsible for Farin's happiness. Looking up at the sky to determine the time of day he decided the brothel would not be full and headed in its direction.

The remaining family members took sips of their drinks in silence after Chastan left, knowing where he was headed. Romnus tapped a rolled up scroll he had been reading earlier on the edge of the table. Such childish resolve. For Chastan to blame his inability to restrain himself on Halfar's strict child rearing was an insult to everyone in the room.

"We must make sure he holds true to the façade for a little longer," Aloni finally spoke. He sipped from his chalice slowly.

"Just like WE would protect Farin, not him?" Kur snapped. He turned on Romnus. "How and when did you know?"

Romnus stopped tapping the scroll.

"Did none of you notice?" All eyes went wide. "She was well rounded when she returned from Lassa some years ago. Even her fair skin had gained some color. Really, you did not see it?"

"To be that observant of Farin speaks volumes about your own feelings for her," Aloni pointed at him.

He glanced up into the ceiling, contemplating it and nodded. There wasn't much he didn't know about Farin. What he found odd was that Chastan never noticed how much time she spent with him as opposed to her supposed lover. Refocusing on the issue, he commented.

"Chastan is going to be a problem at some point. The royal structure is about to be reconfigured."

"Then you will take over rulership?" Kuhala exclaimed. Her excitement was obvious. Aloni turned his head towards him and he saw the gleaming.

"I have made it clear, I do not wish to rule. If I were ruler, I would destroy everything," he paused, "in order to make it better."

That silenced them, taking the excitement out of the air.

Kur made a face.

"When you say everything, what do you mean?"

"Exactly that. I would be deemed worse than Halfar and our fathers combined."

"But you would make it better?"

Aloni explained for him.

"To create a new order with a clean slate, one must first destroy the previous. Lord Romnus would be assassinated within half a century, or less."

"But, you would make it better?" Kur reiterated.

"Eventually the people will see the truth and yes, Azrom would be reborn."

Kur leaned back and folded his arms in deep thought.

Romnus was curious as to what scheme the general had churning in his mind. It would have to wait for now.

"I must go check on our downed females then deal with Chardon when she arrives."

"Oh, I am sure Chardon will not let Halfar live once she finds out," Kur said.

"We have to prevent that from happening, General Kur. If she were to kill him, and on Azrom soil, there would be war between our worlds." Kur seemed to dislike the idea. Romnus got up from the table. As he passed him on the end, he patted the general on the shoulder. "It will be fine. I'm sure you will find a way."

His entourage, sans Biandra, was waiting for him in the corridor. She would be his first visit, then Farin. Ponnae he decided to save for last because if she was unable to survive, he would end her suffering.

The gate atop the main palace burst open revealing a black and purple galaxy swirling inside the vortex before flattening. A single ray of light appeared like a runway and a small group of figures came forward. Chardon was the first to step onto the platform, followed by Chafar, Trinon and Talas. Reita noticed the weariness exuding from their bodies, a sign that great strife had occurred on New Lassa. She sighed. This was not going to make things easier.

"Lady Chardon, it is good to see you."

"Halfar has not come to greet me, yet again?"

"There is an explanation for that. One you won't like."

"I am sure."

"Let us get you some refreshments first and you can tell me what has happened to make all of you so unapproachable."

That jolted the Lassian leader. "You can tell?"

Reita smiled. "Oh, yes. It is deep within you. I can feel it radiating from your core."

They walked in silence until Reita turned to the staircase leading to the first royal house palace. She watched the frown grow on Chardon's face.

"Why are we not staying in the main palace?" she asked.

"That is one place you do not want to be in."

Reita led the group across the courtyard where Kur's mother,

Emalli, held the audience of the royal children. She glanced at the group and bowed her head.

"Who is that?" Chardon whispered.

Reita laughed at the awe in her eyes.

"That is Emalli, Kur's mother. I'd forgotten that you have never met."

"Beautiful," Chardon replied softly.

That made Emalli laugh. "Kur said the same thing when he met me for the first time. Such a perverted child. He takes after his father in that."

"Come," Reita chided Chardon. "We have a small meal prepared for you."

When she returned to the communal hall with her guests, Romnus and Chastan were gone as well as two other members. Only Aloni, Kuhala and Kur remained. A fresh round of food and drink was placed on the table as they all sat down.

"I met your mother, General Kur," Chardon addressed him.

"Hmm. Stunning isn't she? If I weren't mated already, I'd have taken her."

Chardon blanched. "She's your mother."

"A shame about that. We would have remarkable offspring."

"Stop telling such disgraceful things," Reita snapped staring at him. He snorted and took a sip of his drink. She turned to Chardon. "Now tell me what has happened on New Lassa."

That got the other members attention.

"Modas launched an uprising. Manbeasts against us all."

"That's madness!" Kur yelled.

"Yes, well, it turned out badly. He says it was not supposed to happen the way it did."

"What did he expect? Was there to be no blood shed in this uprising?" Kuhala asked.

"Oh, he expected bloodshed, just not the kind that occurred."

"I am not understanding." Aloni frowned.

"Children were also assaulted, as well as his own mate," Talas explained.

"So New Lassa is not a safe haven at this time?" Reita plucked a round of bread from the tray. "That may be to our advantage then."

"What are you talking about?"

Chardon looked around the room. "What is going on here that we have to be in this palace and New Lassa's predicament is an advantage?"

"We think it is best if Farin stays on Azrom. And, in a short time that her child be brought here as well."

Chardon and Trinon both looked startled. Chardon set down the fruit she was eating. "You know about her child? Does Halfar?"

Reita noted the fear in her voice.

"Yes, there was an incident and all was revealed."

"What incident?"

Reita suddenly felt uncomfortable. Delivering such news was not her forte and she didn't want to have the Lassians restrained afterwards. She watched Chafar continue eating and drinking as if none of this concerned him but there was a glint in his eyes. Something foul, like the one his father had on occasion although the boy resembled a Lassian more so than an Azromian. She took a deep breath and prepared to tell them.

"Halfar lost his mind and gave Farin to his royal guards as a gift."

Romnus' voice boomed into the hall and stopped her before she began. His blunt revelation made her angry. This was not going to go well.

"What?"

Chardon shot up from the table, whirling around to face him.

"I was able to get my guards into the main palace before too much damage was done. She is resting for now, her wounds healing properly."

Chafar stopped eating and also stood.

"Where is my sister?"

Reita gave her half-brother a dirty look. With her stare she asked him '*What now?*'

"There is no need to see her now. She is still resting."

That only made Trinon rise from the table and step towards Romnus.

"It is not up to you, Lord Romnus. This may be your palace, but Chardon is her mother and Chafar her brother. If you deny them access, I will have to be their key."

Seeing her brother and the young manbeast face to face, Reita got up to intercede. Trinon had grown, as he would, to nearly as tall as Romnus. Her brother didn't have far to look down at him.

"You expect me to leave my child here, in a hostile environment?"

"No more than New Lassa from what I overheard." Romnus did not avert his eyes from Trinon's. "Very well," He moved from Trinon's view. "My guards will escort you to her."

Chardon went to stand next to Trinon. "And then you will tell me what is going on in the palace, before I decide whether to kill her father or not!"

"That cannot, and will not, happen," Romnus sighed. "That is not the answer."

As they left, Reita slapped her brother.

"What are you doing? We were supposed to neutralize the situation! You just aggravated it!"

"There was no reason to sweeten it. You agree, don't you, Talas?"

Reita turned around and true enough, the Lassian warrior was still seated at the table sipping his drink. The dark patches around his eyes made him look hollow.

"He'll have to do more than beg for forgiveness this time," Talas replied.

"Halfar? Beg? Those two words are not synonymous."

Kuhala snorted.

"His reign may be over," Romnus added.

Talas set down his drink and laid his arms on the table, hands flat.

"As it should. I have long thought his rule was ill structured, lacking and cruel. But there was something I couldn't see. An element that steered it."

"You are quite observant as well, Lassian. You are correct. Halfar has been manipulated and plotted against by the royal advisors for centuries and he has probably just recently realized it due to this incident."

"You want us to take him." Talas turned his head to them.

"He needs time to heal and reassess what he truly wants."

Reita stood confused by their conversation. It was like they were speaking in a language only they knew. She almost envied them.

Watching her child sleep in obvious pain, made Chardon want to storm the main palace and demand Halfar reveal himself. The chamber was dimly lit, casting soft shadows on the bed. Chafar sat down on one side of her and used a finger to arrange hair away from her forehead. Chardon found the lone seat in the chamber and pulled it up to the other side. She carefully inspected the faded wounds on Farin's arms and face with shaky hands. Trinon stood at the foot of the bed, his fists clenched tight.

"My beautiful child, what has he done to you?" She glanced at the guards. "Who did this to her?"

They shifted uneasily then one of them replied, "Her guard, Batis and his unit."

She remembered him and that she had warned him about harming her child.

"Where is he?"

"Lord Romnus broke most of his bones, so he is in medical being treated."

"He's not dead?"

No one answered. She understood why they were leery to give her any more information. In her current state of mind she wouldn't trust herself either.

A medical servant entered the room then stopped when she saw Chardon.

"My apologies," she bowed and was about to leave.

"No, stay. I need to know her condition."

The servant resumed her advance into the chamber.

"She suffered a lot of damage. She fought hard. But, some bones were broken and there were a few deep wounds which took some time to heal."

"Was she," Chardon couldn't finish the words, let alone the thought.

"Violated? Thankfully, no. Lord Romnus got to her right before it was to occur."

She felt ill and drained. A heaviness came down on her as it echoed in her mind. Right before it was to occur.

"Poor Ponnae was not so lucky. Six royal guards had their way with her. She may not live," the servant continued.

Chardon felt her own eyes widen in disbelief. Even Chafar and Trinon turned to the servant. In the history of Lassa, as far as she knew, there had never been such an incident as that. What had gone wrong on Azrom to allow that kind of behavior?

"Who is Ponnae?" The name rang familiar.

"Lord Chastan's handmaid," the servant replied. "Lord Halfar had her and Romnus' handmaid punished for allowing Lady Farin and Lord Chastan to mate." The servant came over to the bed with an injection gun. "If you please, I must administer more healing gel."

"Of course."

Chardon moved out her way. She looked at Trinon, then her son and made a decision. If Halfar had truly lost his mind, then she would help him regain it. But, if he was just being the cruel dictator the Razznians claim him to be, his natural state, then no Azromian would stop her from ending his life and his reign in one act.

A guard appeared at the entrance to Halfar's chamber, adding to the already small group blocking access from either side of the corridors. Halfar noticed the nervous glance, along with the guard's reluctance to enter the room.

"A message, my lord."

"Speak it."

"Lady Chardon is at the first royal house palace."

Fear gripped him. One deeper than anything he'd ever felt.

"Who is accompanied with her?"

"Your son, Chafar, the warrior Talas and the young manbeast, Trinon."

"Is that all?"

"Yes, my lord."

"Dismissed."

The guard nearly ran into a fellow soldier as he spun around so quick to leave.

I wish I could flee as well.

It was only a matter of time before Chardon came looking for him and he had no explanation for his actions. To tell her he let himself be manipulated into harming his own child would be like crawling into his own grave. He had no doubt she would want to kill him. She was on the list of many who wished for his head. There was chanting from the people demanding a new ruler. Azrom's love for Farin was deeply rooted.

Lost in thought, he did not hear the ruckus outside his chamber until it was too late. He barely had a chance to look up and see the cause. The back of Chardon's hand swept across his face and he saw a blurry haze of starlight in his head before hitting the floor next to the bed. His vision tried to correct itself as he attempted to push up onto his hands and knees. The room tilted. She had given him a powerful blow but he was thankful she did not use her power. He remembered what New Lassa looked like after she had unleashed it. If she did that now she would take out not just him, but every Azromian on the surface.

"Get up!" Chardon commanded. "And look at me!"

His guards had unsheathed their weapons, some morphing and he raised a hand, a signal to stop. Too late. Trinon literally picked them off two and three at a time, tossing them over the veranda. The guards who were left backed away from the chamber's entrance and his reach. Halfar dropped his hand and obeyed Chardon's request. He flinched as their eyes met but she grabbed the sides of his head, refusing to let him look away.

"Why have you done this?"

Halfar squeezed his eyes shut and she shook his head to make him open them. They stayed that way for a long time, him on his knees and she holding his head in a firm grip looking down at him. So much despair filled him and the thought that he might have finally lost her came crashing in.

Feeling weak, and monstrous he took hold of the front of her robe and cried out into her bosom. He found himself doing it again and again, his voice giving way with each one. The room had gone black but he could still hear his own screaming, feel Chardon's hands on his face and smell Lassian earth on her robes.

When he finally stopped, his body slumped down. Chardon moved her hands to the back of his head and stopped him from falling backwards. She held him close to her and he let himself rest there. He understood that he had been too young to rule, many of the elders against his entrance in the battle for ruler-ship. The ones who insisted were his father's royal advisors. Two of whom were now part of his own. He had killed the others for the assassination attempt they manipulated Kur into delivering on Earth.

Am I worse than my father, and his father before him?

He felt Chardon's fingers run through his hair at the top of his head. *I want to stay here, just like this.*

Four royal guards from Romnus' palace charged into the room, ruining his solace. Chardon let him go so he could stand. The soldiers had on their most menacing faces and it almost made Halfar laugh. He could take them all out in seconds.

"Your presence is requested in the throne room," the leader stated.

"I am being summoned to my own throne room?" He yelled. "By who?"

"General Kur."

That surprised him. There was nothing dictating the military had jurisdiction over the monarchy.

"I am supreme ruler and no one summons me." Halfar stepped forward, pincers raised, and the guards backed away. "But, I will indulge him this time. Leave us," he snarled.

Chardon nodded to Trinon as the guards left and the Manbeast blocked the entrance. Halfar turned and came face to face with his son, Chafar. He had not spent much time with the young warrior in training, now nearly equal in height with him. An expression of disappointment was aimed at him. He placed a hand on Chafar's cheek.

"I know. I'm sorry to have neglected you all this time."

"That is an issue, father, but the one I am worried about is your treatment of Farin." He removed Halfar's hand from his face. "I would hear her called half breed in your presence, yet you did nothing to deter it."

Halfar winced, his son's words felt like being run through with a longsword.

"Come, let's go see what your General has in mind," Chardon suggested, holding out a hand.

"Yes, I am curious as well." Halfar took her hand and they waked out into the corridor.

Romnus' guards led the way with Trinon, Chafar and what was left of his own guards trailing behind.

General Kur marched into the throne room, General Rass at his side, just in time to see Halfar enter from the side along with Chardon and her entourage. From his position in the middle of the room, he could tell there was a difference in Halfar. It took a moment but he figured out what it was: defeat. A haggard expression was plastered on his face and his body language suggested fatigue. Kur glanced behind him as the rest of his soldiers came in. He had brought six enforcers and eight guards just in case Halfar had truly gone mad and wanted to battle.

Halfar stood in front of his throne and an attempt to appear defiant seemed to be in progress. Kur waited for his ruler to get himself together. He clutched the scroll Romnus had left on the table earlier in his hands. The document was ancient but it detailed the monarchy and how it was to be structured. This is what he was basing his current actions on.

The royals of the first house and representatives from the other four flowed into the room as well. Kur had taken most of the day to convince them to attend his meeting. He looked back to Halfar who seemed ready.

"What has gone wrong in your mind that you dare summon me, your supreme ruler?" Halfar yelled.

"It is not me that has had something go wrong mentally," Kur replied then added, "My lord."

The royal advisors were huddled in the far corner with looks of despair on their faces.

You should be afraid.

Kur stepped forward and unfurled the scroll. He held it at his waist as he addressed Halfar.

"For your actions against the royal houses and the people of Azrom, by Monarchy law you are deemed unfit to rule."

Loud gasps erupted from the now large audience in the throne room. Halfar's face faltered for a moment then a kind of knowing replaced it. Kur inwardly breathed a sigh of relief. There would be no need to restrain him by force. He raised the scroll up and read the relevant passage.

"In the event the ruler is deemed unfit to rule, the head of military will take control and appoint a ruler." Kur rolled the scroll back up. "I, as General of Azrom's militia, with the consent of General Rass, decree your reign is over." A hushed silence followed and all eyes focused on Halfar. "Due to the nature of your crimes, I recommend that you be exiled from Azrom until a firm duration is set."

Again, loud gasps were heard. He glanced over at the royal advisors and the councilmen who conspired with them. Their punishment was due soon enough. Kur looked to Chardon as Halfar backed into the edge of the throne's platform in a state of shock.

"I know you are angry and it is your decision, but are you willing to accept him on New Lassa as your mate?"

Chardon lowered her head for a moment then raised it.

"I will take Halfar to New Lassa."

"I am grateful to you." Kur bowed out of respect for her decision. She could have easily declined, leaving Halfar's fate in his hands. "With this, I appointed Lord Romnus of the first house as Supreme Ruler of Azrom."

He turned around to the royals behind him and saw the pained expression on Lord Romnus' face. Further in, the other royals stood dumbfounded. No one spoke for a long time and Kur wondered what was going to happen next.

"As the law dictates, I must accept your decision of face a battle for rulership," Halfar stated.

Kur turned back to him, surprised that he knew that. Then he chided himself for not realizing it. Halfar was always searching in the old databases to learn everything about Azrom. He waited for his reply. Halfar regained his composure and walked towards the center of the room and stared at Lord Romnus.

"I know that if you had not backed out of the battle so long ago that you would have ruled Azrom instead, and I cannot defeat you in a true battle." Halfar exhaled. "I accept you as Supreme Ruler in my steed and will go into exile."

Then Halfar did what no one thought they would ever see. He went down on one knee and bowed low to Romnus. Kur was stunned immobile and didn't notice Lord Romnus walk past him and lay a hand on Halfar's head.

"I thank you, cousin. Now, rise. I will give you a few days reprieve, but you must leave Azrom when called."

"I understand," Halfar seemed to struggle with something internally, then said, "my lord."

Lord Romnus faced Kur while Halfar stood up and returned to Chardon's side. "I do not want this. I thought it was made clear, my feelings about ruling."

"Yes, you did," Kur answered. "But you said you would make

Azrom better and that is my only requirement for your reign."

Lord Romnus wiped his face with one hand and stared down at him. "What happens next will be on your hands."

"I will support and protect you." Kur went down on one knee and bowed low. "My lord."

In slow succession, everyone in the room did the same, leaving only Lord Romnus standing. Even Chardon and her people bowed. Kur took yet another glance at the royal advisors and councilmen. He knew they would sprint out of the throne room at the first chance and convene for a new strategy. As if hearing his thoughts, Lord Romnus whispered down to him.

"Make sure they are under close guard. I'll rip them apart if I feel for one moment they have defied me."

"As you request, my lord. I have already made arrangements for such an event." He saw Rass smile beside him. It was his mate's responsibility to see it through.

When everyone rose back up, Kur noticed some of the lower royals frowning. He recognized them from the fourth house. They had eyed the advisors earlier and Kur assessed there was going to be issues concerning them later. Lord Romnus caught this as well and nodded to him. A change in ruler was a harsh transition, especially when no blood was shed in the transfer. Given the current circumstances, he knew the people of Azrom would understand. As battle hungry their race may be going into a losing one was an ill decision for a warrior.

Kur motioned for the royal council magistrate. The man stepped out from the crowd and walked up to the platform next to the throne. Lord Romnus followed, taking each step slowly. At the foot of it, he turned to face the audience.

"I hereby anoint you, Lord Romnus, Supreme Ruler of Azrom," the magistrate announced.

Lord Romnus eased down onto the throne. His body fit perfectly into it, unlike Halfar whose slender frame had been nearly dwarfed by it. All heads bowed low to him and that nagging sense of foreboding came over him. He could see it in some of the royal guards and the council, their hostile intent. The magistrate went out onto the balcony and made a summons to the royal guards below to assemble the people.

After the throne room was cleared of everyone except those necessary to the royal court, Lord Romnus stepped down and approached General Kur. They stood face to face for a long time, randomly glancing at the royal advisors.

"You do realize what you have done?" Romnus asked Kur. "I will tear this planet apart."

"As you have said many times over, but you also promised to make it better. So I will trust in you as I had Halfar until it is deemed necessary to remove you as well."

"Then let us begin." Lord Romnus turned to the advisors. "Now, for all of you."

The royal advisors snapped their attention towards him. Fear and loathing filled their expressions. He waited for them to approach, which they did, slowly. Kur's eyes narrowed and Romnus set a hand on his shoulder to calm him.

"I want a meeting with the Dreridians within the next lunar phase. And, you will only deliver my agenda, nothing more. They will tell me if you try to negotiate otherwise and your lives end there." Some of them frowned. "Do we have an understanding?"

"Yes, my lord," they cried out in unison."

Kur raised an eyebrow at him. Romnus knew the general was curious about what he had discussed with the Dreridians after Halfar had stormed out of the meeting. He smiled at him. *All in due time.* The royal advisors scurried out of the room and Romnus watched them until they disappeared around the bend.

Mesrod walked at a brisk pace ahead of his constituents as they made their way towards the conference chamber. No one spoke a word until they were inside where he slammed his fists down on the console in the center of the room. Calba and Jabarz flinched.

"This was not supposed to happen! This is a disaster!"

"I never thought Halfar would be overthrown so late in our agenda," Prevcan stated.

"General Kur is more clever than we anticipated," Dondar added.

"Where did he find that scroll?" Mesrod asked himself.

"It would have come from the royal library," Dondar replied.

"What's done is done. Now we must find a way to get in Lord Romnus' good graces and try to steer our agenda back on course."

"He will be a hard one to turn," Prevcan said.

"But it can be done if we are careful," Dondar concurred.

"And determined," Calba added with Jabarz nodding.

"Let's get this whole Dreridian affair over with. The quicker we sever our ties with those creatures, the better." Mesrod straightened his robes as he said it and made his way to the door. He was angry at the outcome but he believed it could be remedied. Azrom's future always relied on the advice and counsel of the royal courts because rulers were so undependable. In his eyes, Lord Romnus was no different. Even so, he felt his skin crawl with anxiety.

Halfar stared at Farin's sleeping form on the bed and his chest felt like it was going to rupture, spilling out his innards. He didn't dare move any further into the chamber for he had no right. The scene of Batis and his men wrestling her to the ground, intent on having their way with her right in the corridor, brought a sharp pain. It stabbed him in his head and he struggled back tears. He wanted to reach out and caress her hair but the way Trinon turned to look at him made him rethink it.

In two days, he would have to leave Azrom and make New Lassa his home for as long as his cousin decreed. At first, he was angry but then he realized it was what he had wanted long ago after the fight on Earth. The current circumstance was not ideal but he needed the break in routine to feel like he could still love. His view landed on Chardon who raised her head and stared back.

"I know I won't be forgiven. All I can do is promise you I would never harm any of you from this day forward."

"You have no idea how right you are," Chardon answered. "When she is well enough, a handmaid will be assigned to escort her son to Azrom."

Halfar felt his blood race. He would get to see Farin's child for a brief while. Then his skin heated up as he thought of the child's father. Chastan was not the type to show endearment for his children and that his fourth cousin did not think to restrain himself with someone so young angered him.

"There will be no retaliation," Chardon chided him.

"I know," he replied.

He smiled, delighted she could read his mind again after fearing their bond had been permanently severed.

"Come, we need to let her rest."

Chafar leaned over and kissed his sister's forehead before easing off the bed to obey his mother. Halfar was the last to exit the chamber and he took one last look back at Farin.

"I'm so sorry, my beautiful child," he whispered.

He turned away and ran into Chardon who stood blocking his path. She caressed his cheek for a moment then walked ahead of him.

FOUR:
NEW ORDER

Negotiations

Traveling to the Dreridian system gave Romnus time to settle his nerves and steel his resolve. General Kur had insisted on accompanying him for the meeting. Prevcan and Dondar sat in their seats with sour expressions. Romnus snorted and leaned his head back against the bulkhead. He had decided not to use the giant royal ship for the journey because he wanted to appear humbled in the eyes of the Dreridians. Halfar wanted to convey might when he came, Romnus was going to negotiate.

"Approaching Dreridian outpost," the pilot announced over the commlink.

Romnus opened his eyes and lifted his head up straight. Biandra held a fruit in front of him. She didn't even look to see if he acknowledged it. He took it from her and shoved the whole thing in his mouth. The juices squeezed out onto his lips as he chewed.

"Azrom vessel cleared for descent to hangar B-I-4-4-V. Please secure your ship once docked," a voice from the outpost satellite instructed.

The landing was not very smooth and Romnus almost had a mind to strangle the pilot. His body had been jerked sideways then pitched forward from the ship maneuvering into the docking clamps. Biandra was gritting her teeth against the pain caused by the rough movements. Her body, though healed of wounds, was still sensitive. The advisors seemed flustered by the jarring and then there was General Kur, sound asleep as if nothing had occurred.

As they exited the ship and stepped onto the platform, the same group from the previous meeting stood waiting patiently to escort them. Lord Greggor appeared to be in a jovial state and smiled. The craggy mounds of his face made Romnus think the whole face would come apart and crumble to the ground.

"Lord Romnus," Lord Greggor exclaimed while spreading his

arms wide open. "Or should I say Supreme Ruler of Azrom?"

"Whatever suits your taste would be efficient," Romnus answered.

"Not quite settled in your new role? Well, you have plenty of time for that. Come, now. We have much to discuss."

Romnus noticed Lord Greggor cast a side glance at the two royal advisors.

Did everyone in the known galaxy harbor distrust for the Azromian advisors? He asked himself.

It was true they had been in the royal court for nearly three centuries, a third of it during the time of Halfar's father. His entourage was strangely quiet and he wondered if it was due to the nature of the meeting. The heavy debt laid on Azrom by the Dreridians would cripple a lesser civilization. Greggor looked back at him as they walked and smiled again. Romnus could tell what the scientist was thinking; it was payday.

"Oh," Lord Greggor piped up. "I forgot to inform you. This will be a joint meeting. We need to clear up a few things with Razzna and New Lassa."

"Is that so?" Romnus frowned and the effects of the fruit kicked in, easing his anxiety.

"No need to worry, your former ruler is not present. I heard you exiled him to New Lassa. Very lenient of you."

"He is first and foremost of my bloodline."

Lord Greggor waved a meaty hand in the air.

"Of course, of course."

They had reached the palace and were now heading up to the conference room. Romnus and company were ushered through the archway into the open layout of the room. The floor to ceiling panoramic window gave them a view of the massive hangars bustling with ships coming and going. Off in the horizon were great cities blinking with multicolored lights.

Dusk was upon them.

At the table sat Sars, with three soldiers from his unit, and Chardon with Talas and Mota. The Lassians looked weathered, perhaps even defeated somewhat. He had heard about the uprising led by Modas. Owing a debt was just adding insult to injury. As for the Razznians, Romnus saw optimism in their demeanor. He sat down at the table, General Kur to his right and the advisors to his left. His guards stayed near the entryway accompanied by Biandra.

Lord Pondur was already seated at the head of the table sipping from a fragile chalice while his treasurer sat hunched over a tablet deep in concentration. There was no doubt the lean creature was crunching numbers in favor of the Dreridians. Romnus just hoped the burden would not be too far leaning. A fair transfer of goods was his goal.

"Now that we are all settled, I want to clear up an important matter," Lord Greggor announced. "New Lassa was willing to send a large group of manbeasts to assist with Razzna's situation. That will no longer be necessary."

Relief came over Chardon and Romnus was glad for him. Sars had a confused look on his face and he concluded the Razznian did not know of the Lassian's proposal.

"In exchange for shipments of a new product we will upgrade and bring online a new mining system for Razzna. This way, we can get their resources back on the market faster."

"Product?" Chardon asked. He turned to Sars. "What product? From where?"

Lord Greggor grinned and answered him. "Why, something new and exciting that they developed on Earth. I believe they are on the verge of exceeding Halfar's organization."

Chardon went pale and Romnus knew why. The last thing the galaxy needed was another recreational drug for thieves and smugglers to get in on. All the Dreridians saw was revenue, a new commodity driving commerce.

"As for New Lassa, we would still insist on an ambassador to oversee," Lord Greggor paused, "to work with your science council on our joint projects."

"And I have stated before and will again that is not up for negotiation. With the current state of our planet, I do not need or want a foreign entity in the mix." Chardon had leaned forward, resting his elbows on the table.

"Our race has been peaceful and thriving for a very long time," Talas added. "This current setback is merely a tiny blemish in our history. We do not need your input." Mota nodded in agreement.

"With that settled," Lord Pondur said, "there is now the issue of Azrom." He set his chalice down and sat even straighter in his seat. "Please," he gestured to his treasurer.

The intense Dreridian cleared his throat and looked up at Romnus.

"In order to satisfy the ramifications of your planet's actions, in conjunction with Razzna's contribution, you will need to produce and ship one billion kaedirons of Azrom resources. This can include plant life, ore and precious metals. Azrom flowers are a well-known product but the ore and metals are what we most need."

Romnus thanked the gods, and Biandra, for the fruit he had ingested earlier because if not, his reaction would bode badly for Azrom. He could feel the urge to strike trying to stir within him but it was in a losing battle. One billion kaedirons would take nearly three decades at their current rate of production. His hands shook violently for a few short seconds then stopped. A headache bloomed open, its petals reaching every corner of his cranium, making him wince.

"That's insane!" General Kur finally exploded.

His hands also shook but with rage.

"I agree," Chardon interjected. "That is outrageous at best."

"Really?" Lord Pondur asked, his eyebrow raised. "How much do you think the rebuilding of Razzna's trade should cost then? Even with the new product, it will take at least fifty years for it to return to its normal flow."

"There must be a better alternative," Prevcan exclaimed. "This was a result of a battle. The Razznians infiltrated Azrom. We did not start this."

"Was your planet devastated?" Lord Pondur asked softly.

"Of course not," Prevcan snapped.

"Then you see the reason for my course of action."

Silence engulfed the room. Romnus had to agree, the cannon fire sent to Razzna was overkill. He knew Azrom would not suffer much in the battle. Halfar's decision had cost everyone dearly.

"What is the time line?" He asked.

"Since Azrom has the capabilities for mass shipments, once we lift the embargo it should take two decades."

"And during that time we have no bargaining position for trade?"

"Correct," the treasurer spoke. "After the shipment of one billion kaedirons in Azrom product, you will be able to resume normal trade commerce."

"What if we delivered it in less time?"

"Let's not be ambitious, Lord Romnus. Your race can only produce so much in a certain amount of time. Just stick to the timeline," Lord Greggor chided.

"What if we could?" Romnus asked again.

A sliver of irritation moved inside of him. That silence again. He wasn't saying anything unusual. They were here to negotiate and he already had a plan in motion.

"If you did, then a bonus credit would be given and you could start trading within two years of clearing the debt," the treasurer replied.

"Done," Romnus said.

Everyone sat still at the table. Lord Pondur was in the middle of raising his chalice to his lips and halted. His eyes narrowed as the two Lords stared at each other. Romnus forced his mouth to curve into a smile.

"Have you gone mad?" Dondar yelled. "We cannot do such a thing!"

All eyes shifted to him and the color drained from his face as he realized what just happened. Romnus cocked his head to one side and was curious to know if this is how they treated Halfar when he ruled. The fear in the advisor's eyes pleased him.

"I meant to say, it is nearly impossible, my lord," he corrected himself.

"I would have to agree," Lord Pondur said. He set his chalice back down on the table. "How would you do it?"

"That is for me to ponder. You just need to keep your end of the deal."

"My treasurer will compile the necessary documents. They will be transferred within the next seasonal cycle."

Lord Greggor clapped his large hands together, the slapping sound of thick meat echoed through the room.

"Well, since the negotiations are now over, let's have a feast to commemorate our joint business venture."

"More like thievery," Mota whispered to Chardon.

Romnus let out a little laugh. It was true. He glanced over at General Kur who sat with his arms crossed while looking down intently at the floor.

I warned you.

Kur had promised to protect him from any assassination attempts for the next fifty years if need be, but what he was about to put in motion would test that loyalty. He guaranteed it. Azrom was going to be thrown into chaos by his own hands.

With the informal festivities over, Romnus' entourage was escorted back to their ship. During lift off, Prevcan leaned closer to him and began to whisper.

"My lord, you can't mean to adhere to such a short time table. Even if we were to match the Razznians in production, it would take decades."

"Advisor Prevcan, are you insinuating that I do not have Azrom's best interest?"

"No," Prevcan replied. His eyes went wide with shock. "I just simply cannot fathom how you would achieve such a feat."

"You shall know soon enough."

Romnus watched the advisor sit back against the bulkhead and exchange a look with his counterpart. The scheming would begin as soon as they landed on Azrom. He contemplated a guess as to what they had in mind. General Kur kept a keen eye on them from where he sat at the end of the row. Leaning his head back, Romnus let out a loud sigh as he closed his eyes. He really didn't want to be Supreme Ruler.

The moment Romnus released them from his care, Prevcan and Dondar headed straight to the meeting room where the other advisors waited. Four council members were also in attendance when they arrived. Mesrod stood from his seat at the head of the table and gestured for them to be seated before returning to his own.

"What news and how do the terms look?" Mesrod asked.

"It is madness," Prevcan answered. "The Dreridians want one billion kaedirons of Azrom production."

"Unacceptable!" The head of the trade council yelled. "That would take…"

"Yes," Prevcan said, "and Romnus has agreed to deliver it in less time than required."

"That's impossible!" Jabarz added.

Mesrod became unusually silent and it caused the others in

the room to follow suit as they turned to observe him. He had one hand caressing his chin and the other tucked under the opposite arm. Then he smiled.

"It seems Lord Romnus has no sense of social responsibility." He planted his hands flat on the table's surface. "To do such a thing would require a great strain on our people and resources. It would cause," he paused, "undue hardship. Strife."

"A rebellion would be imminent within the first few years," the head of science and agriculture stated.

"Yes, he would be despised." Mesrod smiled wider.

Dondar perked up and sat straight.

"The assassination attempts alone could send a message."

"We can be rid of this ruler as well until a more suitable one can be put in place." Mesrod stood up and paced the room. "But, we must be patient. This will take some time although his reign will be short lived."

"It will be the shortest reign in the history of Azrom," the trade councilman snorted.

"Let him do what he pleases. It will only benefit our agenda." Mesrod stopped at the window and looked out onto the palace grounds. "Victorious," he said softly.

"Til death," the others murmured.

Darkness filled the chamber but Romnus' vision adjusted quickly and he found his way to the bed. He was exhausted and wanted to sleep. Letting his garments fall to the floor as he took them off, he climbed under the covers. He eased down against the pillows and wrapped one arm around Farin drawing her close to his body. She didn't stir. His body's internal rhythm slowed, matching hers, lulling him to sleep.

Images flooded his mind. Dissent of the people, betrayal, senseless acts of violence and blood flashed before him in quick succession. His brows furrowed as he tried to force them away but they were relentless. Suddenly, a sense of calm swept through erasing it all and he was left with the beautiful Farin smiling at him. A soft glow surrounded her and in the background behind her was the palace square full of Azromians cheering.

Romnus jolted out of his slumber and for a moment forgot where he was until Farin moved. He looked down at her sleeping face and breathed a sigh of relief that the dream was over.

Or was it a premonition? He asked himself.

Long ago he had a vision of being Supreme Ruler if he had gone through with the battle for rulership. That was why he backed out and Halfar became the one victorious. Now he felt his actions had only delayed fate. If that was the case then he was the one meant to change Azrom and make it flourish once more.

Beams of light spread across the chamber landing on the bed. Morning had arrived. His body demanded a few more hours, deeming the sleep he had as insufficient. Soft fingertips brushed his cheek. Farin stared up at him and smiled.

Time to get up, he chided himself.

Although they slept in the same chamber, in the same bed, he refused to touch her in any sexual manner. It was for both their sakes because there would be no turning back. He wanted her more than anything in the galaxy but that had to wait.

"I see you slept well."

He leaned down and kissed her softly on the lips.

"I don't think you did," Farin whispered. "You were holding me so tight. Was it a night terror?"

"Hmm, not quite."

"How did the negotiations fare?"

"As expected."

Farin frowned and a sadness came over her.

"You will go forward with your plan?"

"I must."

"You have to tell them. Kur, the royal family and maybe some of the council."

"I can't do that. It won't work that way."

"I don't want you to be hurt," Farin whispered in his ear. "The people won't understand and some will try to assassinate you."

"I know, but that is part of the plan."

Farin sat up to sit on her knees.

"Then you have to stay with me. Do whatever I want until this is over."

"Are you going to lord over me for the next decade and a half?"

"Absolutely!"

"I can't play such a dangerous game with you," Romnus said.

Farin didn't seem to like that. "Chastan played with you when he shouldn't have and I have more sense than that."

"That's not what I mean."

"Yet true."

"You don't want me?"

"Farin." Romnus sighed. He gazed into her eyes and she grinned. "We must get ready for morning meal."

"Will you announce your first decree today?"

Farin had a serious expression which nearly startled him.

"I haven't decided yet."

"Don't. Wait a little while longer." Farin brushed her lips across his for a brief moment then gave him a quick kiss before jumping off the bed. "Let's go take a bath!"

Kur paced his chamber barefoot so not to wake Rass who was still sound asleep. Ideas about what Romnus had in store for Azrom swirled around in his head and none of them were mild. The planet and its people were going to suffer. There was no way around it. Whatever his new ruler decreed he would not appear shocked, because drastic measures were necessary.

Growing up in the training camps, he knew firsthand how bad the social structure was. Whenever he traveled to the different sectors for inspection, it made him cringe to see the poverty.

Yet, no one complained because we were a mighty race. Victorious until our last breath.

Beyond the corridor, sunrise was in full swing. He stood in the archway of the chamber and watched the rays sweep across the surface. A mighty race. Yes, one that deserved better. Halfar became ruler so young and did not think to repair the damage done by his father. Then a new war came and nearly crippled them again.

He thought about the deal with the Dreridians as the sun rose to the same level as the balcony, forcing him to shield his eyes. All of Azrom's secrets were going to see the light of day as well. Kur turned away and found Rass just about to sit up from under the covers. He would tell her about the meeting later. For now, he just wanted to be near his mate so he crawled back into bed and wrapped his arms around Rass.

Just a little longer, he pleaded, *before the chaos.*

There was debate on whether to inform Halfar of Romnus' deal with the Dreridians and Chardon was on the side of not doing so. Back in female form, she waited by the doorway watching him play with Farin's young son. Only a few years old the little one was quite intelligent and never able to keep still, like his mother. Halfar was actually laughing. His first moon cycle on New Lassa was a lesson in heartache for both of them. Chardon left him alone most of the time for two reasons: she was furious with him and he needed to understand the weight of his actions.

In two weeks, the little one would be back with his mother on Azrom which was probably for the better. Her initial feeling was insult, thinking Romnus had no faith in her race keeping mother and child safe. As time passed, it became clear that it was unfair to Chastan. He should have the option of getting to know his son.

"Is he behaving?" Chardon pushed herself off the door frame and entered the room.

Halfar looked up, startled for a moment at her appearance, then his attention went back to his grandchild. The smile on his face faded away and Chardon could feel his sorrow.

"As well as one could hope. He has so much energy."

"And we know where he gets it from," Chardon laughed as she ran her fingers in the little one's hair.

"I don't think he should be on Azrom."

Chardon looked over at him. "Why do you say that?"

"Chastan is not who you think he is and with the sudden change in rulership, there could be chaos. I know the royal council and the advisors were none too happy with Romnus' appointment. They could decide to assassinate him and everyone around him, including Farin."

"That is a given. But I am sure Romnus will protect her with his life and Kur will protect him."

"You seem so optimistic."

"Why are you not?"

The little one squirmed his way out of Halfar's grip and made a straight away to the door, giggling the whole time. He ran right into Und, who appeared blocking his exit, and went down with a soft "oof". Und picked him up by the armpits and carried him off down the corridor.

Halfar stood up and came face to face with Chardon. She searched his eyes for something that may resemble happiness and found none. It was still too soon for that. An awkward silence came between them. Not able to tolerate his hesitation any longer, she grabbed him by the sides of his head and brought him to her. Their lips touched lightly and she waited for him to engage. He was tentative at first, then finally kissed her with the hunger she knew he had been keeping inside for so long.

As they disengaged she whispered to him. "Just because I'm angry with you doesn't mean I don't love you."

"I can't act like I didn't cause such grief for you and our children. I feel as if I've lost everything."

"Not yet." Chardon held him. "And, Farin is not helpless. She's more ferocious than you think, or have you forgotten?"

****☼****

Sparks flew as two longswords clashed together, making a loud clank that rang in the air. Farin sat leaning forward on her knees while she watched a group of royal guards spar in the training arena near the courtyard. Her hands gripped her thighs, the fingers digging into the fabric of her robe, remembering her fight with Batis. Knowing she wouldn't win but determined he would not come out unscathed. As great a fighter as she was, Batis was battle seasoned and twice her size. Like a newborn against a giant. Her teeth clenched together in frustration.

Lady Emalli came out of the archway and settled down beside her. Farin flinched when she felt her fingers slide across her back and rest on her shoulder. When Emalli drew her in, Farin relaxed and laid her head on her bosom. She smelled nice, like fresh flowers just blooming.

"Do not chastise yourself so brutally," Lady Emalli said softly. "No one expects a child to be able to defend themselves against such violence." Farin reached out and circled an arm around her waist. "That being, you holding your own with such a beast like Batis is quite telling. You are a formidable adversary, young Farin."

Farin felt a smile creep on her face. She and her brother had trained with manbeasts and Lassian warriors becoming well versed in fighting techniques. The proof of her short lived success was that she was still here and not broken. The sounds from the sparring soldiers called her attention back to them. This time, she would learn how Azrom fought.

From the balcony above the courtyard, Romnus watched Farin stare intently at the guards in training. Knowing how she felt, he agreed with her assessment of her own fighting abilities. It was time for him to set his plan in motion and she would have to defend herself now more than ever. Of course, he would not let anyone get that close to her but just in case, she needed to do her due diligence.

Thinking of Batis, he had not decided what to do with the soldier still being held in the dungeon after his wounds had healed. Romnus wanted to tear him apart one more time for good measure before debating his fate. A thought occurred and shocked him yet, it was also a very productive one that dealt with both issues simultaneously.

Going over the details in his head, Romnus turned away from the balcony and headed down the corridor towards the dungeon entrance. His entourage fell in place behind him and Biandra held out his favorite fruit. He glanced down at it and pondered if he would need it when facing Batis. Taking the fruit, he bit into it. Better safe than regret killing the soldier.

Seeing Batis dirty and wretched, bound to the wall of his cell made Romnus a tad giddy. The steeled look he gave made it even more priceless. Such hatred should not go to waste. He stood at the cell's entrance and his stare bore down on Batis. They engaged in a silent contest and Batis was the first to severe eye contact.

"At least you still have some pride intact," Romnus scolded him. "Now, address your Supreme Ruler."

Batis turned his head to him and spat. The glob of saliva landed just inside the cell's threshold.

"My Lord," he said, bowing slightly. His restraints only let him bend so far.

Romnus' guards grabbed the hilts of their longswords, ready to draw but his raised hand signaled them to stop. He gestured for the dungeon guard to open the cell and Batis stiffened, his eyes wide with trepidation.

"I have a proposal for you," Romnus said as he stepped into

the cell to tower over him. Batis cocked his head. "Since you have such an affinity for Farin, you are going to train her in combat."

"Is that so?"

"That is the only way I would ever let you touch her."

"What if I decide to kill her," Batis asked. His eyes narrowed and a sly smile appeared.

"Oh, she's not that easy to kill, you should know better than that. And I will tear you apart."

Batis let out a hoarse laugh that made him cough.

"So she's being given to me after all."

Romnus deactivated the restraints and Batis fell forward in a heap.

"Get up," Romnus ordered.

"What about the rest of my unit?"

"They will have a different task to complete with a new leader." He knelt down by the soldier and whispered, "If you truly want Azrom to be beautiful and glorious once more, you will swear loyalty to me."

"What makes you any better than Halfar?"

Batis still sat with his forehead touching the filthy cell floor, his breath causing dried debris to move around his mouth.

"You shall see." Romnus stood back up and left the cell. His entourage halted halfway down the corridor and waited for Batis to stumble forward and catch up. "This will be quite entertaining."

☼

Hordes representing every province on Azrom was assembled within the wall surrounding the palace that separated its land from the rest of the sector. Tension was thick in the air. Romnus scanned the multitude of faces full of curiosity about why they had been summoned. Across the planet, haloscreens hovered above villages displaying his image as he stood on the palace balcony. Behind him were Generals Kur and Rass, Lady Farin, his entourage and Batis.

"People of Azrom," his voice boomed out. "I know you have heard rumors of our debt to the Dreridian conglomerate and I am here to confirm your fears." Loud murmurs rose up. "Due to this debt, I have made a decree that you will abide." From a vid feed farther in the horizon he could see everyone behind him tense. "As of now, all able bodied citizens will work the mines and the fields. Those soldiers not on campaign will also contribute to the work load."

Cries of outrage spanned the crowd and the decibel level was almost too much to bear.

"Tyrant!"

"Monster!"

"You're no better than Halfar!"

"Slaver!"

Romnus took all of it in. He expected as much.

"Those of you who do not comply will be stripped of status and confined to the dungeons." More yells of profane language this time in their native tongue. "Those who rebel," he paused, "will have their entire horde sentenced to torture and confined to the mines until the end of our debt."

A hush flowed like a wave over the people as they stared back in confusion at him. He could see them affirming his resolve by trying to find some solace in his bright green eyes. His were not the murky forest green like Halfar's and they shone like gems in the vid feeds.

Yes, I am serious.

From various sections in the crowd, fighting erupted between the guards keeping peace and outraged citizens. Chaos was imminent and he felt something break inside him as blood flew. With fists clenched so tight he could feel his own blood seeping in his hands, Romnus looked down into the melee.

"Enough!"

The fighting was brought under control and he waited for the rebels to be removed.

"Shifts will be determined through allotments. It will begin at daybreak tomorrow. You are free to disperse."

Romnus turned his back to the crowd and the vid screens. He came face to face with General Kur who just nodded. He unclenched his fists and wiped the blood on his robes as he strode off into the throne room ahead, his entourage following. In the right corner of his vision he saw the royal advisors gloating.

He sat on the throne and let his head fall back against the top ledge. When he lifted back up at his newly formed entourage, he found worry and despair.

"Now the real strife begins," he laughed. Then regretted it.

"Yes, there will be discontent across the planet," Kur said.

"You didn't want to rule or live long, did you?" Batis scoffed.

He tensed when a blade settled across his neck.

"You forgot something," Rass whispered in his ear.

"My apologies, my lord," Batis addressed him.

Romnus waved his hand and Rass sheathed his short blade. It was more than just tension running high, there was a sense of doom in their eyes. Sighing, he leaned forward until his elbows rested comfortably on his knees then glanced around to make sure the royal advisors were still outside and out of earshot, before speaking.

"This agenda is to better Azrom. I know the timetable seems impossible but there is a reason for it. I need you to trust that what I am doing is only for the sake of our planet and our people. There will be many attempts on my life as well as the royal family that all of you standing here before me have sworn to protect. I will hold you to that."

"I promised and so I plan to do so," Kur said.

"What are we committing?" Batis asked. "Ten, twenty, fifty years?"

"I want to clear the debt in fifteen years."

"My lord!" Prevcan exclaimed as he entered the throne room with the other advisors. "That is impossible!"

Romnus sat up straight and eased back into the throne.

What impeccable timing.

He fought the urge to snap all their heads off. Mesrod had a smug expression and the other three exchanged shifty glances.

"It can be done."

"At the expense of citizens dying from over exposure in the mines or toiling endlessly in the fields?"

"Lord Prevcan," General Kur purred. "Are you implying that our Supreme Ruler is using his agenda to murder our people?"

The advisor went pale.

"Of course not," he snapped. "I believe this is undue hardship."

"Forgive me, my lord, but I find it irresponsible," Mesrod added, bowing low.

Romnus could feel the juices from the fruit ebbing away inside him.

No, you find it intriguing.

Like an open invitation to further your own agenda.

He caught Biandra's eye and she stepped up to the throne, presenting a fruit from inside her robes to him. Kur, along with his personal guards had their fingertips on the hilt of their longswords. He assumed they felt the same towards the advisors.

"It is a means to an end. I would advise that you put your faith in my plan."

He watched Mesrod's face scrunch up before relaxing then raised his head up to meet his gaze.

"I understand, my lord. We are behind you with strength and conviction."

Batis burst out laughing, causing everyone to flinch. He went on for a few seconds then cleared his throat. The advisors gave him looks of disdain.

"Leave me," Romnus commanded.

They all dispersed, leaving him alone in the throne room. General Kur halted at the entrance and turned to give him one last look. Romnus nodded in acknowledgement. Azrom was being broken in preparation for its revival.

Necessary Pain

Farin's black talons sliced through the column in addition to the soldier hiding behind it. Blood arced straight out like an asteroid belt just as another soldier came up behind her. She turned, feeling the air being cut inches from her face, and leapt backwards. Her body sailed in an arch as if weightless before twisting ninety degrees so that her feet could land on the still toppling column. Using it as a launch pad, she dove right for the solider.

He was still in the process of advancing towards her when a fortuitous slip of his foot on a pool of blood increased his momentum, leaving him vulnerable. His eyes went wide with fear as there was no time for him to dodge. Farin morphed her right hand into a giant pincer and snapped them shut, slicing him from his left underarm to his right shoulder. His torso and lower body slid away at an angle, his mouth still open from a battle cry.

Landing in a crouched position, she slid backwards coming to a full stop and hurried to Romnus' side. Without hesitation, she pulled the longsword out of his shoulder and flicked it hard, sending blood splatter across the throne room floor. This was the fourth attempt on Romnus' life in the past twelve years since his decree regarding the debt. The only difference this time was the assassins had gotten close enough to harm him. Farin bent down and formed a small ball of energy, using it to cauterize the wound.

"It's not so bad," she quipped.

Romnus smiled and brushed some of her hair away from her face. He seemed defeated somehow, long ago resigning to his fate. It made her angry. Taking a look around, she counted the number of bodies staining the floor. Batis shoved a dead soldier out of his way with one foot and sheathed his longsword.

"They were more determined than I have ever seen," he

said while advancing to their side. His hand grazed across her backside. "Nicely done, Lady Farin."

She smacked his hand away with her free hand. The other she pushed harder into Romnus as she felt him try to rise and get to Batis. This was not the time or the place for domestic fighting.

"Stop that! We have a dire situation here!"

"I taught you well."

"It wasn't just you," she snapped.

Learning all the Lassian techniques along with Azrom's was a great benefit. By combining Talas and Trinon's signature moves, she had created her own, becoming deadly. Her mother had always said she was ferocious as an infant and now she could claim that title. At thirty four, which was still considered child years, she felt accomplished for her age. Most talents or powers didn't manifest until the age of fifty. Farin grinned.

I'm just special.

She snapped out of her self-indulgence and focused on Romnus.

"Can you stand?"

"Of course, I can stand. I just need to catch my bearings a moment."

"Good. We are moving, now."

Batis cocked his head to one side and listened for anything that may set off a warning sign. Satisfied there was none, he waited with her for Romnus to get up.

"How many?" Romnus asked.

"Eight," Batis replied.

"All dead?"

"Yes," Farin answered this time.

"I don't want to kill my own people," Romnus said through gritted teeth.

"I know," she said.

In Romnus' chamber, Farin ripped off the sleeve of his robe, exposing the wound to light for better scrutiny. Batis turned away and walked out of the room, leaving them alone. She got within millimeters of the wound and frowned.

"Damn, it's deep."

"Hmm."

"We need to get the medics in here."

"Where is my entourage?"

"Ambushed in the corridor. They handled the second wave."

"A second wave? It has gotten worse."

"You have a meeting with the Dreridians next moon. This is almost over."

Farin went to move away from him on the bed but he caught her by the wrist and pulled her closer. She felt his nose embed itself in her hair and heard sniffing. He did that often yet still refused to touch her sexually. It frustrated her sometimes, the reason why, but as far as the people of Azrom were concerned, she was mated to Chastan.

"We don't have time for you to sniff me all day." She disengaged from him and went to the entryway. "Where is Kur?"

"Come back to me," Romnus demanded softly.

Farin looked over her shoulder at him.

"After we get your wound treated, I will let you hold me until sunset."

Romnus frowned but then rested his head on the cushions. She giggled, surprising herself. She hadn't done that in a long time since there was not much to laugh at in the past twelve years. Her mother probably felt the same.

☀

New Lassa

Chardon took one look at the itinerary Ganna had laid before her and grimaced. With each year of them finding new ways to clear off their Dreridian debt, Ganna dove deeper into the planets nether regions to find precious morsels to exploit.

"You have no idea what is out there. For all we know the Ginge Ocean could be treacherous."

"That's the beauty of it," Ganna exclaimed. "Have I not produced many new things to the Dreridians' liking?"

"You have, but it is getting a bit dangerous. Plus, we are still in the process of social restructuring for our race." Chardon placed both hands flat on the console and stared at the itinerary again.

"That is something you can handle on your own. I need to satisfy my scientific agenda."

"Then you will take a large crew?"

"Naturally."

"Then safe journey," Chardon said as she rose up from her position.

As Ganna left the conference chamber, she went to the cushion on the end of the console and plopped down. It contoured to her body and she relaxed into it, closing her eyes. Movement from the entrance caught her attention and she opened them. Modas walked into the chamber and stood just inside the doorway.

He looked haggard, like he had aged too fast or not slept in days. A great rift had formed between the manbeasts who joined the rebellion for change and the ones who just wanted to harm others. Being the leader of his kind was no easy task from the start and his agenda had made it nearly impossible. She almost felt sorry for him. Almost. The past years have been hard on everyone. Halfar was finally settling into a more peaceful life letting Chardon rest easy. She missed Farin but knew she was dealing with her own chaos on Azrom.

"What is it Modas?"

"I would like to have Una moved to a rehabilitation facility closer to our home."

Una.

Chardon propped herself on her elbows and contemplated the request. His daughter had fell into a dark place after realizing what she had done in the throes of her madness, combined with the injury inflicted by her brother Und. The female manbeast was mostly catatonic and rail thin, having to be fed intravenously which provided little nutrition when factoring in how much a manbeast consumed on a daily basis.

"That should be better, I think. I will let the medical staff know to transfer her."

She saw the relief on his face. The mighty manbeast was less of one now in her eyes but she also saw his strength peeking out every now and again. He was by no means defeated.

"Thank you, leader." Modas bowed to her and left the room.

Chardon frowned, hating the way he said it. With all that had happened, he should be able to speak with her candidly. The withdrawal was painful.

I will fix this.

Ocean skimmers sailed across the Ginge Ocean at leisurely speeds. They were a new addition to New Lassa's transportation agenda their design pilfered by Ganna from some of the schematics in the Dreridian archives. She had added her own ideas to them and her scientists were more than a little thrilled when the first fleet was built. Ten ships headed towards the eastern side of the planet for a science expedition so she could find out what their new home was hiding in its corners.

Each vessel was operated by a crew of twenty manbeasts who resolved to their fate after the rebellion. Ganna made the proposal to have all manbeasts, regardless of their involvement or lack of, perform labor in conjunction with planet reparations. Chardon did not like the inclusiveness and forced her to revise it. All she wanted to do was make sure none of the manbeasts sat idle. There would be no telling what horrors they'd come up with if left to think.

On this journey, she had Chafar and Und as bodyguards in case something unexpected happened. The younger child of Halfar was too quiet for her taste, his deadpan demeanor making it difficult for her to gauge what he's thinking.

"How long before we reach landfall?" she asked the manbeast at the helm. Her eyes squinted as she looked out through the panoramic window.

"We should see land before nightfall," he answered.

Ganna nodded in approval and turned to the blinking signal to her left from the communications console. Only one person would be keeping tabs on her. Especially since she was hundreds of miles away with a large group of manbeasts. She reached over and touched the link icon. Jaron's face appeared on the screen.

"And how are things going so far?"

"Really, Jaron? Is that what you wish to know?"

"Of course, because I know you would not be stupid enough to try and take out that many manbeasts. I would personally come for you."

"I have been informed we should reach land by nightfall."

"Are the ships holding up?"

"I created them, so yes. They are superb."

"That's good to hear. I will check back with you in a few days then."

The screen went black and Ganna sighed. This expedition was on the tail end of their debt to the Dreridians. She hoped to find yet another resource suitable for bargaining and get them one step closer to fulfilling the quota. Twelve years was not a long time by any means, but it was still too long to repay a debt. After hearing what Lord Romnus had done to speed up Azrom's timetable, Ganna insisted they do the same. Only a few more years were left and both New Lassa and Azrom would be free of the Dreridians. She almost felt bad for the Razznians who were locked into a fifty year contract.

Ahead of the fleet she noticed the water swell upwards like a giant bubble. At first she thought it might be an anomaly of the ocean current until she saw it get bigger.

"Full stop!" She cried into the fleet intercom system. All the ships halted, hovering above the waters.

The bubble rose higher and when it towered over the fleet tenfold, the water broke away to reveal a creature of black oily skin with a bulbous head baring six rows of pointy teeth. Large grappling tentacles, four in all slapped the water and send fifty foot tidal waves towards them.

"Eva…!"

The crews were already taking action to get the fleet out of harm's way. Und stood with his arms crossed next to the navigator and Chafar leaned against the bulkhead. She couldn't tell what either of them were thinking and was shocked, no confounded, when Und finally spoke.

"We should take it down and serve it for evening meal."

The navigator nodded as did Chafar. Ganna found herself standing legs wide apart with her mouth gaped open. She felt her eyes straining as they nearly bulged out of their sockets. Even in her sometimes maddened state of research, she knew this was a moment of danger. This was no time for capture and experimentation. She turned her head towards the vessels on her left and witnessed a new form of madness from the manbeasts. They had heard him via the still open intercom and went about attempting to try and do just what Und suggested, by any means necessary.

All the skimmers were equipped with weapons, one being a harpoon for catching large fish. A reinforced net was attached to the ship and could be released when their prey was caught to drag it close for easier lifting onto the deck. The manbeasts were going about making ready these two items.

"Has Lassa's wisdom fled your minds?" she yelled, still wild eyed.

"What? You dissect it, we claim the meat as you go," Und said.

"Isn't this part of your scientific curiosity?" Chafar added.

She chastised herself for being surprised. Manbeasts would take on any opportunity to show off their prowess. The ship rocked and just as she turned to the observation window she saw a giant tentacle slap one of the vessels down into the ocean's surface. The impact caused another wave and this time, they were engulfed by it.

Lucky rodents!

Ganna threw her torn and ragged travel bag onto the sand and looked back at the remaining vessels cruising onto the beach. She had lost three ships but not any of the crew, to her amazement; and disappointment. They had done the deed in a uniformed effort, bringing the giant creature down piece by piece. The main body was being kept refrigerated for her until she could muster the strength to start dissecting it.

Her body ached all over from being tossed around her ship by waves created from the thing thrashing about. Some of the manbeasts had taken one of the tentacles and was in the process of slicing it up. Barbarians. She was surprised they didn't just bite into it, eating it raw like the animals they were.

"Only you would think we are a bunch of senseless animals," Und snapped, jarring her out of her thought.

"I didn't say anything of the sort!"

"No, you were just thinking it. It was so obvious, you may have well said it."

Ganna pursed her lips. "Fine, but look at what you are doing. None of us are sure it is even edible."

"Oh, I'm sure it is. It never stopped us from eating any of the other creatures we encountered."

"THEY are not that," Ganna pointed to the giant tentacle, "BIG!"

"Look at it this way. We now have enough rations to last for months on end."

Ganna went pale and her stomach felt queasy.

"I will not eat that thing."

Und laughed, backing away from her before turning to go help with slicing the tentacle.

Seeing the vid feed of the manbeasts conquest, Jaron slapped a hand across her mouth to subdue her laughter. Ganna's face appeared in the foreground and she didn't look too please. It was more fodder for Jaron so she squeezed her eyes shut for a few seconds and inhaled deep before letting it out between her fingers.

"Does this amuse you? I lost three vessels! And those heathens did not make it any better."

"So, you found a new food source in the process?" Jaron asked, her voice muffled by her hand.

"In a way and much more."

"Oh?" Jaron removed her hand. "Do tell."

"It seems the creature's bodily fluids have another use. I am not one to condone hunting of a species, but we may need to acquire another one for a generous supply."

"Yes, you seem so out of sorts for suggesting it," Jaron dead-panned.

"I think the Dreridians will like it as much as we will. And, they are not getting rights to it."

"A battle against the Dreridian treasurer?"

Jaron raised an eyebrow.

"This find is ours and they can negotiate trade. I will not just give them every resource we come across."

"Well said. I agree. As I used to say on Earth, they can suck it."

"What?" Ganna reared back somewhat confused.

"It means they can suffer in the flames of Lassa's light."

"Oh. Then yes, indeed."

"Hurry back."

"No rush. My team still has to explore the terrain we landed on."

"Then do it and hurry back. The quicker we get to see your new find and peddle it to the Dreridians, the better."

Jaron touched the icon to deactivate the vidscreen and sat down in the nearby cushion. She used her fingers to wipe away strands of fire red hair from her face and let her head drop back. Almost there. Then she could focus on Modas and how to fix what he had broken. Their relationship was strained but she knew deep down, she still loved him. Getting rid of the obstacle called Dreridian debt was first on the list.

⁎⁎☼⁎⁎

This time, Romnus traveled to the Dreridian home world in his royal ship with a small fleet in tow as guardians. He knew only the main ship would be permitted to land but he wanted to show Azrom's might. They did not need to tip the Dreridians on how torn apart and in shambles the planet was, positive they had heard rumors. He sat in the lounge of the ship surrounded by his entourage. Farin was asleep with her head resting on his shoulder. Next to her was Batis pretending to look bored but Romnus saw his eyes zeroed in on Farin's bosom.

General Kur was seated across from him in silence and he always wondered what the military elite thought about in those moments. Scanning the lounge he counted twelve and realized his group may be too large. A moot point now.

"We are cleared for landing, my lord," the pilot announced over the commlink. "We will be there shortly."

Romnus did not reply. He had faith in the crew's expertise. Nudging Farin awake, he stood up and made his way to the hangar. His four royal guards fell in formation, two ahead and two behind, with Farin and Biandra on either side of him. Batis stayed in the rear along with Kur to oversee Mesrod and the head of agriculture who basically demanded he attend the meeting.

The hatch opened and the ramp extended down onto the docking floor. Romnus didn't even feel the ship land, let alone dock. He wanted to reward the crew but couldn't think of one thing off hand. Down below, standing in triangular formation were Lord Greggor and his faithful entourage. The Dreridian looked as if he had gotten bigger in girth. Romnus had some ideas of what the creature was eating but decided not to dwell on it. A quick glance to his left found him staring at a ship he had never seen before. Lord Greggor noticed his interest.

"Ah, yes. The Lassians arrived in that beautiful machine. I am quite impressed with Ganna and her team's ingenuity."

Romnus gaped at the giant ship with its sleek oval design and muted tones of color that reminded him of New Lassa's surface. He drew his attention away and silently congratulated them on finally getting ships to travel with instead of relying on the vortex so much. Once his people set foot on the tarmac, Lord Greggor turned away and walked towards the elevators. Without needing to be told, Romnus and his entourage followed.

Inside the conference room, Romnus saw Chardon already seated at the table flanked by Ganna and Talas. Modas stood nearby and his appearance was shocking. The manbeast had seen better days. A deep weariness exuded from him. Moving along the edge of the table, Romnus noticed Sars seated with both elbows on the top, hands templed in front of him. They made a quick nod of acknowledgement to each other and Romnus sat down.

Farin had a huge smile on her face as she nodded to her mother. Chardon smiled back. They would have to reminisce later after the meeting. They all waited silently for Lord Pondur and the treasurer to arrive. Romnus felt his fingers tapping the tabletop and stopped. Biandra held out the small fruit and he took it from her slowly. There was no reason to be on edge for this meeting. Then he realized it wasn't the meeting, it was what had to happen afterwards on Azrom.

Lord Pondur strode in posture erect, looking dignified, his treasurer right on his heels carrying the tablet containing every transaction made in the past fifty years. A servant appeared with a chalice and poured liquid from a carafe into it. Lord Pondur waited until the servant slunk away before raising the drink to his craggy lips, taking a delicate sip.

"This is quite unprecedented, all of you demanding a meeting so soon before your quotas' timetable is up." He set his chalice down. "But, I do like to be updated on the flow of commerce."

The treasurer activated his tablet and began going through the uploaded data from all of them. He frowned after some time then nodded in approval. Looking up from his screen, he addressed Lord Pondur.

"It seems, my lord, that Azrom has indeed met their quota ahead of schedule."

Lord Pondur and Lord Greggor both halted their drinks in midair.

"Are you certain?" Lord Pondur glanced at him.

"Very. Would you like to see the data?"

Lord Pondur waved a hand at him.

"That is not necessary. The others?"

"Almost for the Lassians, but they do have a proposal. Razzna has also ramped up production and close to the end."

"How prolific all of you are. I never would have guessed the depths of your convictions. Well done."

Lord Greggor set his chalice down on a small stand near the entryway and cleared his throat.

"What is this proposal that you deem with erase the rest of your debt, Lassians?"

Ganna smiled. Romnus reared back from it and noticed everyone else did as well. It was never a good thing when Ganna was this happy, but this time he thought it may be warranted.

"Your kind has had some difficulty creating apparatus for research of your acidic oceans. The deep crevices of your bodies are susceptible to irritation and corrosion."

"Yes, but we have wonderful mobile suits that are impervious to the harms of our waters."

"But you still would like to able to touch your findings and know the actually texture of the water."

Lord Greggor stroked the rocky mounds of his chin.

"That would be ideal. Continue."

"We have found a new resource that is capable of attaching and sealing itself to organic subjects and can be easily peeled away. The remnants can be reconstituted for up to four uses before it breaks down."

Lord Greggor's eyes went wide and his hands started to shake. "Show me! I want to see this new compound."

"Is this something extraordinary or just good?" Lord Pondur asked seemingly unimpressed.

"It is more than extraordinary!" Lord Greggor exclaimed.

Ganna reached down by her side and produced a clear circular casing that housed a black slush. It moved extremely slow inside the bubble, clinging to the edges for a few brief moments before receding. Watching it, Romnus thought it looked like Azromian blood, only thicker.

"Come," Lord Greggor huffed, gesturing Ganna to the door.

"You're testing it now?" Lord Pondur frowned.

"Of course. I will bring her back before the evening banquet and give you my decision."

"Very well."

As Lord Greggor left with Ganna and his guards, Lord Pondur turned his attention to Romnus.

"What do you want?"

Romnus heard a sense of resentment in the Dreridian's tone. Having the debt cleared ahead of time meant there would be no interest collected. That was part of his initial plan. He glanced at the councilman and Mesrod. His request had to be cryptic but nonetheless understandable.

"I want access to the outer rim so we can barter for supplies."

"Is that so?" Lord Pondur's eyes narrowed into slits. "What could you possibly want from the outer rim?"

"They have commodities beneficial to Azrom."

"You're not going to divulge the reason then?"

Dreridians were highly intelligent and Romnus knew he couldn't hide his reluctance to tell him his plans. The treasurer was hunched over his tablet again.

"What is your timeframe for bargaining?" The treasurer blurted without looking up.

Romnus tapped his fingers on the table then replied, "Five years."

"That's all?" The treasurer was perplexed.

Lord Pondur gave him a glare making obvious his wariness towards Romnus.

"Yes, that is all I need to acquire what I want."

"Shall I authorize it, my lord?" Lord Pondur nodded, not turning his gaze from him. The treasurer's fingers went flying across the tablet. "Very well, Lord Romnus. I have cleared Azrom's debt and releasing access for trade."

"I give you my gratitude," Romnus said as he bowed his head to Lord Pondur.

"And you?" Lord Pondur snapped, addressing Sars.

Sars looked towards Romnus as if asking for permission then smiled. Or what passed as one for a reptile.

"Your overseers off our planet within ten years. We will have our debt cleared by then and there would be no reason for your presence on Razzna."

"Bold aren't we, reptile?"

"Now that we can bargain on the outer rim, I can also negotiate goods for Razzna," Romnus spoke.

"Are you not enemies?" Lord Pondur barked. "Did Razzna

not invade both New Lassa and Azrom? What am I missing in this scenario?"

"We were made enemies based on lies and someone else's agenda," Talas answered. "We all understand this and have decided to negotiate a truce."

"This stemmed from you suggesting trade in parts of the galaxy not charted." Kur continued where Talas left off. "I had never heard of Earth until the council informed me of it by way of your race."

"We are just three primitive races trying too hard, remember?" Romnus smiled.

"Yes," Lord Pondur grinned. "I will keep watch and see how your kind progresses. Please," he picked up his chalice, "prove me wrong." He took a small sip and glared over the rim at them.

The moment they all filed into the banquet hall, Farin ran to her mother and flung herself into her arms. Chardon steeled herself to take on the onslaught. Farin found that amusing, knowing her usual lunge would probably hurt due to her being taller and more filled out.

"I missed you!"

"Yes, I see that," her mother said. "Now let go before we both hit the floor."

Farin did as she was told and for the first time was able to look her mother in the eyes on the same level.

"Are you doing well?" Her mother asked.

"Everything is fine."

"Then why do I get the feeling it's not. What is Romnus planning?"

Farin lowered her gaze. "I can't tell you that."

"Farin," her mother said in a warning tone.

"He's making Azrom better. That's all there is."

"How?"

"Can't we just enjoy being together for this short while? Please?"

From the corner of her eye she saw Talas frown. He had been listening and her heart sank. He was so intuitive that she could tell he was figuring it out. Bringing her attention back to her mother, she threw her arms around her mother's neck.

"I want to tell you about the good things. Like how my little one is no longer so and a pain."

"Because he is just like you."

Farin laughed. "You think so?"

She stole a glance at Romnus who just gave her a forlorn look as she and her mother laughed. Until Azrom was whole again, not even her mother could know of his agenda.

After the banquet, Romnus and his entourage were escorted immediately back to the docking bay and sent off under scrutiny of Lord Greggor's guards. Inside the ship, Romnus hurried to the lounge and took to a floor cushion that barely handled his size. He laid an arm across his face and exhaled.

"And now?" General Kur raised an eyebrow at him.

"We move on to phase two."

"What is this phase two?" The agriculture councilman exclaimed. "You have made many decrees, sending Azrom spiraling down into the depths of despair! We deserve an explanation!"

"You deserve nothing," Romnus spat. He lifted himself up and stared at him. "Have you forgotten? I am Supreme Ruler. You do as I decree regardless of if it suits you."

Mesrod smiled. "I beg your pardon, my lord, but General Kur can remove you from rulership if he so inclines."

"Which I do not," Kur interjected. "I back his agenda fully. You should do the same."

The smile faded and the councilman seemed unsure of himself. Romnus didn't like them in his circle and especially not on his ship. His trust in them was nil and he had no doubt they were entrenched in their own agenda with him in their way.

"Preparing to enter vortex," the navigator's voice announced.

Romnus got up from the floor and went to his seat to strap in. Once he was back on Azrom, the real pain would begin.

They will forgive me when it's over and I am dead.

He felt truth in that.

There was no fanfare when they arrived back on Azrom. No royal guards in splendid arrays of color to greet the Supreme Ruler but Romnus didn't expect any to begin with. He made his way to the throne room via the staircase that wound down to the main level and curved into the secret corridor.

The entire royal court stood in wait for him in the throne room, speech withheld until he was seated.

"The initial start of phase two is going slow but there is progress," Kur began. "Rumors are circulating that some of the royal family members, namely Chastan, have been overly zealous."

"Excuse my ignorance, my lord," Mesrod interrupted. "But, what does phase two entail?"

"We are negotiating with the territories to have them vacate their lands and move into sectors I have prepared for temporary living," Romnus replied.

He saw the rest of the advisors and two other councilmen enter at that moment and what he said registered on their facial expressions.

"That borders on slavery. Why would you remove our people from their homes and imprison them?"

"Because I need to destroy the villages and I cannot do that if the people are still there."

Sharp intakes of air resounded.

"Madness," someone said. People turned to see who had spoken but no one seemed to fess it.

"The only way to ensure the safety and wellbeing of our race is to keep them within close proximity of my reach. Order must be maintained."

"Have you not had enough rebellion?" A councilman cried out. His face was flushed with anger.

"They can rebel if they want. They know the consequences of such actions."

"Destruction will start in the north," Kur continued.

"I want it to commence in two locations at once. The quicker we get the ground levelled, the faster we can get the citizens in the confinement sectors."

"Why?" Prevcan yelled. "Why are you doing such a thing? The people are working the mines and fields nonstop to keep to your timetable."

"Exactly. They are rarely in their villages and so have no need for them."

Many of the royal court went pale as if ill and Romnus fought to keep his composure. He could hear the harshness in his voice. It was necessary to convey his will.

They despise me tenfold.

Locking eyes with Kur, the general gave him a reassuring look.

"Continue with negotiations. I don't want bloodshed."

"That is inevitable," Mesrod stated.

"No," Romnus roared back, "it is not!" He turned to Batis. "See to it."

"As you wish, my lord," Batis answered, bowing low.

"You all know what needs to be done. You are dismissed."

There was hesitation in the movement of the crowd then a sudden stream of people fled from the throne room. Romnus gripped the sides of the arm rests and Farin placed a hand on top of his. As much as he adored her, it would take more than that to ease his anxiety.

Mesrod removed his gloves as he entered the advisors' meeting room and slapped them down on the center console. He laid his hands flat and leaned over with his head hanging down. After a moment, he turned towards his comrades.

"This would not be happening," he started softly, "if he were not still alive!" he shouted.

Calba and Jabarz flinched while Dondar and Prevan sat further back in their seats. He scanned their faces for some explanation even though he was certain there was none.

"Each attempt has failed. Why is that?"

"He's not easy to kill, Lord Mesrod," Calba replied. "We were close this last time. My men were able to wound him."

"Close does not make him dead."

Mesrod slammed his fist on the console.

"No, but getting that close to him means he has let his guard down somewhat," Jabarz said.

"Which he will no longer do since it was so close," Mesrod reminded them. "He is now more wary than before and we have a crisis on our hands."

"But, you said his actions would give us reason to form a coup." Calba seemed perplexed.

"A coup, yes. That is not possible any longer. He is about to enslave the inhabitants of our planet, throwing it into a form of chaos I do not know how to reverse."

"How could he get away with this? How does he get them

to comply?" Jabarz questioned.

"It's obvious. Brute force," Dondar quipped.

"Kill him! I do not want to hear about another failure," Mesrod ordered.

"It will take some time. He will be prepared for one so soon."

"You have less than five years. Get it done."

Mesrod took a deep breath and exhaled slowly. He was getting tired of trying to steer insane rulers onto the right path that benefitted Azrom. From Romnus' father to Halfar's father and the two sons put together, he concluded that the royal bloodline must have been tainted somewhere along the way. It was time to cleanse the palace.

✡

Reports from across the planet came in droves, all disheartening yet some sense of accomplishment could be felt. Every second phase of the moon a new shipment arrived on Azrom and the goods stored in a secret location underground not far from the palace.

Romnus walked along the outer corridor by himself and smiled a little. The royal advisors probably thought he would use brute force but instead he had each village gassed before transporting all its citizens to the designated sectors. Bloodshed was not an option. Of course, there was hostility when they awoke in a new environment stripped of most of their belongings.

Movement to the right of him on the ground below caught his eye and he took a quick glance. Batis stopped walking and looked directly up at him, an eyebrow raised up. It was a bold move for him to stroll the palace unguarded but he refused to be deterred by yet another assassination attempt. He nodded to Batis and continued down the corridor. He was the Supreme Ruler. If he couldn't walk safely in his own palace, then who could? Then he grinned. There is no safety if you're hated.

A messenger came bearing towards him, skidding to a halt to slow his advance. The young soldier was winded with beads of sweat lining his forehead. He gulped a few times to catch his breath then spewed out his message.

"My lord! You have to stop Lord Chastan. He has gone mad."

"What do you mean, gone mad? Where is he?"

"He went to negotiate with one of the eastern villages. It's one of the last few still holding out but not rebelling. Lord

Farregun and his three brothers rule that territory, I believe."

The soldier frowned.

"Yes, they are from the fifth royal house. What is the problem?"

The messenger's face went rigid and it gave Romnus a sense of dread. Hands clenched at his sides, the young soldier blurted, "He has resorted to unprecedented measures of persuasion."

Romnus reared his head up high and looked down at the young soldier as if he had given him something rotten. That description could entail anything but he knew it had to be bad. Maybe worse than he thought. Chastan was a bit rough and ill equipped to handle others. He could not see it being anything of horrors.

"Fine, I will send Aloni and General Rass to see to it."

"Of course, my lord," the young soldier bowed, "but they must hurry."

Turning on his heels, the messenger sprinted off from whence he came, leaving Romnus to ponder what was so dire about Chastan's behavior.

From a distance Aloni could see the village through his surveillance goggles and adjusted the lenses with a side tap to zoom in. He nodded at General Rass to do the same. They were on open land skimmers for their speed and the weather was mild enough. The high velocity created forcible winds that sent their hair straight back as they leaned forward to be more aerodynamic. Six royal guards on their own skimmers were keeping up behind them. The more the distance narrowed, the more they both saw what was occurring and they pushed the skimmers to full power. It was true. Chastan had gone mad.

Chastan's guards held the crowd back and struck down anyone who tried to break into his makeshift arena. On his left was Lord Farregun, nearly cut to ribbons tied to a stake embedded in the ground. Lying belly down with his face turned to one side was his younger brother, barely able to stay conscious. To Chastan's right was the older brother, decapitated. The man had tried to stop him from getting at his daughter so had to be put down. Behind him was the daughter, impaled by two rods in each arm to a board propped up at a forty five degree angle.

Her gown was ripped open down the middle and he

had already raped her in front of everyone. Lord Farregun's daughter had been the first and she too was on the board next to her cousin, unconscious.

"Please," Lord Farregun whispered. "Stop this."

"You could have prevented this if you had complied with my demands. All you had to do was leave the territory as instructed and give your daughters to me. They would have been a great addition to my royal court, but now."

Chastan flipped the short dagger he had used to cut open the gown in his hand then turned back to the dead brother's daughter. He ran the blade deep into her womb, the screams coming from not just her but the crowd as well. He smiled at his work.

"No one will have her."

Pain blossomed through his chest and looking down found the source being the blade of a longsword sticking out of him. He tried to cry out but only ended up choking on his own blood, falling to his knees on the ground. The dagger slipped out of his hand.

General Rass came around him and pulled the longsword out of his back. He saw his own blood spray in the air around him before darkness consumed him.

"What in all of Azrom has happened here?" Aloni cried.

He observed the crowd then turned his attention to the royal family members in front of him. General Rass stood at the semicircle of guards. This could be bad. He had no doubt Rass could cut down every last one of Chastan's men but it went against Romnus' decree of no bloodshed. Blood. Aloni squeezed his eyes shut and tried not to think too far ahead on what to do in their current situation. The people would blame their Supreme Ruler because he had sent Chastan there.

"You will take your master to the medical wing of the palace and wait there. You do not venture anywhere else or I will cut you down faster than I did him. Do you understand?"

Rass had a demonic look in his eyes and Aloni was convinced of the threat. Apparently so were they, for they immediately dispersed, taking a nearly dead Chastan with them. They loaded him and themselves into the transport ship near Farregun's palace, taking off quickly.

Aloni held his breath for a brief moment watching the crowd, waiting for any kind of hostile reaction. Instead, the servants and handmaids rushed forward and tended to the daughters and the surviving brothers.

"You must know that this was not Lord Romnus' agenda," Aloni spoke. "His decree specifically forbade bloodshed. I do not know what Lord Chastan's reason for this was."

"He came to take our land and enslave us like the rest," a handmaid exclaimed. "Isn't that Lord Romnus' order?"

Aloni sighed and addressed Rass.

"I will tell them, and only them." Rass nodded.

He moved further into the middle before the crowd.

"Lord Romnus is not enslaving you. He is trying to make Azrom better. In order to do so, he must level everything. He asks," Aloni paused, "we ask that you please be patient with us during this transition. You can hate your Supreme Ruler, even wish him death, but in the end you will see he was right."

"So, we are to trust you? After this?" Lord Farregun's advisor pushed through the crowd and came face to face with him.

"Yes, even after this. As I said, this was not part of Lord Romnus' decree."

"Then you have royal family members with their own agendas?"

"I hope this is the worse and last of such things."

General Rass tapped the earbud in his right ear.

"Send a medical team and the transport ships."

"Immediately, general," a muffled voice replied.

"Do we really want to show this feed to Lord Romnus?" Aloni asked Rass.

"He must see it!" Farregun's advisor demanded. "He needs to know what his own blood is doing!"

Aloni found himself staring up at the sky to see the small blip that was Chastan's ship disappear into the horizon.

What have you done, cousin?

"Romnus will not like this."

Fury filled Romnus as he watched the simultaneous feed from both Aloni and Rass. The two holoscreens were far enough away from him that he could see every detail on each one. This was far worse than madness. He could never have imagined Chastan capable of such heinous behavior. Seeing what he did to the daughter of the now deceased Lord Than with a dagger nearly made him retch. Even when repaired, the girl would still know that pain, never able to find a mate she could trust. The feed ended and the throne room was silent.

"Where is he?" Romnus boomed.

"Still being treated in the medical bay. I figured you would not want him dead, although I nearly did kill him." General Rass tapped the hilt of his longsword. "I wanted to kill him."

"What else has he done?"

"I was able to get a good amount of information out of his guards. He has been terrorizing the territories and acquiring what he sees fit to have before sending the gas."

"Acquiring?" Romnus was puzzled at first, then remembered what Chastan said to Lord Farregun. "Women? He was acquiring women? For what…" Romnus held up a hand. "No, wait. I think I know. Sex slaves."

"Yes, his own personal brothel. He had even requisitioned a chamber and I was led to it." Aloni pursed his lips and exhaled. "It is more like a brothel of debauchery. I don't think I have ever seen," he stopped short of explaining and Romnus was grateful for that.

He suddenly felt ill. "Does Farin know?"

"She will soon enough," Rass replied. "She heard he was injured and is rushing to his side."

"Well, she might just kill him for you," Romnus stated.

Running at top speed, Farin careened down the halls of the first royal house palace towards the medical bay. She had no idea what had happened but it must be bad if Chastan was so hurt he needed emergency attention. When she came to the clearing of the great hall, a royal guard held up a hand signaling her to halt. At first, she was going to plow right through him but something in the way he did it made her comply.

"Why have you stopped me?" She bent over to catch her breath, letting her arms dangle by her sides, the sleeves of her black robe nearly touching the floor. Her eyes went wide. "Has something happened? Has he?"

Her vision blurred and the sound went down to almost mute as he relayed what happened at Lord Farregun's palace.

Her body stood frozen in a slump as her mind tried to process it. Chastan had turned into some kind of monster? Half drunk, mating crazed Chastan who backed away from a fight most of the time? It hit her hard, the disgust, forcing her body erect.

With everything that Romnus was setting in motion, she was still adored by the people of Azrom, being Chastan's mate to keep up appearance. But now she had ample reason to sever ties with him. All would understand her decision. She suddenly felt weary, nodding her head when he finished then turned back. She wanted to lie down and not think for a long time.

⁕⁕☼⁕⁕

New Lassa

Halfar watched the sun set in the horizon from a hilltop above the compound he lived in with Chardon. Each day was peaceful to him but a series of tension and small episodes of chaos for the Lassians. He understood their disbelief at the rebellion, not being a race of warriors always fighting like Azrom. They did not know centuries of strife as he did. Off in the distance below, he saw the gate open and Chardon's giant oval ship come through. Ganna had outdone herself with that piece of technology.

Pushing himself up off the ground, he turned away from the harsh glare as the last remnants of sunlight glinted off its hull. He headed down the side of the hill to go welcome his mate back home. Halfar smiled at that sentiment. Not being Supreme Ruler was a gift he planned to cherish for as long as he could. In the first few years, he was resentful, finding Chardon's faith in him condescending. Now, he had a better grasp on why she felt that way.

Meeting Chardon's group on the trail leading to the temple, he searched their faces for a sign of what may have transpired with the Dreridians and the hideous smile from Ganna told him plenty. It must have been a success. He reached for his mate and pulled her into a long embrace. Chardon smelled of burnt air, the result of space travel through the vortex. That didn't deter him from burying his nose in the crook of her neck.

"So it is done?" He asked her softly.

"Yes. They agreed to clear the debt early due to Ganna's new find."

"Greed does have its advantages at some point."

"Well, we are grateful they are very greedy." Chardon moved her hands up his back and squeezed before letting go. "We have to address the council. Want to sit in?"

Halfar disengaged from her and cocked his head. Joining in on council matters was something he rarely did because it reminded him that he was no longer a leader of anyone or any race. Chardon knew this, so for her to ask him meant there was something else that needed his specific attention.

"I will, since you have requested it."

"I saw Farin."

Chardon spoke it nonchalantly, taking him off guard.

The group continued their advance towards the temple and Halfar kept in stride with them.

"How was she?"

"Taller, more rounded."

"Does she have more offspring?"

"No." Chardon seemed to find it just as odd as he did by the expression she gave.

"You learned something you didn't like when speaking with her." It wasn't quite a question but he expected an answer.

"More a combination of what Romnus is doing and what she didn't tell me."

"Hmm?"

"Talas has a theory and he's usually right. I want you to hear what he thinks and see if you agree."

"Has he told you this theory?"

"No, he wants to make sure you hear it with us."

A tightening in the pit of his stomach forced him to inhale sharply. Exhaling didn't help ease the tension so he decided to steer the conversation back to Farin.

"So, how tall is she?"

"Taller than the both of us. And," Chardon slowed down her pace, "she seems to be quite strong. Like she is fighting all the time. I could tell how well toned her muscles were by her body movements."

That did disturb him. Farin had been trained by Lassian energy users and manbeasts but it was not for her to become a warrior, only a means to defend herself if necessary. Whatever was happening on Azrom could not be good. They had abided Romnus' wish to not open the pathway to Azrom, sacrificing their ties to Farin. If Talas' theory proved a dire need, he would break that promise, consequences be damned.

Arriving at the temple's side entrance, the entire group formed a single file line in order to enter the narrow hallway. The walk was quiet, devoid of speaking. Inside the council chamber were all the representatives of Lassian divisions. With Chardon's group adding to the numbers, the chamber was nearly filled to maximum capacity. Halfar barely had time to settle down into a seating cushion when the session began. He only heard half of what they were discussing but he got the gist of it. Hearing Lord Pondur's reaction to the three races putting aside their differences for the time being made him laugh along with a few others.

Most of this side of the galaxy was comprised of bipedal lifeforms with similar biological structures. It was when you ventured out towards the outer rim that it got strange and frightening. Razzna was not quite on the verge and had variations of their species. Halfar had only seen one or two beings from the outer rim and didn't care to see them again or any others. Then he realized they were indeed talking about the outer rim and Romnus' bargaining request. His hands clenched into fists.

The council meeting over, everyone dispersed except Chardon's inner circle. Jaron, Kelin, Talas, Ganna, Trinon, Mara and Und sat sipping the last of their drinks, taking a breather from the constant barrage of questions and answers. Chafar just stood leaning against the wall with arms crossed, mimicking Modas. Halfar sat still, not finishing his beverage, lost in thought. He then turned to Talas who caught his eye and halted his cup as it touched his bottom lip.

Talas set it down and made himself comfortable in his seat. The others saw this and did the same.

"Romnus has cleared Azrom's debt in record time," he blurted out. Halfar felt his own eyes widen at the implication. "I have an idea of how that occurred, but I would like to confirm it with you."

Halfar frowned and rested his still clenched fists on the

table. "It would mean mines and fields production at a rate five times the normal output. It would put a tremendous strain on the worker population."

"Unless," Talas stated.

"Unless he made a decree to force the entire population to work them on a constant rotation."

"That's insane?" Jaron spurted. "It borders on slavery."

"Which would turn Azrom into a hostile planet, a race against its own self." Halfar tried to control his breathing before continuing. "It's not worth it. Everyone Azromian would try to assassinate him to alleviate the strife."

"That is what I believe is happening. He is moving on to a second phase that involves bargaining with the outer rim. He is restructuring something but I can't put my finger on it."

With that notion, Halfar's mind tumbled backwards into his memories and landed on a conversation he and Romnus had regarding rulership. His cousin had told him and the rest of the royal family that if he were to become ruler, he would destroy everything in order to make Azrom thrive.

The beings on the outer rim specialized in materials used for building elements of worlds, including structures.

"He can't possibly mean to do this," Halfar said to himself.

"Do what?" Chardon asked.

"Level the surface. Raze the villages and start all over."

Talas flinched at that. Halfar couldn't blame him. It was an extreme measure.

"Then that means the entire royal family is in constant danger, Farin included."

Halfar nodded.

"We have to find a way to Azrom. He's locked the pathway for the main gates."

Ganna snorted at that.

"I have other ways to get to Azrom."

"If what you say is true and assassination attempts on Romnus are high, then with Farin by his side she has no choice but to defend both him and herself," Trinon spoke up. "I don't like that."

"Neither do I." Chardon glanced at Halfar and they silently agreed.

"Travel takes time and it has already been over a year

on Azrom since your return. If you can get a new pathway opened fairly soon, we can get there before his five year mark." He addressed Ganna specifically.

"It shall be done. Excuse me."

Ganna got up and left the chamber.

"Can they hold much longer?" Kelin caressed his chin. "With such an implementation, the attempts will become much more frequent."

"And more brutal." Jaron added.

"Oh, sweet Farin. She has so much to deal with. At least she has the backing of the royal family," Mara said.

"Not necessarily," Halfar unclenched one hand to wave a finger at her. "There are some from the lower houses who wish to ascend to the throne by unconventional means."

"Are you going to reclaim your throne?" Chafar asked mildly.

Halfar looked up with a jolt and found all of them staring at him. "No. I do not wish to rule any longer. That said, I will not let Azrom be destroyed or ruled by yet another tyrant if that is what I find Romnus to be."

"Then it's settled," Chardon declared as she stood up.

"We leave for Azrom as soon as possible."

Halfar let his other hand rest, the stiff numbness slowly subsiding.

Please wait for me.

He hoped his plea would reach Romnus and Farin.

End Game

Dungeon cells overflowing with royal guards and soldiers who rebelled against Romnus' decree made cleanliness next to impossible but the servants did the best they could. Kur was not enjoying the sight of Azrom soldiers trapped in an underground cage because they refused to trust in their supreme ruler's vision. It was almost over and he was sure they would see the outcome as a great thing for Azrom. He couldn't lie to himself and say it was not a challenge to keep the faith. There were times when he questioned even his own judgement in naming Romnus the new ruler.

An imprisoned royal guard rammed himself against the beams of his cell to try and grab a servant bent down a few inches from the bottom with a vacuum tool. The servant was quick on his feet and leaped backwards out of reach. The royal guard let out a frustrated roar, hit a beam and cursed as his skin sizzled where he had made contact. Kur saw them turning into barbarians, regressing to primal instinct. Not wanting to stay longer than needed, he left the observation to his unit leader and went back up to the palace courtyard.

He strolled along deep in his own thoughts and ended up at the first royal house palace's courtyard. His mother, Emalli, was there tending to the royal children. Farin's precocious son was among them, though he was now of teen years. His blond hair was straight like Farin's and hung just past his shoulders. He was a beautiful boy.

"When do I get to hold a child of yours and Rass'?" She asked him, meeting his gaze.

"Your intuition is extraordinary. Very soon. I wanted to wait before announcing the news."

"There may not be anything left when this is over, my son."

"Rass also brought that to my attention."

"You cannot protect him forever, no matter how great a warrior you may be."

"I have been successful so far."

"Mmm, but the advisors is getting desperate. They have the backing of some of the council members too."

"You are assuming they are the ones responsible for the constant attacks."

"General." She only called him that when she was angry. "Even you are not so naïve."

Kur dropped his head. The anger inside of him crept back up and he had to force it away. He was well aware of the advisors attempts to end not just Romnus' life but his, Rass' and Farin's. A thought came to him.

"I need you to do something for me. Something that requires immediate attention."

Emalli raised an eyebrow and smiled.

"What do you need?"

"Someone who can protect Rass and the first royal house."

"Oh? There is such a being who is stronger than Rass and yourself?"

"Yes, Rass' father." His mother sat up straighter, a shocked look on her flawless face. "I need you to find him."

"That may take resources you cannot hide."

"I don't wish to hide it. If asked, the reason would be to connect with Rass' bloodline as I have with you."

"Then I will do this for you. For our family line."

His mother stood up to her full height, just shy of his own and placed a hand on his cheek. He leaned his head into it and closed his eyes.

Just a little longer.

☼

A poisoned dart came sailing across the outer corridor as Lord Romnus walked it with his entourage. He reacted before his guards, hearing it cut the air and caught it with his bare hands, thus letting the tip enter flesh. The effect was instant, bringing him to one knee as he clutched his chest. Farin had already pulled the dart from his hand and tossed it over the ledge. Biandra knelt next to him and rammed an injection rod full of antidote in his neck.

They were prepared for almost every scenario lately and he thanked his entourage silently as the pain subsided. Glancing back he saw Batis lowering a crossbow and followed the guard's gaze to a soldier falling down towards the ground below. Romnus stood up brushing off his robes and took a few deep breaths.

"Are you alright, my lord?" Biandra concealed the rod back into the folds of her robe.

"For now." He turned to Farin. "Did you touch the tip?"

"I was careful, unlike you," she snapped. "What were you thinking?"

He cowered from her anger. It didn't suit her at all.

"That was quite reckless of you, if I can add to that," Batis said.

"My apologies, it was instinct."

They continued on, heading to his royal chamber in the main palace. At the entrance, Batis and Biandra stood guard while the others split up to patrol the corridor from each direction. Farin went inside with him. He rubbed the injection site on his neck and planted one hand on the wall by their bed for leverage. Looking out at the afternoon sky, his mind felt cloudy and knew it could only be a residual effect of the poison.

Farin stood on the other side a few feet away from him. The thought of not being closer to her stirred something within. A deep desperation that had always been there but pushed away every time. Reaching out with his free hand, he snatched her from where she stood and drew her to him. His lips found hers and he kissed her, deeply, hungrily.

Time stood still.

When he finally pulled away, he said, "Rule with me."

Batis' head peeked around the entrance. Romnus paid him no mind and kept his stare locked on Farin's eyes. They were wide with what he could only describe as a stunned look.

"You....I," she stuttered. Her eyes searched his. She wriggled out of his embrace and stepped backwards towards the entrance. "You don't want someone like me," she whispered. "I'm too young."

"I need you. Rule with me."

"I agree," Batis stated. "You are the only choice to be by his side." Biandra nodded.

Farin turned and ran from the chamber, he heard the guards cry out in surprise as she ran past them. Romnus found himself standing in the middle of the chamber, dejected.

"She needs time to think it through. I wouldn't worry, my lord. She will say yes in time."

Batis' reassurance irritated him because he was probably right. Farin may be young still but she had grown far beyond her years physically and psychologically. Her advice was always relevant and never steered him wrong when he implemented them. Taking a few steps back, he bumped against the foot of the bed and sat down on it. Time was something he had little of these days.

Royal guards crowded into the first royal house palace court-yard, forming a semicircle around the center. A vortex had suddenly appeared nearly sucking some of the royal children into it. Emalli and her fellow handmaids were able to get them rounded up and safely into the palace. She then returned to see who could be coming through at such a remote location far from a main gate console.

Kur was at the forefront with Romnus and the other members of their royal house behind him. Whoever was coming either had no clue that an alarm had been raised the moment the vortex was detected, or they did know and were prepared to defend them-selves. Emalli was not surprised and started laughing as the group stepped out of the vortex.

Chardon, Halfar, Trinon, Talas and Chafar were already in fighting stances, weapons drawn, then hesitated when her laugh caught their ears. Emalli stopped and wiped tears from her eyes. She saw the incredulous look on her son's face and nearly started up again but restrained herself.

"What are you doing?" Kur demanded, addressing Halfar.

They all straightened their stance and concealed their weapons. Halfar came forward and nodded towards Romnus.

"I came because he has lost his mind just as I had. Did you think we would stand by and wait for Farin to be killed after you put her in such a dangerous situation?"

"You don't even know what the situation is," Romnus hissed.

"Process of deduction," Talas spoke up. "I brainstormed everything you said at the meeting and ran it by Halfar. He came up with the logical answer."

"You are too intelligent for your own good," Kur snapped at Talas. "And you," he stared at Halfar, "are supposed to be exiled. How do you think we are to explain this?"

"Who says I am here?" Halfar cocked his head.

Emalli erupted into laughter again, breaking all their trains of thought. She let herself get it all out of her system then walked up to Halfar.

"This is advantageous for us all. Now, I won't need to drudge up useless information to fulfill your request, my son." Kur eyed her questioningly. "Who would know better where to find Rass' father than the former Supreme Ruler?"

Romnus turned and mirrored Kur's expression. The two warriors had a stare off before Kur spoke.

"Rass is with child. I need someone who can protect her and the first royal house. As competent as you all are, the next attack may be bigger than we anticipate."

Halfar locked eyes with Emalli.

"I do know where he would be. It would have taken you a long time to find him and I believe none of you have much of that."

"Excellent! Now," she slowly turned to Kur. "Tell the guards to back away so we can continue this discussion inside."

"Disperse!" Kur ordered. "You tell no one of this event. It stays within this courtyard."

Weapons were sheathed and fists slammed into the left side of breast plates in acknowledgement. The guards bowed to Romnus and emptied out of the courtyard. Emalli grimaced at the display of discipline.

She found it insincere.

"Where is Farin? I thought she was part of your entourage?" Chardon asked.

"Hiding from Romnus with her son," Batis answered.

His presence registered for the first time with Halfar and Chardon and they moved towards him.

"Wait!" Romnus held up a hand. "He is now a part of my entourage as well."

"What madness is this?" Halfar demanded.

"I made him an offer and he is Farin's combat trainer."

"A very quick learner, the beautiful Farin," Batis added.

"After what he did?" Halfar roared.

"At your behest." Batis smiled wickedly at him.

That silence everyone. Emalli sighed heavily and grabbed Halfar by the sleeve.

"Come, we have much to discuss."

She addressed Kur and Romnus as she walked away, her back to them. "I'm sure you can manage entertaining our guests."

Aloni was the first to speak. "We need protection? Really?" He toyed with his longsword.

Kur gave him a sideways glance.

"Yes, you all do. I cannot be in two palaces at once."

"And Rass' father is what?"

"I have no idea, but knowing how powerful Rass is gave me a clue."

The entire group headed into the palace and entered the main banquet hall. Reita summoned servants into action and drinks were brought instantly. As they all sat down at the giant wood table, Chardon looked around at each of them.

"Where is Chastan?"

Drinks halted in midair. Kuhala frowned. An ominous cloud of anger filled the hall.

"My brother is no longer part of the royal house at this time. He has behaved," Kuhala stopped.

"Chastan dove into a higher level of madness that I could not have fathomed," Aloni finished.

"Did it have anything to do with Farin?" Chardon asked.

"No, but their mated status was severed on that day. She will have nothing to do with him and rightly so."

"That's a relief." Chardon set her drink down. "Now, you need to let us help you. This is not something you should have tried to do on your own and in such an isolated manner."

"In hind sight, you are correct," Romnus stated. "At the time I thought it was the best course of action."

"Will you go over it in detail then?"

"Are you giving me a choice?"

"No."

Everyone then took large gulps of their drinks before setting them down on the table. Not even the royal house knew the plan in any detail. This would be the first time they heard it in its entirety. Romnus looked uneasy but settled into the cushion at the end of the table and began explaining his agenda.

"My timing could not have been any better and I feel fate has intervened," Halfar said to Emalli as they sat in her private chamber. A handmaid set down drinks and hurried from the room.

"How so, my former lord?"

"Halfar is sufficient." He glared at her.

"My apologies, please continue." She picked up her drink and sipped daintily.

"If my timetable is correct, in two moons a fleet sent on campaign decades ago will be returning. Rass' father is a commander on that ship."

"Oh? Where did you send this campaign?"

"Why is that relevant?"

"What are they bringing back?"

Halfar sat startled for a moment then tried to remember. When it came to him, he smiled.

"Advantageous indeed," he finally replied. "Seeds. To diversify our crops. The harvests have been lacking."

"That is an understatement. With the heavy burden from constant turning of crops, the soil won't yield what it used to."

Halfar rubbed the bottom of his chin. "Then the soil needs treatment as well before we can plant them."

"I will let the council of agriculture handle that. I have work to do in regards to my mission." Emalli stood up and gestured for Halfar to exit her chamber. "I'm sure they are waiting for you."

The meeting was brief and to the point which suited him fine. He arrived at the banquet hall just as Romnus started to explain his agenda. Instead of interrupting by taking a seat at the table, he held up a finger to the servants to stay where they were and sat on a cushion just inside the archway. He listened to every word.

"Are you going to finally join us, cousin?" Romnus asked him after he finished talking.

"I was trying not to be rude in your palace," he replied. He rose up and made his way to an empty spot at the table. "That is some agenda, cousin."

"You both say cousin as if it's a dirty word," Talas interjected.

"On the contrary, it's a term of endearment," Romnus said.

"So, Halfar. What exactly is Rass?"

"There is a village on the far North of the planet where the people grow larger than normal. We use them as second wave soldiers because of their mass and," he paused, "their incredible speed despite their size."

"Those monstrosities we clear a path for and do not fight alongside?" Reita cried out.

"Yes, those."

"Rass is nowhere near that size. How do you conclude that?"

"In each species there is always an anomaly. Rass would be considered a runt. He was conceived by a whore in the brothel. His father rarely frequented the chamber so it was pure luck that he impregnated his selection. Since Rass was born in the palace that is where he remained."

"To be made a whore in the brothel like his mother," Kur spat angrily.

"I had no say in that. I didn't even know of Rass until," Halfar stopped himself. No one else needed to know more than that.

"Then, this warrior would be ideal in charge of our safety. No assassins would dare come at him," Kuhala said.

"Don't be so sure," Aloni added, raising a hand.

"The advisors are getting bolder. It's only a matter of time." Batis crossed his arms.

"By the way," Chardon interrupted. "Why is Farin hiding from you?"

Romnus' head snapped, surprised that she had remembered what Batis stated earlier. Halfar was not and had decided to wait until later to ask the same thing. He should have known Chardon was not going to let it slide.

This time Batis laughed out loud.

"He asked her to rule with him."

Romnus gave him a warning look but the soldier just met his gaze and smiled.

"Rule with you?" Chardon asked unsure.

"As in Queen?" Halfar yelled.

His fists slammed down on the table and his brow furrowed.

"Oh?" Chardon slapped a hand across her mouth.

"So what?" Chafar leaned on the table resting his elbows. "If she bonds with a Supreme Ruler, that's what happens, right?"

"There has not been a Queen of Azrom in over five hundred

years," Halfar replied.

"That's preposterous!" Chardon exclaimed.

"No. My father never bonded with my mother," Halfar explained.

"And neither did my father to my mother when he reigned," Romnus continued.

"For that matter, neither did their father, if my history is correct," Aloni added.

"Why would you put such a burden on her?" Chardon yelled at Romnus.

"It's not a burden!" Romnus slapped his hand down on the table. It shook from the impact. "I want her and no one else."

There was a silence.

"You finally decided to be honest with yourself," Reita laughed. "Good. Now all you have to do is convince her."

"Because she is of royal blood, it would solidify our bloodline." Aloni turned to Halfar. "You have no objection?"

"For her to be mated to Romnus, no. It's the Queen part I am objecting to. You have no idea how our race would respond to having a Queen after so long."

"She is adored by all of Azrom. I think she will be well accepted," Kuhala said.

"That being if we pull this off without all of us being assassinated," Talas quipped.

Farin sat in her son's chamber deep in her own thoughts. She had let him go play with the other royal children and leave her to be alone for a while. The kiss Romnus planted on her that day kept repeating itself in her mind. He had never kissed her like that before. Worse, SHE had never been kissed like that before. Chastan's were a bit rough and sloppy, Batis' resembled being assaulted by some starving animal, but Romnus left her warm and lightheaded. Her insides had tensed up, especially between her thighs. She knew then, unequivocally, how much he wanted her.

The sound of boots striking the floor outside in the hallway, caught her attention and she stood up, her muscles flexed. She let the short blade concealed in her sleeve slide into the palm of her hands. Only a few people knew where she may be and they were not in the vicinity to her knowledge. The tip of the boot appeared at the entryway and she lunged.

Chafar blocked her strike with his own longsword, pushing her back further into the chamber.

"I heard you were hiding," he said.

Shocked at his presence, she stood in a defensive stance staring at him.

"Are we really going to spar in this tiny space?"

He sheathed his weapon and leaned against the entrance's frame. That deadpan look on his face irritated her.

"What are you doing here?" She yelled at him. "How?" He shrugged. "Chafar!"

"Farin?"

She dropped her guard and slid the short blade back into the hidden sheath in her sleeve. They would get nowhere. Her brother always had that demeanor, never smiling, his words minimal reminding her of Modas.

"What's happening?"

"Talas had an epiphany."

Farin went rigid. She had known he would figure it out in short time.

"And what does that have to do with you being here?"

"Not just me."

"You can't mean?"

She shook head, hoping he would follow suit.

"Father has returned as well. It must be kept secret."

"Does Romnus know?"

The look on her brother's face told her the answer.

"So now what?"

"We are going to help you see this through. To the end."

"I guess there is no other way."

"Mmm. At least you will be Queen after this."

Farin's head shot up and she stared at him.

"What did you say?"

"Did he not ask you to rule with him? That would make you Queen."

"I have not given him an answer!"

"Then you should do that. He has a right to know what you're thinking."

"You're talking a lot, brother."

"Only when it's necessary." Chafar pushed off the frame. "Walk with me, sister."

And she realized this may be the first, last and only time they would be able to talk.

Romnus, Kur and Halfar watched the massive command ship settle down onto the hangar dock and the clamps grab hold of it, securing it to the surface. A handful of royal guards stood behind them, their numbers low to ensure there would be no breach of information. The hatch opened and the ramp came down as one hundred Azrom soldiers came marching down it. They made four neat rows, one behind the other, in front of the three leaders. In the middle of each row stood the commanders and the one in the last row was unmistakable, twice the size of the soldiers in his unit.

Kur was just over seven feet tall but the monster he saw was clearly a foot taller than him. Thick jet black hair spilled across the shoulders and tanned skin from many suns was visible at the face, neck and hands. His uniform was different as well. A black cloak with animal fur lining the lapel and edges was combined with black leggings and boots. His waist held no longsword and Kur understood why. Morphed, the commander would be gigantic, his sheer size instilling fear among enemies.

"You have been gone a long time. We commend you on your campaign's success." Kur addressed them while the crew unloaded the ship's cargo. "In your absence, there has been a change in rulership. Halfar has," Kur looked over at Romnus.

"Abdicated," Halfar offered.

"And Lord Romnus has graciously accepted the title of Supreme Ruler."

The soldiers slammed their fists into their chest plates and bowed down on one knee. Romnus looked down on them in what Kur interpreted as disdain but then the ruler smiled.

"Rise, warriors. You need rest and I know you would like to go home to your villages, but." Romnus wiped his face with one hand then sighed. "In lieu of restructuring the planet, temporary sectors have been established. Everything you need awaits you as does your families. Please, accept my apologies during this transition."

As the soldiers filed out, Kur called out the commander in the back row.

"Commander Abras. A word with you."

The giant stopped so suddenly, he created a small gust of wind. *Impressive.* Kur stayed where he was, not daring to get any closer, feeling dwarfed by the warrior. Commander Abras pivoted gracefully towards him and stood at ease.

"Please accompany us to the royal palace. We have a situation to discuss."

"As you command."

The deep baritone of his voice boomed in the air and sent shivers down Kur's spine. He glanced at Halfar and Romnus. They too seemed to step back from the sound and Kur suddenly felt fear. What if finding out he has a child made him extremely paternal? The soldier would tear him apart if he so much as yelled at Rass during one of their many arguments.

The three of them led the way but went faster than normal because one step from commander Abras was like three of their own. By the time they reached the conference chamber in the palace, Kur's chest had tightened and he was by no means out of shape. Abras stood just inside the entrance waiting to be instructed as a good soldier should and Kur relaxed at that a little.

"Please, take a seat."

Romnus, who was a hair taller than Kur, barely fit into one of the seats so when the giant commander sat down, the chair bowed, changing shape to a near flat surface. He made the chair look like it was for a small one yet showed no sign of discomfort. Kur nodded to Halfar. The former ruler blinked in confusion. Kur tilted his head towards the commander then Halfar understood, but not happy.

"When you last visited the brothel some centuries ago, you impregnated your choice. The child was raised in the palace." Commander Abras' eyes shifted to Halfar. He saw nothing registered in those eyes. "I eventually brought him into my care."

Kur's face heated up and his eyes narrowed at Halfar. That is not what he would call it but kept this to himself. Rass' father may actually become angry if he knew the real story and the three of them would not be able to handle the monster.

"You would know him now as General Rass." Something glinted in the giant's eyes and Kur wasn't sure if it was good or bad. "Also, General Rass and General Kur are bonded."

"Hmm."

The sound vibrated through the room, ringing their ears.

"Lord Romnus has put forth an agenda that is not popular with the people of Azrom. More importantly, some of the heads of government and the royal courts are also against him. I would like you to protect and defend Rass along with the first royal house."

"Why are royal guards insufficient?" Commander Abras asked, making them wince at his voice.

"The assassination attempts are getting bolder and we are not sure who is involved. We try to keep a small number in the know. Also, Rass is with child and not at full strength."

"Then eliminate the threat."

"That is where you come in. If it comes down to it, the advisors, the councilmen and any guards on their side must be dealt with. They will come for all of us in due time."

"What is their agenda?"

"To remove any within Lord Romnus' circle and find a more 'suitable' ruler they can control."

"Understood."

"You will be escorted to the first royal house palace from here." Kur gestured for him to follow the guards outside the entrance.

When he was gone, Kur slid down in his seat and breathed a sigh of relief.

"Were you frightened, General Kur?" Romnus had a smirk on his face.

"You would be too if that were Farin's father."

"Noted. You must tread carefully from now on."

Halfar stared at the entrance. "He is very protective of Rass." Kur sat up.

"How do you know? He made no indication of such."

"During battles, he made sure Rass' unit was protected on all sides. He must have a natural instinct."

Romnus burst out laughing. Kur frowned at him. This was not humorous for him.

Being pestered by the royal family to say yes to Romnus' proposal was getting tiring. Farin could not sit and eat meals in peace because of this. And then there was Romnus not saying a word to deter them. She was almost furious at him but realized it was her own fault for not giving him an answer. That had been over a year ago and time was running out.

Earlier, when she went out to survey the last of the villages to be destroyed she saw Azrom was a wasteland. There was no sign of life. The sectors where most of the population was being held were littered with large white squares easily mistaken for power plants. No windows, just vents at the four corners of the roof and one in the center.

The role of Queen took on so many connotations that it made her head feel like it was spinning. She thought about this as she walked down the outer corridor of the main palace, not paying attention to her surroundings. Her head butted into something firm and she looked up in surprise, ready to apologize.

Romnus towered over her and his expression made his intent clear. Before she could back away, he pulled her to him.

"Stop running away from me," he whispered in her ear.

His kiss set her body on fire and her hand automatically went to his chest and grabbed a handful of his cloak. The other just hung to her side lifeless. She gasped for air and the kiss went deeper. Lightheaded, she felt her body go limp but he held her firm.

"How barbaric, my lord." Batis' voice cut through the fog. "In broad daylight on the veranda."

Romnus released her and his lips pulled from hers as if sticky. She shuddered.

"Be more careful," Romnus chided her.

He stepped past her and continued down the corridor with Batis and two guards behind him. Batis smiled at her and brushed his hand across her hips.

"You should just say yes," he laughed softly.

☼

It was time to move.

Mesrod could feel it. His plans were in full swing and he would finally be able to wipe the royal slate clean, getting control of Azrom back into the hands of the government officials along with the royal courts. Each advisor had a group tasked to eliminate their targets. Once that was accomplished, he would signal the soldiers he had turned to his side decades ago to release the people of Azrom.

He had noticed strange and elaborate structures being erected where the villages used to be and seeing how beautifully done they were knew who the recipients would be. He had long heard the royal families complain about the lack of territory they controlled and being confined to the palaces.

Mesrod went over the plans in his head. The first act would be to get rid of that halfbreed. Her child was mostly of royal blood so he could be contained and raised properly. Next would be the Generals and their offspring. There was no need for it in the palace. Killing infants was not ideal but he wanted to eliminate any events of retaliation from the child when it reached maturity. Romnus was his responsibility and he had a full arsenal to handle him and his entourage. The very last part would be to infiltrate New Lassa and kill off Halfar and the other half breed. If Chardon got in the way, then she would be dealt with as well.

The chamber door opened. Dondar and Prevcan walked over to him with looks of great resolve and he approved. Their agenda would not work if they didn't have murderous intent. A council member had been assigned for each group to bear witness and record the historic events. The hostile overthrow of a Supreme Ruler had not been done in two millennia and needed to be noted for prosperity.

"Are we ready? Is everything in place?" He asked them both.

"All units are heading into position now. We are just going over some last minute adjustments and will wait for your signal." Prevcan gave him a short bow.

"The councilmen are ready and the poison is being loaded into weapons as we speak," Dondar stated.

"Good. There will be no signal. At mid dawn on the second moon, we strike. There is no turning back, no aborting the agenda. Understood?"

"Yes, Lord Mesrod," they replied together.

"Let's see it done."

The two left him alone in the chamber and for the first time in ages, he genuinely smiled.

Biandra set her basket down on the ground and stretched. The field was brimming with fruit and the stalks were high, just shy of her own height. They were denser in the row she had chosen to do her picking but that didn't stop her from hearing the strange whisking sounds coming in her direction. Not a moment too soon, she leapt upwards, keeping her eyes on the space below.

As she arched backwards, a view of the assault was made clear. Tiny needle like shards pierced the fruit stalks in the surrounding area where she had stood, killing them instantly. The stalks withered, crashing to the ground and the fruit decayed to rot, turning into a thick liquid that stained the soil black.

There was no place to hide so while in midair she calculated the distance from her location to the palace courtyard. Lord Romnus was able to clear it in mere seconds but she was not as fast. Some of the poisonous shards would hit her which left little time to administer the antidote. She saw the second wave coming at her as she landed into a launching position. This would be close. Using every ounce of muscle, she shot forth towards the palace.

Six guards were taking a break with Chafar and Trinon just outside Farin's chamber for a game of virtual cards. Trinon laughed at the looks of frustration whenever he or Chafar won a turn. The sun was just barely peeking over the horizon. Trinon waved a hand across the holodeck of cards, erasing them and stood. His eyesight adjusted on the fields beyond the courtyard and landed on the needle like spray following a blur which could only be Biandra for she would be out in the fields around dawn.

Sensing that something was wrong, Chafar and the guards rose up.

"No! Don't!"

Trinon tried to push them all back down but not before four of the guards were struck by multiple shards. From his view he could see the attack had come from the rooftop of the palace across the way. The four guards convulsed then lay still as tiny shards dissolved from their body heat into them. He had heard about the poison darts but this was a new way to administer the deadly fluid. No need for injection, just high velocity projectiles capable of piercing the flesh. Each volley spewed out dozens at a time.

"We're sitting open like easy prey," Chafar noted.

"Shall we jump?"

One of the remaining guards glanced over the ledge, gauging the descent.

"You would not survive it intact," Trinon replied.

Another onslaught of poison projectiles came over the veranda, missing them by millimeters. Trinon cautiously lifted his head to spot the culprit and found no need to act. A long rod stuck out of the assailant's neck and he fell head first down to the ground below. Trinon turned to his right. Batis was lowering his crossbow, a look of pure malice on his face.

"They think Farin is asleep in her chamber," he announced.

"So they've come to get her first." Chafar took a glance around. "Where to now?"

"This would be a first step. If for some reason she would not be here, then they would be ready at the second most likely site. With her son."

"That's inside the first royal house palace." Trinon stood up and pivoted towards that direction.

"Let's go," Batis ordered.

As they rounded the first corner, bodies lay in their wake. A few shards of poison were melting on the platform. From where they stood all the way down to the staircase that led into the courtyard, royal guards were frozen mid death throes. Then a trans-portal opened and an entire unit of soldiers spilled out to surround the group of five. Batis tsked and dropped the crossbow, unsheathing his longsword instead. The other two guards and Chafar followed suit. Trinon extended his claws.

Screams from all sides made commander Abras wince in fury. He knew something was amiss when one of the hallways ahead of him had become silent. Arriving at the foyer, he found dozens of royal family members along with their guards and handmaids dead in various forms of agony. He stepped on something tiny and moving his foot off it found a tiny shard crushed and melting.

Four blades came into his immediate view and he swerved using his speed to dodge and his massive size to pummel the soldiers whose hands were attached to them. They went flying into separate sections of the foyer, hitting the walls with simultaneous crashes. That didn't deter them for they were back on their feet and coming at him again. The one on his left finally got a good look at him and hesitated for a split second. That was all Abras needed.

Snatching the soldier by the legs, Abras used him as a weapon, swinging him like a longsword against his comrades. Blood splattered as flesh and bone met each other in a blur of lightning fast strikes. When the three were down, crumbled in bloody mounds, he dropped the wilted broken body of the first and advanced further into the palace. He could hear swords clashing ahead in the vicinity of Rass and Kur's personal chamber. Instead of using the corridor, he launched himself through the walls, creating a shortcut.

It wasn't just Rass fending off intruders, but Aloni and Kuhala as well. They were struggling from the sheer number of soldiers opposing them. Kuhala seemed dazed and he found melting shards of poison on the chamber floor. In the far corner was Rass' infant bundled up and shielded by the chest plate he should have been wearing. Abras could see Rass was beyond rage at this point.

The carnage under his feet was no doubt from his offspring general. Limbs were strewn in all directions, ribcages ripped open and heads decapitated. Even Aloni and Kuhala were standing a far distance from him, defending the child from inside.

Despite all the destruction, Rass was not unscathed. Abras calculated his son would not last another hour of fighting and Kuhala would drop any moment, the amount of poison in her system overriding the antidote vaccine. He counted twenty three soldiers left to deal with so made a decision. As the soldiers charged forth, he morphed into his full form.

His uniform stretched in vain to accommodate the shift as the legs formed into giant praying mantis limbs full of muscle and the pincers of his arms grew to the size of two men. The torso widened to reveal the definition of the abdomen. Rows of muscle packs bulged against the fabric. Standing at over ten feet tall, he glowered down at them. Some soldiers screamed in terror while others came at him emitting desperate battle cries, for it was too late to halt their advance. Abras approved. They had to commit to death or victory or both. That was the Azrom way.

He brought down his right claw on the soldiers in reach and heard the wet squishing sound of bone and tissue liquefying. His left did the same on that side, bringing down the total number of soldiers to fifteen. The area was not large enough for him to use his full speed but even at half, he could do damage. Within seconds, he had circled the still charging soldiers. His claws opened from behind them and engulfed an equal amount in each. He snapped them shut, cutting all of his prey in half.

He regressed back to his normal size and form only to witness Rass falter. He dashed forward and caught him before his body hit the floor. Rass' longsword slid from his hands as Abras cradled him.

"It is over," Abras spoke. "It is done."

"For now," Aloni said. He grabbed Kuhala by the armpits and dragged her into the far corner on the other side of the chamber. "If they were bold enough to ambush Rass here, then that means the rest of the palace, including the main, is under siege."

"Those," Kuhala managed to breathe, "poison shards. Problem."

"Yes, they took out most of our guards and anyone else in their path instantly."

Abras had no suggestions on how to combat that. He too would have been taken down if enough of the shards had gotten into him. He pawed the hair from Rass' face and looked over at the sleeping infant. Nearly two years old and already showing no fear in the midst of a battle, made Abras proud.

Biandra purposely overshot her target and ended up past the courtyard into the first foyer of the palace. She crawled to a wall and propped herself up. From her sleeve, she brought out an injection rod and pushed the needle into her thigh, releasing more of the antidote. Footsteps came closer to her position but her vision had failed her. Warped colored shadows came into view at the entrance in the corridor. If it was the enemy, she was doomed. Her body gave in and she slumped unconscious.

Everywhere around the palace, chaos had broken out. Chardon used her energy to create a shield whenever any poison projectiles came at her. Halfar was cautiously cutting down soldiers who came within close proximity but out of range of the poisonous spray. The enemy was smarter than she thought which posed a great hardship on the three. Their guards were long since dead and no sign of reinforcements so far. Romnus had lost all sanity for a brief moment when his royal guards, who had been a part of his entourage for nearly a century, were mowed down like insects. It took everything Chardon had to talk him back down and see reason; they had to move.

On her left was the hall leading to the courtyard and to the right was a banquet hall. Its smaller size seemed ideal for a short break to recalibrate their strategy so she steered their escape towards it. Once inside the hall, Chardon removed her outer robe already torn to shreds then tossed it aside. It was covered in blood and in the way of her fighting.

"Hurry, they will be coming down this way shortly."

When no one answered her, she turned to yell at them again. Romnus was standing still, his gaze on the floor against a wall. Halfar had grabbed his cousin's arm and held it in a death grip. Biandra lay crumbled, her body seemingly devoid of bones by the way it lay limp, but there was a rise and fall of her chest. Something in Romnus' eyes told her that this hall was going to be their last stand. Biandra was the only survivor of his original entourage and she knew he would not leave her to die.

"I will not run any longer. Let them come," Romnus said softly.

"Agreed," Halfar added.

Light spilled into the hall as the sun rose shining down on the blood soaked soil and white walls of the palace. The sound of metal clashing from the outside could be heard. Over that were boots stomping down the corridor just around the corner. Chardon wiped flecks of blood from her forehead.

"Here they come."

The stomping moved in succession then slowed as they approached the hall's entrance. At the archway, Mesrod appeared followed by a councilman and Chardon counted nearly thirty soldiers. He smiled at the three of them and she felt a sickness in her gut.

"Lord Romnus. I came to personally see to it that your reign ends today before sunset. But, I never expected you to have our former ruler here along with his off world mate. This is glorious!" Mesrod's eyes narrowed and he looked up at them from a downward stare. "I don't have to infiltrate New Lassa now to get rid of them."

Chardon saw Halfar's arms form into giant pincers and Romnus grew in height and girth. She noticed the councilman was wearing recorder goggles and a wide grin. Channeling her energy into both hands, she formed two orbs of red light that crackled in the air. Mesrod stepped out of the way and the thirty soldiers charged in.

She had never seen Halfar truly fight so it surprised her when instead of going into the soldiers before him, he jumped a foot in the air and spun. The momentum added to the swipe of his claw and cut a large gash across the chest of four soldiers, cutting through the breast plates and flesh. He didn't bother to land, using one of the bodies as a launching pad into the next wave.

Two soldiers were nearly upon her so she broke out of her awe to smash the red orbs of energy into their heads. There was a loud sizzling pop as they dropped and Chardon found her hands covered in sticky, cooked blood. Disgusted, she wiped her hands on the sides of her tunic and formed two more orbs, this time blue. They had less power than the red ones but just as effective. She decided they would be enough for this battle.

"Stay still, you disgusting halfbreed," Dondar screeched.

Farin crouched further onto the floor of the meeting hall. The beautiful multicolored sheers that lined the ceiling were now in tatters and blood smeared the walls and floor. Her bodyguards had been murdered, while surrounded protecting her, with poison shards. One had nicked her in the bicep but the antidote took care if that. She gave the councilman with the recording goggles a dirty look while she kept a view of Dondar. He had sent ten soldiers to deal with her and he himself, a former royal guard, would join in the fight. So be it. She was going to take him down as well and send him to Romnus for true punishment.

Her movements from one end of the hall to another was infuriating him and she liked it. The strategy was to allow time so she could figure out a way to get rid of them with one blow. It was proving difficult due to Dondar's involvement. He was a seasoned murderer and she was out of her league. She then remembered her training with Batis, also a well-seasoned killer, and found the answer.

Since her claws were heavier than the rest of body it would normally be a hindrance. But with the right momentum, she could destroy her prey with one movement. Speed she learned from training with the manbeasts meant Dondar could be taken down with an energy orb. Timing it just right and knowing when to morph was key. To do that, she would need one of her arms not morphed. Running it through in her head, she nodded to herself.

"End game," she sneered.

Dondar laughed. "For you, half breed, it is. Kill her!"

He came at her from an angle as the soldiers came head on, three on either side ready to split off and surround her. She smiled. That's exactly how she wanted it. Backing up a little, her body tensed, then sprung forward up in the air. Dondar leapt up to match her height but she was already curving down towards the soldiers. Her left hand became a shiny black pincer the same length as her legs and she spin. It hit the soldier from the left and continued on across the line until it reached the last on the right of her. Blood sprayed over her like rain.

As her body came around in rotation to face Dondar, her right hand formed a blue glowing orb. He was coming down fast from his descent, longsword poised to skewer her. The weight of her pincer dragged her down as expected, giving her leverage and she released the energy orb. He veered to dodge it but was hit, a large chunk taken out from his side. Dondar slammed into the floor, a smoldering piece of meat, not yet dead.

Farin landed on both her feet and whirled on the councilman. He inched closer to the wall with nowhere to go. The carnage of soldiers blocked the entryway. She was on him in one flash step and her fist connected with his head, bouncing it off the wall behind him before he too fell in a heap.

Bloodied, hurt and angry, Farin grabbed him and the bloody mess that was Dondar by their robe collars, one in each hand. She dragged them out of the hall and headed towards the throne room. A laugh erupted from her and she figured maybe she had finally lost her mind.

She found, upon her arrival, the idea to converge in the throne room was not an original one. Her brother, Batis, Trinon, Aloni and Abras were all there with a half bloodied advisor and their accompanying councilmen. Batis turned to her and looked down at Dondar. He raised an eyebrow and she nodded.

"Very good, my pet. That is impressive. He won't live long, you know?" He walked over to her and stood less than an inch from her.

"I'm hoping he lasts until Romnus gets his hands on him."

"Hmm." Batis grabbed the back of her hair and kissed her ravenously. He let go and she smacked his arm down. "You're such a natural killer. Makes me want you more."

"Stop that! This is not the time for your amusements."

She caught Chafar and Trinon eyeing her in obvious dissent. The two would never understand the explanation for her dynamic with Batis. For the training sessions to work, they had to know each other's strengths and weaknesses, mentally and physically to put them at equal advantage.

A loud rumble from above made her look up and hairline cracks began to spread across the ceiling. She looked to the others, then up again. The fissures grew larger and pieces of the ceiling came crumbling down. At the last second, everyone leapt backwards, dragging their prizes with them, towards the walls as it caved in at the center. Along with the giant chunks of debris came bodies.

Clouds of dust swirled in the air dispersing out from the middle and settling on the floor. Farin counted at least eight figures, maybe more. One of them she was certain of. Romnus rose up out of the debris holding his right side with his left hand. Blood blossomed from the wound to match the one across his left shoulder. Her mother sat up from landing on her back, a nasty gash along her temple. Blood dripped from a mangled pincer on her father's morphed arm. Before she could move to their aid, Romnus' body shimmied and the battle resumed in a blur of movements.

Not wasting any more time, Batis hefted his short blade in his hand then drew back and sent it into the fray. The bodies of soldiers came flying outwards and in the center stood Romnus, her mother, and father. Mesrod lay on the floor twitching and screaming with the hilt of Batis' short blade sticking out of his right eye. The royal advisor's hands hovered over it, not sure whether to pull it free or leave it. Batis eliminated his options by going over and retrieving his blade. Only half the eye came out with it, spilling bloody tissue onto Mesrod's face.

The throne room looked like hell on Earth. She had seen footage of the battle on Earth and that is how her mother had described it. She went to Romnus' side and tried to help him up but he was just too heavy. They both slumped down to the floor.

"We brought you presents," Farin quipped. Romnus looked at her in a disappointing way. "See." She pointed to the royal advisors laying on the floor unconscious. Some of the rumble had knocked them out.

"Where's Jabarz?"

Farin looked around at the advisors and realized that yes, Jabarz was missing. But then again, so was General Kur.

Soldiers loyal to the royal advisors kept vigilance over the sectors housing Azrom's people while waiting for the signal to break open the seals and release the occupants. Jabarz was stationed at the main hub closest to the palace that housed the workers of the mines and fields. The councilman who had been assigned to him had already documented the different sectors and was now also waiting to see the outcome of an enraged people crashing into the palace only to see that vengeance had already been done on their behalf.

So engrossed in their glee, that they were taken by surprise then terror as the soldiers around them were snatched up and ripped apart by modified enforcers. Jabarz turned towards the palace and off in the distance stood General Kur with an entire squadron of royal guards behind him. A second set of enforcers bounded across the terrain heading in the direction of the other sectors nearby.

"No!" Jabarz screamed in a rage.

This was not going to happen on his watch. He had not been a soldier on the front lines in sometime but he still knew how to wield a longsword and use his pincers for murder. That is what he had in mind for General Kur as he confiscated a longsword from the severed waist of a dead soldier. Pushing the councilman out of the way, he sprinted headlong to Kur's position. The general did not move an inch, standing with arms crossed at his chest, then his eyes narrowed as he understood Jabarz's intent.

Good! Face me, coward.

Jabarz used his lower body to flip until he was flying feet first.

His boots struck the blade of Kur's longsword and pushed the general back a few feet. He had not seen the general unsheathe and was impressed with such speed. Pushing off the blade, Jabarz jumped back and landed on his feet a few yards from Kur. Even at this distance, the general appeared quite large. Behind him, he heard the crunching sound of bones being snapped.

"You would kill your own kind? Because they do not agree to our insane ruler's ideals?"

"It was your collective agenda that started this," Kur answered. "You started the killing first. If a soldier decides to join in the murder of his own people then they should be prepared to receive the same treatment."

"You're out here alone," Jabarz laughed, "while inside the palace, your precious mate and all of Romnus' people are being slaughtered."

General Kur cocked his head.

"Do you really think it would be that easy to take down Lord Romnus, or General Rass for that matter? I assure you, even if you get some of them, the wrath from those who survive will have made you wish for death sooner."

Jabarz didn't wait for him to continue. He lunged at Kur with all his fury but the general dodged it. Not to be taken lightly, he went for another attack. Kur blocked it with his longsword again and they stood face to face, blade to blade. They pushed away from each other and Jabarz immediately went for a low blow. His blade swung, missing Kur by mere millimeters as the general bend forward while leaping back. Frustrated, he called out to him.

"Why are you dodging me, great general? Are you afraid to shed blood?"

"Sectors are secure, General Kur," a royal guard reported from behind Jabarz.

Startled he moved sideways in case it was an ambush. Kur's blade struck him from behind, piercing the meat below his ribcage. It caught on the bone and Kur was able to lift him up in the air like a barbarian showing off his prize. With a flick of the blade, Kur released him into the air and let his body crash to the ground. On impact a glob of blood bubbled up and exploded out of his mouth. General Kur came to stand above him, looking down in disgust.

"Shallow words," was all he heard Kur say to him. Darkness took him then.

The throne room was a nightmare. Servants cleared away the rumble as best they could and medical personnel treated the wounds of everyone in the vicinity, even the traitors. Romnus was being helped by royal guards into his throne, the only thing in the room still fully intact. At the base of the throne lay the other four advisors and the councilmen who had conspired with them. Kur gestured to the guards dragging Jabarz by his armpits to set him alongside the others. They dumped him like the trash he was.

"I had a feeling you would all come out victorious," he said.

"Til death!" Royal guards cried out, stopping their tasks to do so.

Halfar cringed at the display. Kur grimaced and made a note in his mind to change that battle cry. It no longer rang sincere. Just a slogan to recite whenever the word victorious was uttered.

"Get them on their knees," Romnus demanded. "And bring out the magistrate along with the rest of the council."

A small group of guards forced the culprits to their knees while another group went to fetch the requested others. Time felt like an eternity and Kur was relieved when they returned. Upon entering the throne room, the magistrates drew in sharp breaths and surveyed the damage ahead of them. The other council members did the same as they stepped over the threshold of the room. They all bowed low to Romnus as they neared the throne, not moving any closer to the half dead men kneeled down in a row before him.

"My lord, what has happened here?" The head magistrate asked in awe.

"You had no knowledge of this?"

"This? What is this? What madness has occurred?"

"The royal advisors and councilmen before you have been staging an agenda for quite some time. It involved my assassination, the murder of Lady Farin and Generals Rass and Kur."

"Preposterous! No one is that daft! What reason could they have?"

Calba, the least injured of the five, spoke up.

"Our reason? The bloodline is tainted! Halfar and Romnus have both dove into madness. Even that drunken man whore Chastan, went insane. We have some unknown half breed with free reign of the palace and our people enslaved in sterile sectors to make way for more royal housing."

Stunned silence followed.

"Yes, I did lose my mind," Halfar began, "but that does not constitute my bloodline to be deemed tainted."

"I'm curious." Kur turned to Calba. "Where did you come up with the idea that we are building housing for the royal families?" He asked in the sweetest tone.

Prevcan answered instead.

"We saw those new structures with splendid homes and access to the trade networks. We are not stupid."

"Oh, but you are." Romnus leaned forward, wincing from the pain in his side. "Bear witness, magistrates and councilmen." He nodded to Kur.

Kur went and stood in front of the two rows of traitors, advisors in front, councilmen behind them.

"For the act of treason against Azrom, the death of innocents and the attempted assassination of our Supreme Ruler, it is by Supreme Ruler Romnus' decree that you be executed for your sins."

Mesrod spit on Kur's boots and an onslaught of profanity erupted from the accused men. Kur stepped away and allowed Commander Abras to stand in front of them. He unsheathe his longsword, a ten foot blade made special for his species' size, and made one slash across the air before them. He sheathed his sword and stepped back.

The curses and yelling abruptly stopped. Some of the accused open their mouths in surprise but nothing came out as the top portion of their bodies slid to the left, tumbling onto the floor. For a millisecond there was no blood, then it flowed like a river forming a pool of red around them.

"The decree has been handed down. Are there any objections?" Kur asked.

The magistrate tapped a button on his wristband and opened his hands. A virtual tablet appeared and he began entering data into it. When he was done, the virtual tablet disappeared.

"The decree has been noted and there are no objections to this ruling. We should have seen the warning signs, my lord. Please accept our deepest apologies." The magistrate bowed low.

A New Era

Farin had been dodging the royal family for weeks since the attack and could find nowhere to run. Due to this, she was in a state of distress, constantly in tears. Her mother warned her not to run away and face the problem head on. It was not a problem, but a very heavy decision for her. Even her brother kept asking why she didn't just go to Romnus and say yes. If she had not heard about there not being a Queen in five hundred years, she might have been more open to the idea.

She had been ambushed four times this very day and her heart beat was elevated to the point where it was hard to catch her breath. Her usual black robes felt heavy as she ran down the outer corridor, looking behind her for anyone who may have followed her. It was a mistake. She forgot to look ahead as well. Farin ran right into Batis' arms.

"There you are, beautiful Farin." He clasped his hands behind her back, pinning her to him.

Farin stared up into his eyes, pleading with them. He laughed at her and wiped away the tears forming at the corners of her eyes then held her again.

"Please, let me go. I just want to go to my room. I just want to," she looked down, trying to think of something.

He leaned down until their lips were barely touching.

"This will be the last kiss I give to you."

To her surprise, it was not his usual brutal savage kiss, but a passionate one. He kissed her more and it seemed to go on for a long time. When he finally pulled away, there was a look of regret and longing. He unclasped his hands then grabbed hers.

"What are you?" She didn't get to finish her question.

Batis pulled her behind him by one hand all the way to the throne room and as he entered, released her like a ragdoll onto the floor in the middle of the room. She stared up at the base of the throne, not daring to look up.

"Supreme Ruler, Lord Romnus has approved you as a candidate to be his bonded mate. It has been cleared by the magistrate and the royal council. Do you accepted?" Batis yelled out.

Romnus had moved to the edge of his seat when Batis showed up with her and he remained there now. She could feel his anxiety drifting down to her. A quick glance and she noticed the magistrates, the royal council, her mother and father, her brother, the royal courts and even Chastan waiting for her reply. She balled her hands into fists and let them rest on her thighs as the tears fell down her face, staining her robes. Taking a breath, she let out a high pitched cry then looked up to find Romnus had come down from his throne to stand over her.

"Yes!" She cried out in defeat and hung her head.

Romnus knelt down, gathering her in his arms and held her while she continued to cry. She didn't even know why she was crying because feeling his arms around her always made her feel better.

"We will have a Queen," the magistrate announced, excitement in his tone.

"It's a perfect day, my lord," the head of social affairs commented. "This is also the day you release the people from the sectors."

Farin raised her head and stared up at Romnus. "Is that true?"

"It is," he replied, wiping away the rest of her tears.

"Did you plan this?"

"No. I found myself surrounded by everyone and then Batis brought you her." He squeezed her closer. "Are you sure? Do you want me as much as I need you?"

"I'm sure."

"We shall send out the announcement after the people have settled in," the magistrate declared.

The villagers exited the transport in a single file and stepped out onto fertile land. Gone were the dead trees that had marked the entrance of their territory. There were now tall healthy ones, fields bursting with vegetation they had not seen before along with familiar ones and a waterway instead of the giant well. What truly mesmerized them were the homes that sat scattered throughout the village. Beautiful, pristine buildings waiting to be claimed by their new owners.

"They are all identical but can be recolored, the insides customized to your liking. You will no longer need to live impoverished. This is Lord Romnus' gift to the people of Azrom," Lord Aloni announced.

"What is that building at the end?" A man asked.

"That is the marketplace where you can barter your wares with other villages on the planet. It has full interface so you don't have to limit yourself to one territory."

Loud exclamations of "Oohs" and "Ahhs" filled his ears, making lord Aloni happy. This had been the reaction of every village so far. And every time, they expressed shame and regret for not trusting the Supreme Ruler. Some did express anger at how the transition was executed and Lord Aloni had to agree with the people of Azrom in regards to that. Twenty years of strife was nothing in their life time but it was more than they should have endured.

As word spread of a new Queen, the planet became a plethora of well wishes and gifts for Farin. She didn't understand what she had done to deserve such adoration, amazed at how beloved she was. The cabinet members of New Lassa had arrived last week and Mara was making a fuss over the bonding ceremony gown with Emalli. Farin fled all of it to find a place of peace and quiet.

The library looked fairly dark so she ducked into it and found the first seat. She didn't bother turning up the glow orbs above so hadn't noticed the seat was already occupied. She let out a yelp as her hands press down on firm thighs then arched her body back up. Large arms wrapped around her, pulling her back down.

"What are you running from this time, my love?" Romnus' voice breathed into her hair.

She relaxed and leaned back into him. "I thought the fuss over Rass and Kur's bonding ceremony was overwhelming. This is madness."

"Hmm. It is tiring. What colors are you leaning towards?"

"You may not like it."

"Whatever it may be, I will love you."

Farin twisted her body so she could face him in the dim light. He had a small tablet in his free hand and was reading. She suddenly felt jilted and annoyed.

"Are you even going to pay attention to me?"

Romnus set the tablet down, grabbed her by the buttocks and drew her to him. He kissed her.

"Is that better?"

"Are you going to finish reading while I'm here?"

"Farin, my love. You dropped onto me in a dark library."

"Don't ignore me," she said softly.

"I am not Chastan. I would never ignore you."

She laid her head on his shoulder listening to the inner workings of his body, each beat strong.

Sunlight flooded the throne room from the entrance and the newly structure ceiling now showing the sky. All the adjacent rooms above had been torn out to accommodate it. The room was close to maximum capacity and from what had been reported, a mass of nearly two hundred thousand people were outside the palace. Romnus couldn't understand why so many had come when they could witness the bonding ceremony on the planetary communication network every village had.

For prosperity. He had forgotten about that.

Sitting on a cushion in the far corner by the entryway, he waited for the ceremonial entourage to bring Farin to him. His leggings were a light lavender color like the winter flowers and matched the sash around his waist. The robe was black with blood red trim and he wore the longsword he owned but never used. His hair had been washed, tugged at and brought to shiny jet black waves; it's natural state. He had no idea his hair was dull and dried out from mistreatment over the past few decades.

"Now you look like royalty," Halfar laughed.

"Really? And how do you keep your hair in good condition?"

"After you've been on Earth a while, you find it is imperative when holding a higher state of authority."

"I am bonding with your child."

"Yes." Halfar folded his arms. "But better Farin than someone from the lower royal family. I think she is too good for you, personally."

"You may be right."

Chimes began ringing and the first group of chaperones entered the throne room, Farin behind, followed by the tail end of them. Romnus sucked in a deep breath and forgot to exhale. The dream he had years ago of Farin wearing that gown waving to the people of Azrom flashed before him. Time stopped and he watched her come closer to his position near the entrance. He exhaled and everything resumed at normal speed.

She wore a lavender gown with a red sash, her hair piled up high at the front with the rest spilling down her back. The flowers entwined in it were flowers from spring and winter; red and purple. Romnus stood up and made his way to her. He took her hand in his and together they walked down the aisle. They went slowly up the stairs to the two thrones of equal size and style signifying one was no more important than the other.

The magistrate stood between them and cleared his throat. A councilman stood in wait.

"Greetings, my lord," he said, bowing low to Romnus, "and honored guests. This day we rejoice in the bonding of our Supreme Ruler, Lord Romnus, and the beautiful Lady Farin."

The aisle created by the masses filled in with the royal families and other guests followed by a hush.

"Do you swear devotion to each other, and to Azrom, even in death?"

"We swear this," they both said together.

"You shall now demonstrate proof of your will." He nodded to the councilman on his left.

The councilman produced the ceremonial knife and the couple held out their wrists. He sliced both with a smooth swipe, preventing blood splatter. The blood dripped down into the chalices placed directly beneath each arm. A second councilman came with a bundle of red fabric folded in his arms. Seeing the chalices half full, he unraveled it and bringing the two wrists together, bound them with it to stop the blood flow.

The councilmen each picked up a chalice and handed one to Romnus, the other to Farin. They stared at each other and without breaking eye contact, downed the contents of the chalices then handed them back. The official nodded proudly and placed his hand on the fabric covering their wrists.

"As royal magistrate and by Azrom's decree, I present to you Romnus Supreme Ruler and Farin, Queen of Azrom!"

He removed his hand and let them turn to the guests. They bowed deeply and the thunderous clapping began. The fabric was removed so the councilmen could check to make sure the wounds were sealed, then cut the red fabric in two and wrapped one on each wrist. They sat down on their thrones with their hands still joined together and smiled at the audience.

"The bonding is complete!" Loud roars and cheers resounded in the hall.

Music erupted and food on giant trays carried by servants came filing into the room. Drinks were poured in sloppy succession to make sure every cup, mug and chalice was filled. When that was done, Romnus and Farin stepped down from their thrones and walked the length of the throne room to the balcony. Farin let go of Romnus' hand and turned to him. The smile on her face was the same as in the dream.

"I present to you, our new Queen!" The royal announcer's voice boomed over the communication feed.

Below, two hundred thousand Azromians cheered and she burst into laughter. Not the halfhearted one he always heard, but a real one full of joy. Romnus turned to Halfar and he too recognized the real thing. As she waved to her people, Chardon stepped up behind him.

"If you harm her, Romnus."

"I know. But you won't need to worry about that."

"The people would kill him first," Halfar said.

"True." Chardon slid an arm around Halfar. "So, my love, would you have ever wanted to bond with me?"

Romnus stifled a laugh as Halfar stiffened and turned to her.

"You want that now? After I am no longer ruler?"

"Because you are no longer ruler."

"Father," Farin called to him without looking back, still waving. "We are both free now." She finally turned around and with a smile more beautiful than anything they had ever seen said, "Find your joy!"

~END~

ABOUT THE AUTHOR

Maquel A. Jacob has had a passion for the written word since the age of seven, reading everything she could get her hands on which included encyclopedias and the thesaurus. At twelve, she had her first encounter with a Stephen King novel and was hooked. She became inspired to write her own brand of fiction, combining multiple genres to keep things interesting.

Always ready to learn new things, her search for knowledge never ceases. She has an AAS in Accounting, an AAS Business Administration, went to Cosmetology school and studied Digital Film and Video for two years.

She is a huge Anime fan, loves a great bottle of wine and rocks out to heavy metal music. Green and lush Oregon is where she works part time in accounting and spends her free time spinning tales of imaginary worlds in her head, daydreaming.

If you feel inlcined to help out the author, please consider leaving a review on your favorite platform. Thanks

Follow on Twitter and Facebook: MaquelAJ1

Find her on Goodreads

Visit the website:

WWW.MAQUELAJACOB.COM